BIG BOSSY SURPRISE

MANHATTAN BILLIONAIRES
BOOK 4

LILIAN MONROE

Cover design by Maria at Steamy Designs
Editing by Shavonne Clarke at Motif Edits and Paige Kraft at PK Edits

ONE

BONNIE

IT'S WORSE than I thought. And I thought it would be bad.

I'm *so* not ready for this.

Craning my neck, I draw my gaze up, up, up the height of the Lusso apartment building. The penthouse sits at the top of the glass-and-steel giant, surveying Central Park and Manhattan from its perch at the pinnacle of the world.

My friend Leif's company designed and built this building a few years ago. I saw pictures of the penthouse when it went up for sale. It's beyond anything a mere mortal like me would ever gain access to in her puny little lifetime.

Until now.

My heart thuds.

Last time I was in one of these buildings, in an apartment just like the one towering fifteen hundred feet above my head, my career died a horrible, grisly death. My ego did too. Now I'm here. At the very bottom.

How fitting.

Is it too late to turn around and run away?

I touch the bag slung over my shoulder, where my phone lies dormant. My sister would kill me if I flaked on her newest client. Even worse, she'd be disappointed in me. For that matter, so would my bank account.

It's been ten years since I last worked for Linda, and her business has exploded since then. Just look at this building, this client. The Delmar Nanny Agency has a platinum reputation, and that's due to my sister's efforts. I can't let her down—especially not after everything she's done for me.

The doorman nods as I enter through the tall glass doorway, its tinted panes reflecting the bustling street behind me. I step across the threshold and into a different world.

Geometric wood shelves separate the lobby into two distinct spaces. A café with bowtie-wearing baristas and hissing espresso machines takes up the far wall, with my side of the partition strewn with plush sofas and intimate conversation nooks. As soon as the door closes behind me, the noise of the outside world disappears, and I know I've entered a new realm. A woman in a silk top and camel-colored trousers sips a coffee and flicks the tablet on her lap, oozing wealth from the crown of her shiny hair to the very tip of her red-soled designer shoes.

Once upon a time, I lived in a place like this. Well, not like *this*, but it was this apartment building's distant, less opulent second cousin twice removed. My home was a beautiful condo, a three-bedroom, three-bathroom paradise that made me feel like I'd made it. But that was before. Now, I know on what shaky a foundation my previous life was built. I know how easy it was for it all to crumble to dust.

I should have learned my lesson the first time, shouldn't I? But I've learned it now. I need safety nets for my safety nets. I need to trust no one but myself, and maybe Linda. I need to stand on only two feet: my own.

This job will help me do that.

Clutching my bag to my side, I make my way to the reception area, give my name, and wait for the woman behind the gleaming black desk to contact the resident of the penthouse. She's a tall, slim woman with black hair and red, red lips, and she gives me a nod as she hangs up the phone. Her beautifully manicured hand sweeps out in an elegant gesture. "Take the elevator up to the one hundred and twenty-ninth floor. Mr. Noble is expecting you."

"Good thing I'm not afraid of heights," I quip.

The woman gives me a polite smile but doesn't laugh. My nerves ratchet tighter. A staff member by the elevator swipes his card and presses the number for me, then steps out of the elevator, giving me a short nod before disappearing behind the closing doors.

I shoot upward, feeling like Charlie in the Chocolate Factory about to burst through the roof and into space. Floating through the cosmos would be about as comfortable as the penthouse I'm about to step into.

The ride up the elevator gives me time to tuck in flyaway hairs as I check myself over in the mirrored doors. I'm wearing a white tee tucked into a calf-length pleated skirt that feels silky beneath my fingertips, my shoulders covered with a cropped leather biker jacket I got at a basement thrift store six years ago. When I left my house, I thought I looked cool and approachable. Now I feel frumpy and underdressed.

My palms begin to sweat. The elevator shoots up and up, and I feel like my stomach is going to splatter at my feet. Gripping the handrail, I take three deep breaths and curse my sister for doing this to me.

I could have found a job on my own. I had almost figured out a plan. I didn't need this. Yes, my life had slid down a steep embankment and I was approaching the *splat* at the bottom, but I could have fixed it. I was going to fix it any minute. Linda just happened to walk into my roach-infested subleased apartment at the wrong moment. It was all under control.

Lies. Lies. Lies.

Another inhalation, and the elevator slows. I blink my eyes open and square my shoulders just in time to hear the faint ding before the doors slide open.

A woman is waiting for me on the other side. She's blond, like me, but her hair is cut in a short, sharp, chin-length bob while mine hits me mid-back. Her eyes are shrewd, and she looks me up and down as if she can read every shortcoming written right there on my face. "Bonnie Delmar?" she asks.

"That's me."

"I'm Laura Mason, Mr. Noble's household manager. I oversee all the staff on the premises. If you have any issues, please come to me first. Follow me."

She's wearing sharp, pressed pants in charcoal gray that hit her just above the ankle and show off her stylish sneakers. On top, she has a crisp white tee. An earpiece hangs from her ear, disappearing behind the collar of her top. I let out a small breath, happy I'm not entirely underdressed. Tees are acceptable.

I know nothing about Arlo Noble, other than his name and the fact that he has a five-year-old boy named William. Linda gave me his file to review this week, which I didn't do. I glanced at it for four or five seconds on the subway this morning, because I'm a coward who doesn't want to face the reality of her situation.

He's a big-shot billionaire with a reputation as a shark. Big whoop. Before my career imploded, I used to rub shoulders with those men all the time, and I learned most of them walk around high on their own inflated egos. If I had a choice, I wouldn't ever have to speak to a wealthy man again.

But the reality is this: Linda gave me a temp job as Arlo

Noble's fill-in nanny. It's one month of work, after which I'll have a bit of padding in my bank account. Enough to get out of the city and start over.

Could I ask Linda for money? Of course. But I also saw the bags under her eyes, and I heard her assistant talking about the length of the waitlist for new clients. She's severely short-staffed, and Arlo Noble is one of her biggest clients. There's a one-month gap in coverage that could lose Linda his patronage.

My sister is as desperate as I am.

But I still spent the week looking at the folder like it would explode if I opened it. It's one month of work, but it's also an admission of failure. Taking this job is me agreeing that my career is well and truly dead. I've exhausted my network. I've applied to every finance job posting in the five boroughs.

I am officially blacklisted.

So I'm here, entering a billionaire's lair, doing my sister a favor, shining a light on all the ways I've failed.

Laura the household manager leads me down a hallway toward distant windows, where I can see a slice of green and the first peek of autumnal colors that must be Central Park. The floors are wood, arranged in a parquet pattern that looks stylish and upmarket rather than dated. We emerge into a living room filled with tasteful, contemporary furnishings and a gorgeous glass staircase in the corner. Behind the curving staircase, two walls of glass meet in the corner. Light bounces and reflects off of every surface, shattering across the room like an art installation all on its own.

I try to modulate my breath. This place is *beautiful*.

This was *such* a bad idea. I should not be here. My heart has already started to thud a bit harder. Memories lurk at the edges of my consciousness, searching for a crack in my shields. I shore up my mental defenses, trying not to think of the event that ruined my life.

That event occurred in a swanky place just like this one. It was the beginning of the end.

"This is the guest floor," she explains. "This room is sometimes used as a reception room for more intimate events than the salon upstairs."

Intimate. This room. Right.

We walk over plush rugs and step onto the staircase. Laura moves with sharp, efficient movements, as if she has no time to waste on anything but doing the best job she can. "You'll stay in a bedroom down that hallway," she tells me when we stop on the landing halfway up, pointing to the corridor in question. "Mr. Noble handles nights with his son, but you'll be expected to be upstairs by six o'clock every morning. Your day ends when William is in bed. You'll get every second Sunday off, as outlined in your contract."

I nod. "Understood." Light slices across her in a thousand different angles as we stand in this glass corner, like we're caught in a prism. How is she not in awe of this place every single day?

I manage to actually look out the window as we stand on the landing, seeing the entire world at my feet. Central Park spreads out like a carpet below us, its curved pathways like knife slashes in a bed of green and orange and red. The concrete and steel and asphalt of the city loom at every edge of the park, like a tidal wave of mankind's achievements stopped dead by the might of nature.

I feel like I could stretch my hand out and touch the edge of the world from up here. I'm so high up above the city, the horizon bends at the edges. Down on street level, it's all car fumes and grime. It's dark and dingy and chaotic. This...this is light and life and glory.

I was wrong. This place is *nothing* like my old apartment. This is another league. Another universe.

It's terrifying.

"First, you'll meet Mr. Noble and his son. The current nanny, Alexandra, will walk you through some of the rules and routines you'll have to follow."

"Sounds good." My voice doesn't tremble, but my heart takes off.

When my sister set this up for me, it sounded so logical. I was —am—broke. I'd lost my job and any prospects of finding another one. I was struggling to feed and house myself. She could retrain me and give me a temporary posting here, no problem. I'd worked for her all through college, from my bachelor's degree to the end of my MBA. Getting prepared for this job was just a matter of redoing my CPR and first aid certificates and completing a new background check.

In Linda's typical fashion, the facts were laid out one by one, in a way that couldn't be argued with, like she was pulling cards out of a deck and placing them on the table in front of me. Yes, I needed help. Yes, I'd accept hers. Yes, I'd do the training and make sure I hit all the requirements to take the job. Yes, I'd show up at Mr. Noble's house on the first available day, ready to nanny his kid. That's how I ended up here on a Thursday, staring out at Manhattan like I've never seen it before.

But this residence cuts too close to the worst night of my life. And this Noble guy won't be any better than the man who ruined my career. He'll be another puffed-up peacock, high on his own power.

I shouldn't be here. I should have done something—anything— to claw myself out of the hole I'd sunk into.

But my sublease is up at the end of this week, and after that I'll be homeless. Linda might have been able to sense that I needed help, but she doesn't know how close to ruin I really am.

"Come," Laura says. She gives me a curt nod, then keeps

walking up the art installation staircase, and I have no choice but to follow.

As I climb, my fluttery skirt dancing over my bare calves, I build my strength up, step by step. Brick by brick. It's temporary. It's just another season of my life. It's just a job.

I need money, and Linda needs me to do my best. Once I have a safety net, I'll be able to move on.

I can do this.

Then we emerge into an enormous room with soaring thirty-foot ceilings. More windows. More light. More two-hundred-and-fifty-million-dollar views. The couches are low, the rugs are plush, and the cushions are arranged just so. A billionaire lives here. It's an absolutely drop-dead gorgeous space.

Across the vast room, I spy a man in a button-down shirt with the sleeves rolled up to mid-forearm. Light from those massive windows glints off his hair, which is dark and speckled with silver. His skin is a burnished gold, and his beard hugs his strong jaw, sprinkled with more silver than his head. His profile is regal, commanding.

In his hands, he holds two ankles that belong to a wriggling, pajama-clad boy. He lifts his arms, and the dangling boy shrieks with delight, laughter bouncing off of every hard surface in the room. Mr. Noble's lips split into a smile as the boy trails his fingers over the rug.

"Again!"

With a heave, my new boss swings his son up, then gently back down. His muscular arms press against the fabric of his shirt as he makes his son laugh harder. A low rumble of a laugh vibrates through the air, shivering over my skin. Mr. Noble gently drapes the boy onto the floor. William lies on the floor and laughs, and is immediately picked up and thrown over Mr. Noble's shoulder like a sack of very squirmy potatoes.

Then he turns and notices Laura—and I see the rest of his face.

My heart stops. My legs wobble. I grip the top of the banister and stare, wide-eyed, not understanding what's in front of me.

I know this man.

Motes of dust float in front of my face, illuminated by the sunlight streaming in behind me. For a few moments, I live in a dreamlike world, where nothing exists except my buzzing body, light, a few specks of dust, and this gorgeous man and his child. This gorgeous, *familiar* man.

This man that lived in the Before Times, in the mind palace I built just for him. Before everything collapsed. Before everything changed.

He hikes his kid up on his shoulder as Laura moves across the massive space toward him. Then he shifts his gaze to me.

Those eyes crash into me, exactly the way I remember they did almost three years ago. They're a dark, unforgiving brown—almost black. His gaze hits me like a sledgehammer. I wobble.

My stomach finally drops all the way to my feet. My throat closes up. I freeze.

Because I don't just know this man—I *slept* with this man. In one anonymous night, the billionaire standing on the other side of the room completely shattered everything I knew about sex. He rocked my world like no one else ever had, and probably ever will. He made me question everything I knew about pleasure, became the yardstick against which I judged every sexual experience that followed.

This man changed my *life*. One night of nameless sex three years ago made me pine and wish and hope. It made me fantasize about another conference, another business trip, another chance meeting. Every time I traveled for work or pleasure, I wondered if I'd run into him again.

That night—and the need that built in me after it—is what ultimately led to the biggest mistake of my life and the end of my career.

I've been in lust with this man for three entire years. I've been silly with it. Stupid with it.

And, judging by the blank look on his face as he rakes his gaze over my face and body...

He doesn't even remember me.

TWO
BONNIE

UNGLUING the soles of my shoes from the no doubt outrageously expensive timber floor, I take an unsteady step toward the other side of the vast salon. I skirt around a big gray sofa and join Laura on the far side of the room, where a smaller conversation nook is delineated with a second rug and a couple of armchairs. Toys are strewn on the floor—a plushie, a few action figures, toy cars.

I stop in front of the man as he sits on an armchair, the boy deposited on the floor again. Laura stands next to me, silent.

Mr. Noble watches me for a beat. I wait for recognition to strike.

It doesn't.

He arches a dark brow, and it makes him look haughty, danger-ous, and extremely—unbearably—hot. "Ms. Delmar?"

"Bonnie," I croak, and hey, how amusing, now we know each other's names. Three years after the incident.

Thoughts crowd my mind. I didn't know he had a son that night, but he did tell me he was divorced. Was that a lie? Was I the other woman?

I really should have read that file.

Then I remember Linda saying that he's had custody of his kid since William was a couple of months old. He's as protective of his son as he is dangerous in the boardroom. So, not an adulterer, and apparently a doting father. That's good.

His voice feels like velvet on my skin. "I understand you're Linda Delmar's sister. I've been very happy with her services so far." He shifts those magnetic eyes away from mine and over to his son, and I can breathe again.

But then I watch his face soften as he looks at William. The boy is acting out some sort of intense fight scene with two of the action figures, complete with sound effects. He gives his father an impish grin, and Mr. Noble grabs another action figure and brings it stomping toward the other two. A dramatic fight ensues, and Mr. Noble's toy is defeated by the triumphant heroes in his son's hands.

And oh, I can't do this. I cannot look at this man playing with his adorable child, knowing that I've been intimate with him. Knowing that the experience didn't even register as a blip on his radar.

I thought every scrap of my pride had already been stripped away. When my career imploded, I thought I was building myself from the ground up. Now, I'm realizing that there was, indeed, some self-esteem left to shatter. I can hear it cracking as my new boss meets my gaze again, not a glint of recognition in his beautiful eyes.

I force myself to speak. "Linda's the best of the best when it comes to childcare," I answer truthfully while my mind spins and whirls into kaleidoscopic panic.

A woman appears in the mouth of a hallway to our right, diagonally across from the staircase. "Will," she calls out. "Time to get ready."

The existing nanny. I can immediately tell why she needs a replacement—her pregnant belly looks like it's about to pop. She smiles as the boy stands and comes running across the room toward her, action figures in his hands. She gives me an even brighter smile, then follows the boy out of sight.

I turn my attention back to the man seated on an armchair like it's his own personal throne. All levity is gone from his gaze. The man who grabbed an action figure and played with his son has been replaced with this pillar of stone and masculinity.

Suddenly, I don't know what to do with my hands. I feel somehow too big and too small for my body, like I'm either going to burst out of my skin or shrivel up into a human raisin right before his beautiful brown eyes. I search his face for any hint of recognition, then I let my gaze drop to his hands—hands that were on me, *in* me—and suppress a shiver of... I'm not sure what it is. An echo of desire? Horror that I'm a stranger to him? Utter, bone-deep mortification?

Squaring my shoulders, I give him a bright smile. At least, I hope it's bright. "Your son is five years old, correct?"

If he doesn't remember me, well, I guess I don't remember him either. That night three years ago didn't change the way I think about men and sex and pleasure, because it never happened.

I'm here to work.

Or, at the very least, I'm here to make it through the next half hour, and then I can call my sister and quit before running away to a country far, far away. Maybe a hundred years from now, my embarrassment will fade.

"That's right," Mr. Noble replies, and I remember him saying other things to me. Things like *that's it*, and *just like that*, and low, sinful chuckles followed by, *you like that?*

He was deliciously demanding in bed. All serious and focused and perfect. My thighs clench at the memory. I want to turn to the left, get a running start, and throw myself out of those massive windows.

His dark eyes search mine. "You seem familiar."

You don't say.

He leans his elbows on his thighs. "Have we met?"

"Us?" I squeak. "Y-you mean you and me? Me and you? Nope. Never. Uh-uh." I shake my head in case my babbling answer wasn't enough. "I don't think so."

A wrinkle forms between his brows, and somehow it makes him look sexier. *No.* No, it doesn't. It makes him look like my boss who is displeased with something I said. It definitely doesn't remind me of the focused look on his face when he first touched me below the belt. Because that never happened. The man in the armchair living in this seventeen-thousand-square-foot penthouse has never touched me anywhere.

"When Will is finished getting ready for the day, I can introduce you properly," Mr. Noble says, and pushes himself up off the chair to stand.

I'm not sure if it's my memories of this man naked on top of me, or if my brain is just malfunctioning, or if maybe Mr. Noble is, indeed, the hottest man in existence, but watching him go from sitting to standing is the sexiest thing I've ever seen. His arms stretch the fabric of his shirt as he braces his broad hands on the arms of the chair, those strong forearms flexing below his rolled-up sleeve. His chest strains at the little ivory buttons marching down his torso, that tantalizing triangle of flesh at his throat reminding me of the masterpiece of a man hiding beneath.

He had glorious chest hair that night. Probably still does. It was coarse and not too thick, covering his chest and diving down his stomach like an arrow pointing to a truly magnificent cock. I could probably draw his chest from memory. I could draw most of him from memory, actually. I've gone over the mental image of him a thousand times or more since I left that hotel room.

I can't do this.

"Where's the bathroom? I'm sorry—I—do you mind?"

He straightens, glancing down at me from the few inches of height that top mine. "No problem. Laura?"

"I'll show you the way," she says, gesturing to a nearby hallway on the opposite side of the room as the one Alexandra the nanny used.

My breaths are shallow, barely providing enough oxygen to keep me conscious. As soon as we turn the corner and are out of sight of her—our—boss, Laura glances over her shoulder and frowns at me. "Are you okay? You look a bit green."

"I'm fine," I lie. "Just nervous." And mortified. And...horny?

Her lips curl into a sympathetic smile, the first I've seen. "He has that effect on people, but don't worry, he's a softie underneath."

Oh, there's nothing soft about him. As I am *well* aware.

She leads me to a bathroom, and I barely register the opulence. I flick the lock, run the sink, and splash some water on my face. Then I turn it off and grip the edges of the vanity as I gulp down deep breaths to try to get myself back under control.

Fumbling for my bag, I pull out my phone and dial my sister, then immediately hang up. What would I even say to her? That I'm stuck in the bathroom in her client's house, and oh, by the way, I had sex with him three years ago and *he doesn't remember me?*

Maybe I can call my friend Nikita. She'd laugh and laugh, and I'd feel better. Temporarily. But then I'd hang up and I'd still be stuck here.

This is bad. And in the context of what happened since then, with the demise of my career, it's even worse. I used to make a lot of money working in finance. I elbowed my way into the boys' club of the hedge fund where I worked and showed them that I deserved to be there. I was *good* at my job. I brought in huge clients and managed their portfolios better than any of my peers.

And then...

Old memories press against me so hard they almost feel like a physical weight. Then that night happened, that holiday party, that nightmare. The betrayal. Then I was thrown out of the club and dragged through the mud until I had no choice but to tuck my tail and run. Then I lost everything.

And now, here I am, in a house with a man—

"Everything okay?" Laura's voice calls out.

"Yep!" I answer. Water drips off my chin into the beautiful glass bowl.

I look at myself in the mirror and groan. I forgot I was wearing makeup. Now I have mascara streaked all down my cheeks, like some sort of hysterical crazy woman. Which, to be honest, isn't precisely inaccurate.

What do I do? What do I *do*?

Stay or go? Disappoint Linda? Pretend that night never happened and try to be professional?

I don't know. *I don't know.*

My phone buzzes. I scramble to pull it out of my purse. It's Linda, asking me how things are going. I stare at the screen and close my eyes, shoulders dropping.

I can't back out. My sister needs me. Mr. Noble is one of my sister's most important clients, and her business is everything to her. Her staff shortage is really stressing her out. Even in the dim depths of my rock bottom, I saw it when she came to my apartment —the bags under her eyes, the tension in her shoulders.

She did this for *me*. She told Arlo Noble that I was the best choice. She trained me and gave me work and set me back on my feet. I can't throw that back in her face. Not when she found me at my lowest. Not when she needs me just as much as I need her.

We're a team. We take care of each other. That's how it's always been.

Plus, if I don't move in here and work for Mr. Noble, I'll be homeless. I wouldn't ask Linda to take me in when I just threw this opportunity back in her face. Her couch would be too good for me if I sank that low.

It's just a job, and I'm a grown woman.

I grit my teeth and look myself in the eyes. I can do this.

So what if I had sex with my now-boss? That was three years ago, and I am an adult. I can move on. We made no promises that night; we didn't even know each other's names. He was clear that he didn't do dating or relationships, and I was more than happy to lose myself in the anonymity of our encounter. I got a call before he woke up, and I had to leave. That was the end of it.

I'm mature enough to not let that affect my life any more than it already has. Pining over the man was a ridiculous indulgence, and it stops now. Right this instant.

I use toilet paper to swipe under my eyes, then pat my face dry. Using the few bits of makeup in my purse, I do some damage control and fix my face, then re-emerge from the bathroom and smile at Laura. "I'm back."

She frowns at me. "Are you sure you're okay?"

"I'm totally fine." I smile, hoping it doesn't look deranged. And for all intents and purposes, I am fine. I know what's at stake here: my relationship with my sister and my own stability. I can't give that up just because I've seen my boss naked. That was Before. This is After. I nod at Laura. "Shall we?"

When we reappear in the main room, the force of Mr. Noble's presence doesn't hit me quite as hard. Or, it does, but at least I'm ready for it this time. I brace myself as we walk in, so the sight of that body, that face, those eyes…it only makes me wobble the tiniest bit.

"This way," he says, and nods at Laura to leave us. I fall into step beside my boss, and his shoulder brushes mine. It makes my thighs spasm, but I pretend they don't. I can't afford thigh spasms right now. I'm Bonnie Delmar, the new nanny. I'm pleasant and professional and the perfect woman for the job.

Mr. Noble glances at me. "So. You work for your sister?"

"Nepotism for the win," I joke, then let my smile fade.

"Ah." He nods. His strides are long, and I have to hurry to keep up with him. "I hired Alex, our current nanny, through the Delmar agency. Every interaction I've had with Linda has been irreproachable. She's an impressive woman."

"I'll pass on the compliment," I promise.

He glances at me, eyes unreadable. Has he finally recognized me? Is he going to mention it? Am I going to get fired before I even begin?

My heart jackrabbits in my chest, and I only just restrain the urge to press my hand against my sternum to make sure the organ stays where it's supposed to.

If he finally remembers me, what do I do? Do I pretend *I* don't remember *him?* Do I joke about it? What joke could I possibly make? Do I fess up and ask him to just move on?

Oh, three years ago? In London? At a work conference? Let me see if I… Oh! Yes, I remember you. Haha—I barely recall the six cataclysmic orgasms you gave me in as many hours. They were just so forgettable, you see. No offense.

I stumble, my thoughts crowding in too much for me to pay attention to my feet. I trip on empty air and pitch forward. A strong arm bands across my chest before I can fall, and I find myself engulfed in a scent I thought I'd never experience again.

Because it *is* an experience.

Arlo Noble smells like heaven. For an instant—the barest second—I feel the heat of his arm against my chest and I remember just how much I enjoyed being pinned down beneath him. Then he retreats, his hand moving to my shoulder to steady me. It's an impersonal touch, and it makes every inch of me flush hot.

"Thanks, Mr. Noble," I say. "I'm okay. Must have had too much coffee this morning. I get the jitters if I have more than two shots of espresso."

"Call me Arlo, please," he replies. His voice is pleasantly deep, which I already knew, and it sends shivers coasting along my skin. He drops his hand from my shoulder. "Laura won't, no matter how much I insist. She says it's a bad look when she has to speak in front of 'outsiders.'"

I nod, pinching my lips into a tight smile. "Arlo, then."

"I'll remember not to feed you too much coffee in the morning," he says, then clears his throat, like he didn't mean for it to sound so intimate. Or maybe that's all in my head. Then he sweeps his hand toward the end of the long hallway and starts to walk again.

This corridor is wider than the one downstairs, and we pass lavishly decorated bedrooms, two powder rooms, and finally come to a stop in front of an open doorway that leads to a playroom.

William is no longer in his pajamas and is instead wearing jeans with an elastic waist and a red tee.

He's still playing with those action figures as Alex tidies up the room. He has the biggest brown eyes I've ever seen. After a quick, curious glance at me, he turns back to his play.

There's a door to my left that leads to a bedroom, a Batman-themed comforter covering a bed. The wall directly in front of me is covered with photos of Arlo and William, a woman I'm guessing is a sister, judging by her resemblance to my boss, and a few other people. There's a life-sized plastic statue of Batman in the corner.

The current nanny turns toward us. Her hand moves to her pregnant stomach, her face beaming.

"Bet you can't wait to have one of your own," Mr. Noble says, leaning a shoulder against the wall. Then he straightens and motions for me to approach. "Bonnie, this is Alex. She'll be training you this week before she leaves us."

"You're going to love it here," Alex gushes. "And I'm not just saying that because Arlo is standing there."

I smile. "And this is William, I take it?" I kneel on the floor and smile at the boy. "Hi. I'm Bonnie."

He looks at me suspiciously. "Hi."

"Nice to meet you, Will." I touch one of the action figures off to the side, straightening its arms. "The Joker," I say, humming, looking at the figurine's wide red lips. "Personally, I prefer Mr. Freeze."

Will whips his head toward me and scoffs. "*Mr. Freeze?* No way. Batman can beat him with his eyes closed."

"I just like his little glass helmet thing," I respond, grinning.

Will rolls his eyes, but then he clambers to his feet and pulls a box out from the shelf on the wall. He digs in it, and comes out with a Mr. Freeze action figure, handing it over to me. "You can be him, but Batman is gonna beat you." He picks up his well-worn Batman figurine, facing off against me.

I laugh. A vicious fight breaks out between the figurines, and Mr. Freeze dies dramatically. Will cackles. Then he stands up, whips his shirt off, and flexes like he's Arnie on stage at the Mr. Olympia competition. "I win!"

It's hilarious and weird, and it reminds me how much I love kids. I love this age, when their personalities are so strong and unapologetic. Will turns to the side and points at a triangular birthmark on his rib. "Look," he says, showing off. "I've had it since I was born."

"Oh!" I exclaim, pleased that I might be winning him over so quickly. "Just like your father." My jaw clamps shut so fast I nearly shatter all my teeth. A woman who has never met Arlo Noble would definitely *not* know that he has a triangular birthmark on his left ribcage.

Arlo shifts behind me, a rustle of fabric against fabric. "What did you just say?" His voice is low.

"Huh?" I turn to look at him, hoping my face looks guileless. I'm just the nanny. The professional, competent nanny who has definitely never seen her boss naked.

"You said something about my birthmark." His frown deepens. "How did you know about that?"

Um. Um. Uhh...

My mind is a frantic whirlpool, and seconds are ticking by. I need to say something, anything—

"We do our homework over at the Delmar Agency!" I give him my most winning professional smile, the one that used to get clients to hand over their hard-earned millions to a hedge fund.

"Homework that involves intimate details of my body?" His voice is dark. Dangerous.

My smile creaks around the edges as I widen it. "You'd be surprised what comes up in clients' files."

"Will, put your shirt back on," Alex says behind me, voice quiet.

"I don't want to."

"You have to."

I glance over and pick up his T-shirt, handing it over to Alex so she doesn't have to bend over. She smiles at me, and I risk a glance at Arlo over my shoulder.

He doesn't look happy. "Are you sure we haven't met?"

"I'm sure," I say, brushing my hands down my thighs. "I'd remember you, I promise." That last part comes out a bit...testy.

Whoops. I tweak my skirt to adjust it over my legs as I kneel on the floor just so I don't have to look at my boss's face.

Wouldn't it be funny if I got fired, after all?

I stand, uncomfortable with my new boss looming behind me. It makes me feel small and powerless and panicky. With my back to him, I take a deep breath and brace myself for the impact of his stormy expression, but when I start to turn, I accidentally step on the Batman figurine Will discarded in his bid to impress me with his muscles. Not wanting to crush his favorite toy, I spring my foot back up...and my shoe-clad toe gets caught in my hem.

That's why, when I bring my foot back down onto a clear patch of flooring, it takes my skirt with it. The elastic waist is comfy, but it's not exactly secure when a sharp tug pulls the fabric down. My skirt drops to my feet in a flutter of silver.

I yelp and immediately bend over to grab my skirt. Then I remember I'm wearing a thong. And I still have my back to my boss.

Could this day get any worse?

I'm not sure about Linda's employee handbook, but I'm pretty sure showing a client the full moon within fifteen minutes of meeting them isn't something I'm supposed to do.

My butt cheeks are on full display as I try to wrench my skirt back up, so I also reach a hand back and try to tug my T-shirt down as far as it will go. Unfortunately, the awkward position makes me lose my balance, and my feet are tangled in the fabric that's stupidly clinging to my shoes, tightening around my ankles like a vise.

And I fall over.

So, yes. This day can get worse.

But I've been through a lot of crap over the past few years, and I can always find a silver lining. The belly-clutching laughter of a five-year-old boy almost makes it worth it. At least one of us can laugh about this.

And hey—there's a second silver lining. I probably *will* get fired now. So this whole nightmare will be over any minute. I just have to survive the mortification trying its best to suffocate me, pull my skirt back up, and walk out of this place with my head held high.

While my face is busy bursting into flame, I untangle myself and pull the fabric back up over my hips. Then I stand.

I'm not sure what Arlo does. Until my clothing is back where it's supposed to be, I pretend he doesn't exist at all.

Finally, when I can withstand the embarrassment, I spin around and face my new (soon-to-be-ex?) boss.

There's a long pause. A very long pause. It's torture. I inhale slowly and deeply and bring my eyes up to meet his, trembling all the way down to my toes.

"All right," Arlo announces slowly, staring at me from beneath his furrowed brow. "Come with me, Bonnie. We have a few things to go over, and then I'll leave you with Alex for the day."

That doesn't sound like he's firing me. I don't know how I feel about that, but I'm pretty sure it's not good.

But I'm here, and Linda needs me to do this. And also, I have no other job prospects and my life is in the gutter. So I smile (Professional! Competent! Not so embarrassed I want to die! Not at all imagining Arlo Noble naked and inside me!), then take all my recent thoughts, feelings, and emotions, and shove them all into an iron box. Then I put that box on a very, very high shelf in my mind, and promise myself I'll never, ever open it. My smile widens, as if I didn't just flash him my entire ass. "Sounds great."

THREE
ARLO

BONNIE SMELLS like sweet vanilla cupcakes. As soon as we step into the hallway, the scent of her skin punches me in the gut, twigging something in my memory.

I swear I've met this woman before. Everything about her—her voice, her laughter, her scent—is driving me crazy with remembrance. But I'd remember a face like hers. Those high cheekbones and bright blue eyes. Those pillowy, pink lips. That long, wheat-gold hair.

I'd remember an ass like hers too.

She's not the kind of woman a man forgets. Not by a long shot.

Her skirt, firmly anchored above her hips, swishes around her legs as we walk down the hall toward my office. I find myself entranced by the movement of the fabric, the memory of what it looked like puddled on the floor.

This is bad.

I should call her sister's agency and request a new nanny. Bonnie isn't a good fit.

But Linda was clear when I spoke to her; she's short-staffed, and Bonnie is more than qualified. I'll be put on a waitlist if things don't work out with her, which means I'll have to start the process of finding a new agency. That means new background checks, interviews, waiting, and training.

I don't have time for that. Alex is already working longer than she wanted to, and I know it's to do a favor for me. She should be enjoying the last weeks of her pregnancy with her husband. Alex's replacement, Sofia, isn't available for full-time work until a month from now.

I don't have a month. My newest company is about to go public in three short weeks, and I need every minute I have to work on the IPO, the initial public offering. We need to raise enough capital to take our solar panels to market. Our technology is groundbreaking, but these three weeks are absolutely critical.

Looking for a new, temporary nanny from another agency, which I haven't vetted, will pull me away from my work when I need to be absolutely focused. Today was a rocky start, but I owe it to myself—and Bonnie—to see this through. It's one month. I can do one month. I can resist a flash of lust. I can deal with someone slightly clumsy and more than a little entrancing.

"You have a beautiful home," Bonnie says into the heavy silence hanging between us.

I stop in front of a door and gesture for her to enter. "Thank you."

Her scent wraps sweet tendrils around me as she steps into the study, torturing me with memories just beyond my grasp. How do I know her? When did we meet?

This woman is like a word on the tip of my tongue, a melody faint and familiar. It drives me crazy.

"My friend Leif designed the building, actually," she says, stepping across the room to peek through the windows. The light that streams through silhouettes Bonnie's upper body, her hair a golden cascade. She glances over her shoulder. "And yes, I did just name-drop him." She lets out a self-deprecating laugh. "Whoops."

That laugh. I've heard that laugh before. Where? How do I know this woman?

Suspicion crawls up my spine. Is this Alice's doing? My ex-wife has already tried to infiltrate my life twice that I know of...I wouldn't put it past her to try to gain access to William through the new nanny. If Bonnie is here to spy for my ex-wife—or do something worse—there is no square inch of earth I'll leave unscorched. Even the thought of yet another attempted betrayal makes my hands tighten to fists.

"Your friend Leif?" I grate.

She walks around the far side of the desk while I make my way to the chair, keeping the desk between us. I'm not sure if she does it out of propriety or self-preservation. Maybe she can sense the hair-thin thread of control leashing my temper. She nods at my question. "I guess Leif didn't design it himself. But he owns the company that did."

Why would a woman who rubs shoulders with Leif Sorensen need to work as a nanny? She's Linda Delmar's sister; she should be managing the business, not out in the field.

There's something I'm missing, and I don't like the feeling. Not one bit.

Her hands flutter over the waistband of her skirt, like she's trying to make sure it's still there. Her nails are painted a soft pink, cut short and shaped elegantly. Her wide blue eyes and pink mouth draw my gaze every few seconds. I want to take my thumb and trace her cupid's bow, those two defined peaks on her upper lip calling to me even from across the desk.

I frown. Who is she?

I gesture to the chair across the desk from me and watch her arrange that maddening skirt around her legs as she sits. She folds her hands on her lap, prim and proper, and gives me a slight nod. Her smile is bland, professional, and false.

A prickly feeling lifts the hairs on the back of my neck. I keep my face neutral and lob a question across the desk at her. "How's Alice doing?"

Bonnie blinks, confusion flitting across her gaze. "Alice who?"

Either she's a fantastic actress, or she has no idea what I'm talking about. Maybe I'm just being paranoid. Wouldn't be the first time.

After Alice's initial betrayal when William was born, she's tried to blackmail me and sink her claws into my life at least twice that I know of. My lawyers are good, though, so it's come to nothing. Is this her trying again? Does she want to plant someone in my household to get information? To try to drag me back to court?

Blinking, I clear my throat and sit behind the desk. One thing I've learned in my many years in business is to show no weakness. Give no explanations. I don't have to explain myself to this woman. I can just pretend I never mentioned my ex-wife's name, and it will be as if the question never crossed my lips.

This room is small, with only a white desk and a couple of plush chairs, a single window, and a small bar cart. My main home office is upstairs on the third level, but this is where I take meetings when I'm on this floor.

I pat my pocket for my glasses—then remember I don't need them anymore. Old habits die hard, though. Huffing at myself, I flip open the case for the tablet on the desk and pull it toward me. Navigating to the email Laura sent me this morning, I hum. "I see you've signed the contracts and gone over access and emergency details."

"I have," Bonnie replies, pretty brows drawing together. Her eyes spark as they meet mine, and I'm once again struck by the idea that I know this woman. I've seen her somewhere. She's nervous—especially after the little display in my son's room—but she still squares her shoulders and looks me in the eyes.

I like that. It's unusual. Intriguing.

I lean back, letting my face settle into the mask I use in business negotiations. Let's see how steady this woman really is. If she's here to feed my ex-wife information, I'm going to find out. "Any questions for me?"

She lifts a hand and smooths her hair back toward her ponytail holder, sooty lashes thick around her ocean-blue eyes. She shakes her head once. "Not at the moment, no."

"Good." I hold her gaze. "Because I have one."

A little inhale makes her chest move, but she just dips her chin in response.

"What else is in my file, besides the location of my birthmark?"

She shifts in her seat, not meeting my eyes. She plucks at her skirt again. Her cheeks are pink. "Oh, you know...the usual."

"I don't know what 'the usual' is, actually. You'll have to elaborate."

"This and that." She smiles, but there's something like panic in her gaze. I'm a hound catching the first whiff of an interesting scent. I lean forward. She takes another little sip of breath, her nervousness like a drug to me. She smiles. "Things that might be useful for us to know."

"A birthmark is useful for you to know?"

Her bottom lip gets caught between her teeth, drawing my gaze. Beautiful lips. Maddening lips. I tear my gaze away from them and meet her eyes again, but they're blue as precious sapphires and filled with a delicious kind of fire.

She straightens. "There was a picture," she exclaims, like the thought just came to her. "Yes. A picture. Of you. Without a shirt on. I just noticed the birthmark, that's all."

She's an absolutely terrible liar.

I lean back. "There was a picture of me without my shirt on in my file at your sister's nanny agency?"

"It was...online," she amends. Her face brightens as the words come out of her mouth. "Yeah, that was it. I saw a picture online."

I arch a brow. I know she's lying, but I don't know why.

Bonnie nods vigorously. "Yep. I just saw a paparazzi photo of you, and I noticed the birthmark. That's how I knew. Forget what I said about the file. It was definitely a pap photo. I was confused." She huffs for emphasis, the pulse pounding in her neck, making me want to drag my knuckle over her quivering skin.

I curl my hands into fists. "Confused."

"Uh-huh!"

"You didn't seem confused."

"Oh, well, you know. I'm not the sharpest crayon in the box, as they say. I forget things. And then there was all that coffee this morning." She flicks her ponytail over her shoulder and smiles brightly at me, like she's trying to convince me that she's vapid and easily confused. "But I admit it. I cyber-stalked you. When I said it was the usual, I just meant it was the usual *for me*. It shouldn't reflect on the agency. It was my fault."

Bonnie's airhead act might work on someone else, but I've prided myself on my ability to read a person's character.

She doesn't strike me as stupid and easily confused. I saw her face when she met William. I heard the gears gnashing in her mind when she first walked into my living room. Something startled her so badly she needed to run to the bathroom to compose herself. This woman is hiding something from me—and I'm going to find out what it is.

Then a thought hits me. Is this related to the IPO? Our competitors, Nortley Inc., are racing to bring their solar panels to market before we do. Someone's been feeding them information about my company, and I thought I'd plugged the leak. Is this a new espionage attempt? It wouldn't be the first time they've tried to plant corporate spies in my midst, but a nanny would be a new low.

The timing is suspect. She'll have access to my home for the weeks before I take my company public. It makes more sense than my ex-wife coming out of the woodwork after I paid her so much money to leave me alone.

My frown seems to make her nervous. She wipes her palms on her legs, then wraps her fingers around each other like she's trying to stop herself from fidgeting. Her neck and chest have turned bright red.

She's nervous. Flustered.

A vision pops into my head—all that blushing skin laid out on my bed. Her blue eyes drugged with pleasure. Those fidgety hands twisting into my sheets.

If this is Nortley, they've done their homework. They've given me my own personal temptation come to life.

My lips curl into a smile. She sees it, and her eyes flare with heat.

I no longer want to keep her around because finding another nanny will be an inconvenience. Now I need to know why she thinks she can lie to me and get away with it. The only way to tease this secret out of her is to keep her very, very close.

If this woman has been sent by Nortley—or Alice—I intend to find the evidence and bury them so deep they'll never dare to challenge me again.

I make my decision and lean back in my chair, tenting my fingers in front of my chest. She shifts her weight and clears her throat.

No, I'm not going to request a new nanny. I'm going to keep this one. I'm going to move her into the first floor of my home, and

I'm going to extract every secret, uncover every lie, shine a light on every corner she's trying to darken.

Determination settles over me, relaxing all my muscles. "How did you end up working for your sister?"

Another flash of truth—and hurt—crosses her face before she hides it behind that infuriatingly bland smile. "Serendipity," she answers. "It just worked out. She's a great boss."

"Tell me the truth, Bonnie."

She starts, brows drawing together for a beat, then visibly relaxes, like she's willing her body to cooperate.

This woman is not stupid. I would put money on her being very, very intelligent. And for some reason, she's very, very skittish.

But *why*. Would Nortley really hire *her*?

For a brief moment, I see a real expression on her face. Some dark and twisted memory flashes in her gaze, and she lets out a long breath. "I needed the work," she admits quietly. "But I promise you, I'm good with children and I'll take care of William to the best of my abilities. My boss might be my sister, but she put me through the same rigorous training as everyone else who comes through her doors. I worked part-time for her for nearly ten years. This month will go smoothly, and your son will be taken care of. I promise."

That, I believe.

I nod and unlock the tablet in front of me once more. "Take a look at this picture." I turn the tablet.

Studying her face for any hint of reaction, I see no recognition when she looks at the screen. Her full bottom lip is drawn between her teeth again as she pulls the tablet closer, angling her head as she studies it.

The fabric of her shirt molds to her breasts before nipping in beneath her pleated skirt. A skirt that danced around her legs and clung to her thighs when she walked beside me. A skirt that would feel silky in my palm if I grasped a handful of fabric between my fingers and slid it up her long, lean thighs. A skirt that looks very, very good crumpled on the floor.

Blood flows south, and I wrestle myself back under control. Now is not the time for carnal thoughts. Not when I have so many questions about this woman. Not when she could be playing me.

But that's just it, isn't it? She's more than she seems. She's *intriguing*.

Tearing my gaze away from her lips, I stare at a spot on the wall. What the hell is wrong with me? I'm not interested in staff members. I don't lust after employees. I don't toe any kind of line that could be considered inappropriate. I'm not that kind of man.

Sex is impersonal. Transactional. It always has been.

Other than my mistake with Alice, when I thought I'd found that mirage called love, I haven't met a woman that I've wanted to spend more than a couple of hours with. I'm more than happy to keep things casual.

But that's not quite true, is it? There was one other time. One single night in London, when I was a different man.

I scowl, hating that memory too. "If this woman approaches you," I say, nodding at my ex-wife's face on the screen, "you're to stay away from her and leave the area immediately."

Her eyes grow wide. "Okay. Who is she?"

If this woman is a corporate spy, she's the perfect choice. A lesser man than me would be fooled by the doe-eyed act.

"This is Alice Noble. My ex-wife."

Bonnie straightens, then looks at the photo again. "Oh."

That was a genuine reaction. She doesn't know my ex-wife. I'm almost sure of it. My Nortley theory seems more and more likely.

Then Bonnie's eyes narrow. "Alice? As in, the Alice you asked me about just now?"

I ignore the question. "She's not legally allowed around Will other than supervised visitation, but she's been known to harass Alexandra and other staff members who are out with William. She hasn't bothered anyone in a couple of years, but I want you to be aware. Let me or one of the team know immediately if you see her."

"Is she dangerous?"

"She wouldn't hurt William."

Bonnie's gaze narrows. "That's not a no."

The corner of my lips twitches. I drop my gaze to the picture. "I don't think she's dangerous, no," I admit. "But she has tried to violate our custody agreement on multiple occasions in the past."

Bonnie nods, her lips bunching to the side. "I'm sorry you've had to deal with that."

I jerk back, frowning. "What?"

Her cheeks flush pink once more. "Oh, no, I mean... I'm sorry. I didn't mean to overstep. I just... My sister, Linda, she's divorced, and she had to go through the courts for custody, and I saw how difficult it was. I can only imagine how messy it must have been for you. That's all."

That's all, she says.

And yet she's one of very, very few people who have expressed that sentiment to me. Apart from one friend and my sister, anyone I've talked to about the divorce has reacted like my winning the messy custody battle four and a half years ago was a foregone conclusion.

It wasn't. I had to fight dirty. I'm not proud of myself.

But this woman—this oddly familiar woman—walked into my life, looked at me with those big blue eyes, and stared right into the very heart of me.

All the while, she's been hiding something.

We're out of balance. She can see right through me, but I have only questions when I look in her direction.

Shaken, I clear the gravel from my throat and stand. Time to end this conversation before I do something I'll regret. She'll be living just downstairs, and I'll have lots of time to figure out everything she's trying to keep from me.

I stick my hand out. "Good. Can you find your way back to Alex?"

"Of course," Bonnie says, and slides her palm against mine.

Her touch jolts through me, sizzling the blood in my veins until I'm scorched through. Our handshake lasts only a few seconds, but it rocks me.

I grip her palm before she can slide away. "Bonnie." I taste her name on my tongue. "I know you."

Her smile is tremulous. She blinks rapidly, then shrugs. "I get that all the time. I think I have one of those faces."

"One of those faces."

"Yeah. You know, kind of generic. And I'm not saying that to fish for compliments or anything, it's just a fact."

"Your face is not generic."

A gleam enters her eyes, a sharpness that wasn't there before. "No? Well, then don't you think you'd remember me if we'd met?" She flings her words at me like they're meant to cut.

I want to tug her close and feel her soften against my chest. I want to burrow my hands into her golden hair and feel its silkiness gripped in my fist. I want to find out why she thinks she can lie to me. "Yes, I think I would remember you."

Her lips twist. "Well, there you go. You don't."

I drop her hand, but the scorched feeling remains. "Let me know if you need anything."

"Will do," she replies, then slips out the door.

FOUR

BONNIE

AS I LEAVE the Lusso building in the early evening, I stand on the sidewalk, slightly thunderstruck that I still have a job.

The air is cool now, with the first bite of autumn entering the air. I zip up my leather jacket, fumbling with the fastener with sausage-like fingers. All day, I've felt unsteady.

I'm glad the soupy summer is ceding to cooler weather, and I don't have to stand here, drenched with sweat, feeling light-headed from the heat of the concrete around me. Not that the ground feels solid beneath my feet. I've been wobbly since I saw Arlo Noble's face more than six hours ago.

William is a little rogue and a darling, of course, and Alex is an amazing nanny. I also met the chef, the housekeeper, and two assistants. After my interlude in my boss's office, I didn't see him again, which was good for my overall health and mental stability.

I still remember the way he studied me, reading every reaction with an intensity that made me nervous enough to puke. I babbled like an idiot, and he didn't fire me. Why? I wouldn't trust me with my kid after a first impression like that, that's for sure. But I still have a job, which means I need to pack my bags and move into Arlo Noble's house tomorrow morning.

Wonderful.

Maybe Linda extolled my virtues when she told him I'd be Alex's replacement. Maybe he's desperate enough not to care that I acted like a skittish, idiotic weirdo.

Either way, I'm stuck. I have to keep working for him.

Numbly, I walk to the subway. When I'm about to descend the steps, my phone rings. Standing to the side, I pull it out of my purse.

"Hi, Nikki."

"Hey girl," my friend says. "Still down for salsa dancing tonight?"

I blink.

She must read the slight pause, because she lets out a dramatic huff. "You forgot, didn't you?"

"I've had a rough day."

"Girl, join the club." She snorts. "New plan: we meet up, have really strong margaritas at my place, complain about our lives, *then* we go salsa dancing. I'm almost home. You in?"

Glancing over my shoulder, I can just see a slice of the Lusso building poking out above the neighboring skyscrapers. "I'm in," I answer.

"Good. I'll have the tequila ready."

A little while later, when my head has just about stopped spinning, I show up at Nikki's apartment. She lives in a one-bedroom, one-bathroom place in Brooklyn. It's a rent-controlled apartment whose lease she inherited from her cousin years ago. As soon as Nikita lets me in, I'm assaulted by her maximalist decor. Her place is a riot of color and art and rugs and throw blankets and pillows. It's very her: warm and welcoming and loud.

It makes me miss my old home. I miss having a place of my own, a place that I could paint and decorate exactly how I liked.

"On the rocks, just how you like it." Nikita thrusts a margarita into my hands as soon as the door closes behind me. The salt rim is nice and thick, and judging by the smell of it, the tequila is plentiful.

I drop my bag on the floor. "You're a goddess."

Nikki grins. "Tell me something I don't know." She picks up her own glass, licking a bit of the salt off the rim. "Like, for example, what was so bad about your first day on the job? Is the kid a terror?"

"The kid is great. I need to finish this drink before I tell you."

"That bad, huh?"

I grimace. "Worse."

"Well, it can't be worse than my day. Remember how I told you the shop owner wanted to speak to me today, and I thought it was to make me an official buyer for the store?"

I nod. Nikki has worked at a vintage clothing store for ages. If she were to become a buyer, she'd spend her days sourcing all kinds of cool clothing for the shop. She'd be perfect for the position. Her style is sexy and classy and impeccable. She has long dark hair, which she often wears in pinup-inspired styles, and she loves a vampy red lip. The store she works at is her domain, and I've seen her in action. She is amazing at styling people and at selling clothes, and she's like a bloodhound in an overcrowded thrift store. The woman can spot gems from a mile away.

"Well, that didn't happen," she tells me, flopping onto her teal velvet tufted sofa. "I got fired instead."

"*What?*"

"Yep."

"Why?"

"They brought in an external consultant who determined I

was being paid too much, and it would be cheaper to fire me and get a replacement."

I slump down on the sofa next to her. "I'm sorry."

She sips her drink and leans her head back on the soft cushions. "Thanks. What about you? It can't be any worse than getting fired, can it?"

"Would you believe me if I said I was disappointed that I *didn't* get fired when I left work today?"

"No. Girl, you're broke. You can't afford to get fired."

I laugh. "I promise, it's true."

"Why? Is this Noble guy a creep?"

I close my eyes. The glass in my hands is cold against my fingers, condensation dampening my hands. I rest it on my leg, knowing it'll leave a wet spot on my skirt. "No," I admit.

"So what is it?"

I open my eyes and stare at the ceiling. "Do you remember that guy in London?"

Nikki snorts. "Mr. Sexalicious? How could I forget? You've been pining after him for years, Bonnie. I keep trying to tell you, it's unhealthy. No one is that good in bed. Your brain is lying to you."

"I have not been pining," I lie.

"Right." She slurps her drink. "What about him?"

I take a big gulp of margarita, then meet Nikki's gaze. "It's him."

Confusion draws her dark brows together. "What's him?"

"Arlo Noble is him. My new boss is Mr. Sexalicious."

Nikita blinks about a dozen times. She sips her drink. Swallows. Puts her glass down on the vintage coffee table, on top of a coaster with a delicate floral design. Then her lips twitch.

"Don't you dare laugh."

"I'm not," she protests, but her lips quiver again.

"It's not funny."

"I never said it was."

"You're laughing!"

"Am not!" She giggles. "I promise."

I groan, slapping a hand over my forehead. "You want to hear the worst part?"

"What, he didn't ravage you on sight like you've been dreaming about every day for three years?"

I meet her gaze. "Nikki, he didn't even remember me."

Her eyes widen. She puts a hand to her mouth, her dark-red nails touching her upper lip. "Oh, Bonnie."

"No," I tell her. "We're not doing this. You're not going to look at me with pity in your eyes. I can't handle it."

Her lips curl ever so slightly behind her fingers. "It's not pity."

I groan, putting my drink down next to hers and burying my face in my hands. "That's not even the worst part," I admit, and I tell her about the interlude in William's playroom, when I unfortunately lost my skirt and mooned my boss.

Nikita loses the fight against laughter. She clutches a pillow to her stomach and falls to her side on the sofa. Tears stream down her cheeks, messing up her perfect winged eyeliner, which she fully deserves because her traitorous glee isn't helping my situation.

But soon, I find myself laughing too. "I am never wearing a skirt again," I declare, slashing my hand across the air for emphasis. "Pants and shorts only."

"Really? What if he suddenly remembers you and decides he wants to ravage you? Wouldn't you want something with easy access?"

"No. *No*," I say. I had a workplace romance before, and look how that ended. I'm not doing it again. "I'll be wearing shapeless sack dresses from now on."

"Mm-hmm."

"With granny panties. And leggings. And a chastity belt. With the key thrown away."

She tilts her head, reading me like only Nikki can. The thing about Nikki is she's crazy smart. We met five years ago, when I had to save myself from a creepy client at a cocktail bar. I swooped over to her table, where she sat with her friend Penny, and the two of them pretended to be my long-lost besties. The creep was dispatched, and I met two of the very few girlfriends that survived the implosion of my life.

Nikita and I grew close over the years that passed, since we're the only two in our friend group without kids. And I learned a few things about her. She's hyper-perceptive, very intelligent, and so stylish it almost hurts to look at her. Sometimes I think she uses her fashion sense as armor, because people—and by people, I mean men—dismiss her as a frivolous birdbrain because she wears pretty, retro dresses and she does her hair with more skill than a whole army of hairdressers could muster.

But since I've known her, she's taught herself to be conversant in Spanish in her free time. She helped the owner of the clothing store she manages expand to two more locations and more than tripled his business. She even completed a management course in the evenings. I don't know how she found the time for it all. Nikki has a brain like a steel trap.

And she's looking at me like I'm a two-year-old trying to pull one over on her. Like I have chocolate ice cream smeared all over my face and chest, and I'm telling her I don't know who ate all the Häagen-Dazs.

I go for outraged innocence. "What?"

"He was hot for you."

Rearing back, I let out a snort. "Excuse me?"

"I can see it in your face."

"You can see in *my* face how *he* felt about me."

She nods. "Yep."

"That's ridiculous."

"He pulled you into his office and gave you some inane talk about his ex-wife, but I bet the whole time he was undressing you with his eyes."

"Well, there was no need to do that, because I'd already dropped my skirt five minutes earlier."

"He was hot for you, and you find it thrilling, and now you don't know what to do."

"He literally forgot I existed after we hooked up. I do *not* find it thrilling. The last thing I want is to be forgotten again. Plus, he's my boss."

"Hmm."

"Hmm? What does *hmm* mean?"

"Are you going to sleep with him?"

"Excuse me?" I repeat. My outrage reaches a new peak.

"It's a simple question."

"It is *not*."

"Bonnie, this is Mr. Sexalicious. He made you orgasm so hard, you literally have brain damage from it."

I drop my head in my hands. "This is a disaster." I'm mortified. I'm so embarrassed, every inch of my skin feels hot. He didn't even remember me.

The worst part of this whole ordeal is that the night I spent with Arlo, he kept telling me how beautiful I was. Every part of my body was praised that night, even the soft parts, the stretch mark-covered parts, the parts that I don't particularly love in myself. He was so sincere that I believed him—and I carried those compliments in my heart like little treasures. For three years, I unwrapped those memories like they were precious gems, bringing them out into the light every so often to cheer myself up. He made me feel like a goddess.

And they were all lies, because he didn't even remember me.

I speak into the hands covering my face: "I'm not going to sleep with him, even though he's really hot."

"Okay."

I peek through my fingers at her. "What do you mean, okay?"

"I mean, okay, you won't sleep with him. That's probably wise." She checks her nails, then frowns at me. "What if he was faking it?"

"Faking what?"

"Forgetting you."

"He wasn't, trust me." I think of the blank look on his face when I walked in. The baffled, frustrated way he studied me in his office. "He thought I was familiar, but that was it. And he also thinks I'm an idiot who cyber-stalked him and memorized the position of his birthmark."

"And yet, he's keeping you close. He's not firing you."

"Maybe he'll fire me tomorrow." I don't know if I'm hopeful or despondent.

"Maybe," Nikki agrees. "But I don't think so."

"I have to *move in with him.*" I groan. "What am I going to do?"

She slugs her margarita. "You could have sex with him."

I whip my head around. "What? No."

"I bet the reality doesn't live up to the fantasy you've created. If you have sex with him, you can move on once and for all. And then you can both forget about each other."

"I'm not going to sleep with him. I *work* for him."

"Right."

"Right."

She bunches her lips to the side. "So you're just going to keep pretending you've never met him?"

"Yep. For one entire month. And then I'll take my money and start fresh."

And right now, my only prospect at a fresh start—and at preventing total destitution—is Arlo Noble.

"We never slept together." I say it out loud as if it'll make it true. "There's no attraction between us. He's my boss, and I'm filling in for his permanent nanny for one month. That's it."

"Mm-hmm."

I glare at my friend. "Are we going dancing or what?"

She grins. "We're going dancing."

We finish our drinks and slip on our salsa shoes. Since I came straight from work, I have to borrow a pair of Nikki's shoes, which have a higher heel than I usually wear. I tie the ankle strap over my vertical surgery scar then stand up, putting a bit of weight on the leg. It feels okay, so I test out a few salsa steps.

"Are those too high?" Nikki frowns at my ankle. "I don't want to flare up your injury."

"It's fine," I answer. "I need to dance off my nerves anyway."

"We can stop at your place for some shoes. Or you can wear your sneakers."

"No, I want this," I say, clicking over to where I dropped my bag. "Salsa never feels the same without some sort of heel on. And I need to let loose tonight."

Her dark brows are drawn, but she gives me a nod. Nikki is perceptive, but she respects independence. "Okay. Let's go dance, then."

It's only much later, when my ankle is killing me as I kick off Nikki's heels, that I regret my decision. But my body is deliciously loose, and my skin is covered in perspiration, and I feel like I've danced off the worst of my jitters. When I step into the shower to wash the sweat and alcohol from my skin, I finally let my thoughts drift to tomorrow.

Tomorrow, I'm moving into a penthouse in the Lusso building. I'm packing up the scraps of my life and carrying them into Arlo Noble's world.

All I have to do is forget that we ever slept together...and pretend I don't want to do it again.

FIVE

ARLO

I STARE AT MY PHONE, seeing nothing. Alex is with Will in the playroom, but I'm far too antsy to go to my son. Emails ping one after the other on my phone, relentless.

My career as an entrepreneur began over twenty years ago. My partner and I developed a component for cell phones that increased their range and made cell service more reliable. He and I went to college together; he was the engineer working out the specifics, and I was the business guy. Money came at us like a tidal wave in those days, so much I couldn't even comprehend it.

Since then, I've started and sold over a dozen companies. I've invested in even more startups as an angel investor. That's what I love—the spark. That first, initial, genius idea that needs to be massaged and developed and tested. I like the snarls that come up when you're not quite sure if a product is viable. I like seeing a mountain rise up before me, knowing I can make it to the top if I just take it one step at a time.

My latest venture is in a new breed of solar cells that are thinner and more efficient than current photovoltaics on the market. We recently fixed a snag with fragility—the substrate material tore too easily to make the product viable—but the engineers have fixed the design, and we're ready to take it to market. It's exciting, groundbreaking, potentially fortune-making work.

Taking the company public in a month is nearly the tip of the mountain for me; when I get to that point, I've made it. I'll steer the company for the next couple of years, then hand it off to a successor. Then I'll move on to the next business. Or, who knows? Maybe I'll retire.

Because apart from starting businesses, I've been expanding the Noble Foundation. As I've ramped down business ventures to only projects I care about, I've ramped up philanthropy. I should be happy about it; snarls and red tape are plentiful in this world too. My foundation is led by a fearsome woman called Wanda, who's planning the gala and silent auction that should provide an influx of donations for a local children's hospital.

I should be reaching out to local politicians and reading up on health care policy. I should be reviewing the grant applications piling up on my virtual desk. I should be reading the slew of emails from lawyers and finance departments.

But I'm staring at the clock, waiting for *her*.

After my meeting with Bonnie, I contacted my private investigator. He sent me a report last night with general background information. He found nothing incriminating. She's college educated. She worked at her sister's company to put herself through school, graduating in finance. She got an MBA. She worked on Wall Street. Now she's back to working for her sister.

Maybe childcare is a passion? She tried something else and discovered she preferred working with kids?

The investigator is looking into what happened to make her leave her job. We're reviewing her finances and digging into her family history. I need to know everything about her. I need to find her connection to Nortley, if it exists.

And if she's here for Alice, I'll find that out too. And I'll crush them both.

One of the things that makes me so good at starting companies is my need to find answers to questions even when others would abandon the chase. Presented with a problem, an unbearable itch will form under my skin until I can solve it.

And Bonnie is a problem.

Her familiarity. Her sass. Her hidden little lies that reveal themselves with every panicked, frazzled glance.

Until I know what she's hiding from me, I'm not letting her out of my sight.

I hear William shriek in his playroom. Alex murmurs something. My blood pounds in my ears. Laura's here, somewhere, making my life easier. Fernando is probably waiting in the car, knowing I could call him any minute to take me somewhere. Steve, my chef, will be arriving soon to prep the next three days' worth of meals for me and the rest of the household.

I should be working. Everyone else in this house is working. I should be one of them.

The whole reason I hired Bonnie was so I could put all my attention on the IPO.

Before I know what I'm doing, I stand and head for the elevator lobby on the second floor of my residence, just around the corner from where I'm sitting. The doors are closed, which means my private elevator has been called to the lobby.

She's almost here, and she'll be sent to the 129th floor, which is the first floor of my penthouse. I arrow toward the stairs. I take them two at a time, heading for the lower foyer.

"Sir," Laura exclaims, appearing in the doorway to her office. "Can I help you with something?"

"Clear my schedule for the week," I tell her. "I'm going to be working from home."

She blinks. It's a surprise, because up until today, I've been spending all my time at the office. I *should* be spending all my time at the office. But Laura has worked for me for a long time. She nods. "No problem."

"And talk to Alex about her plan for training Bonnie. I'd like a clear program for the week in my inbox by noon."

"Of course." She nods, taking a step toward the stairs. Then she glances at the elevator bank, and I know she's thinking of Bonnie.

I fold my arms. Usually that's enough to get people to do my bidding. Laura isn't intimidated by me—not the way a lot of employees are—but she still draws her brows together and gives me a furtive nod before disappearing behind me in search of Alex.

A moment later, the elevator doors open.

Arms still crossed, I meet a startled Bonnie's gaze. She blinks at me, gripping the handles of two rolling suitcases, her blond hair tied back in a ponytail I'd kill to pull apart. I bet her hair feels like silk. I bet it smells like sweet vanilla cupcakes.

I could wrap a fist around her ponytail and pull her neck tight. I bet she'd tremble if I ran my lips along the line of her pulse. She'd whimper and melt for me.

She's wearing a black dress that hides every curve. It covers her from neck to knee, and the shapeless sack somehow makes my blood heat, like her trying to hide herself beneath it only makes me want her more.

"Arlo," she breathes, and my name sounds so sweet on her lips I nearly groan. "Good morning." Her voice is raspy, a touch hoarse this early.

This is madness. I should turn around and walk away. Why am I here? I have an empire to run. I have a legion of lawyers and employees who need my input for any number of different tasks. My foundation is planning the biggest event of its history. My son is upstairs. There are a million things that should be demanding my attention right now, and none of them are Bonnie.

My feet carry me forward, until I'm standing in the elevator doorway. I curl my fingers around the handle of one of her suitcases, the edge of my index finger brushing hers. She sips in a tight little breath and lets go of the handle.

In the small space, her scent crowds me, attacking my faulty memory like a swarm of angry bees. Maybe it isn't memory. Maybe it's just arousal. Maybe it's anger at not knowing why she's lying to me. Not knowing what I'm missing. Not understanding why her presence does this to me.

"This way," I grate out, tugging the suitcase out of the elevator and turning my back on her, if only to escape the maddening influence of her gaze.

SIX

BONNIE

MY HEART STUTTERS as I follow my boss down the wide, timber-floored hallway. There's artwork on the walls, photos of abstract shapes and vague portraits. We walk through a kitchen that I suppose is meant to be small and spartan but is actually bigger than my entire last apartment.

This bottom floor isn't as opulent as the floor above, but it's still gorgeous. We turn right out of the galley kitchen and walk down another hallway. Laura said it was for guests, but I also spy a gym and a theater on our way to the far end of the floor, where we finally stop in front of a bedroom.

Arlo strides straight in, like he owns the place. Which, *duh*. He sets my suitcase upright and clicks the handle down into its slot. Then he plants his hands on his hips and glares at me.

Not wanting to meet his gaze, I scan my new bedroom.

The room is amazing. Of course. How could it not be? The bed is a four-poster thing straight out of my dreams. The posts are square and painted black, and the headboard has vertical slats. It's all very geometric and masculine, softened by the luxurious bedding. The sheets are a soft dove gray, and the duvet looks like I could face plant into it and land in heaven.

That is a dangerous feeling.

Big windows silhouette Arlo, framed with pale blue curtains. To my left, I spy a walk-through closet that leads to an en suite bathroom. I don't even need to face plant anywhere; I know I'm in heaven. This is heaven. I get to live in this place for a whole month.

Giddy, I let my gaze drift back to the big man scowling at me, and I almost manage to forget that his fingers felt freaking amazing when they were pumping inside me three years ago. "Well," I say, feeling the word vomit coming already, "I've never had a billionaire as a bellboy before. How much should I tip you? A cool half a mil?"

His gaze is steady, unruffled. He looms at the foot of the bed, and my whole body tingles. It shouldn't be affecting me this much. I promised myself I'd resist his pull. I was so sure I'd be able to do it—until the elevator doors opened and I saw him standing there.

I mean, honestly. It was one night. I can't believe I even remember it in such vivid detail. It was just sex.

But it was so much *more*.

"You're hiding something from me," he declares.

Ha. I bat my eyelashes. "Am I?"

"Don't get fresh with me."

"I'm not fresh," I promise. "I'm stale. I'm the stalest bread you could imagine. Stale white bread, not even good for French toast."

He takes a step toward me, and I feel it in my nipples. This has got to stop. He's not even that hot.

Okay—that's a total lie. He is that hot. And this whole menacing, mysterious, suspicious thing is really getting me going right now. I can feel his energy boiling in the air between us, trying to swallow me whole. It's so violent and masculine and powerful that

I feel like I would do anything he asked me right now. I would drop to my knees and service him if he said so. I would lie back on the bed and let him do what he wanted with me. I would beg for it. I am absolutely feral for him, and when he looks at me with those dark, dangerous eyes, I can't even be mad at myself for it.

It's an unspeakably bad situation to be in, because he one hundred and twenty percent does not feel the same way. Or if he does, it's not because he's reminiscing about our first time together, overcome with joyful lust that we're finally reunited. That's purely a *me* problem.

That night we met, I was in London for my company's annual business conference. It was hosted by the hedge fund for which I worked, but attended by lots of bigwigs in the finance world. I had to be *on*, fully, all the time. It was exhausting. That day, I'd screwed up with one of the European powerbrokers, got their name mixed up with one of their competitors. A small thing, maybe, but it felt like a really big misstep.

I'd slipped away to the hotel bar for a self-pity drink that turned into three, and Arlo arrived when I'd ordered my fourth. I didn't know he was Arlo at the time, but he sat two stools down from me, pretending he hadn't chosen that stool exactly because it was two stools down from me.

I spoke first. I remember every second of it. I said, "I like a man who's not afraid to take a risk with his socks," because he'd been wearing a black shirt, black pants, black tie, and black leather belt, but his socks were a pink paisley pattern.

Today, his socks are navy. He's not wearing any shoes. That makes my nipples feel oversensitive all over again, which is further proof that I've lost my mind.

He takes another step closer, and I retreat until my back hits the corner of the four-poster bed. The edge of the wood digs into my spine as he prowls closer, eyes like black fire.

"The only reason I haven't fired you is because I haven't figured out what you're hiding," he says.

"Oh. Goody."

He crowds closer, and he smells freaking divine. It goes straight to my head, then that feeling dive-bombs between my legs. I'm being clobbered with arousal for this man, and I absolutely do not want to be. All I want to do is work this month, help my sister, make enough money to secure a soft landing when I get out of the city, and forget all about the billionaire in front of me.

I chant Nikki's words in my head: The reality won't live up to the fantasy. It can't. It's impossible.

My breaths are shallow. It's all I can manage right now. He takes another step, and the space between us is alive. I meet his gaze. "If you think I'm so evil, why are you trusting me with your son?"

"Because you work for the Delmar Agency, your background check came back clean, and I'm not letting an unanswered question walk out of here." His eyes drop to my lips then climb back up to my eyes. His gaze causes heat to unfurl behind my bellybutton. "And because until I figure out what you're hiding, I'm not letting you out of my sight."

"Oh." Not the cleverest answer, I know. But two little letters are all I can manage when he's this close to me.

It's almost a relief that his presence is as powerful as I remember. What if I'd made it all up? What if I'd met him again, and it was ho-hum? The past three years would have been a lie. I would've been judging perfectly adequate men against a fantasy yardstick.

But it's also awful that he's living up to the memory, because I have to spend a month with him. Because he's here, in the flesh, and I want him so badly my body hums with need for him. Because he doesn't remember me.

I am so pathetic. So utterly pitiful, it's not even funny. He can never know that he has this impact on me. Never, ever, ever.

I believe him that he'll figure out what I'm hiding, if I let him. I can sense the determination pulsing off him, a hint of it at the edge of that wall of energy that surrounds him. He'll figure it out, and it'll be humiliating.

I can't let it happen.

A breath fills my lungs, and I use it to build up my walls. I slide a stupid smile over my face and make myself look bland and professional. I'm a good, qualified nanny. I'm here to take care of his kid. Nothing more, nothing less.

A frown draws his brows together. That hot, boiling energy recedes ever so slightly as he rocks back on his heels. I can still smell him, so I take only the shallowest breaths.

"I'll leave you to unpack. Alex will talk to you about the schedule for the week upstairs when you're ready."

When he walks out the door and his steps disappear down the hall, I fall backwards onto the bed, arms out, heart thumping. My body is a wet noodle. My legs aren't functional.

I am in so much trouble.

SEVEN
BONNIE

UPSTAIRS, I find Alex in the grand living room with William. He's kneeling at the coffee table by the armchairs in the corner, trying to write his name in wobbly block letters.

"Good job!" Alex coos. "Your 'W' looks so good."

"How do you spell your name?" he asks, marker poised above a blank sheet of paper, gripped awkwardly in his fist.

I come closer. "Hi," I say, giving her a little wave. The redness in my cheeks has receded, and I feel almost human.

While I was unpacking, I had a serious talk with myself and reaffirmed that I can never tell Arlo how we met. No matter how hard he scowls at me or how intensely his forcefield of energy presses against me, I just can't go through with that humiliation.

I played the situation out in my mind as I hung up my clothes. He'd realize who I was. It would take him a while, because a one-night stand three years ago is obviously a minuscule blip in his past. If it finally came to him, he'd be surprised, then pitying. He'd know that I knew. And I'd know that he knew that I knew. And it would be mortifying.

When my career collapsed, I had a whole lifetime's worth of embarrassment and shame heaped onto me. I can't handle any more.

So, I can't let Arlo know about our night together. Simple as that. It just won't happen.

And, really, I think I can do it. Sure, he's hot. So what? Lots of men are hot. It doesn't mean I'll melt into a puddle of hormones like a horny Wicked Witch of the West whenever one of them comes near me. I'm better than that.

"Laura told me you were here," Alex smiles. "Do you want coffee? There's some in the kitchen." She points her chin toward the hallway leading to Will's room and the office. "Last door on the right. After that, we can start running through this guy's schedule, can't we?" The last two words she says to William, who nods absentmindedly as he writes his name again, tongue sticking out of the corner of his mouth.

"Okay," I say. "You want one?"

She puts her hand over her stomach. "Can't," she says. "Thanks, though."

"I'll be back in a sec." I duck down the hallway and find the last door on the right, then step through into the main kitchen.

This one is grander than the one downstairs, a huge room with a big island in the middle. The cabinets are dark blue with sleek silver hardware. The fridge is built-in, hidden behind its own dark-blue cabinet, so the whole kitchen looks elegant and refined. It's almost strange to see a kitchen that's just a kitchen. Most homes these days are open plan, but this residence has the kitchen tucked away at the back.

I guess wealthy people have staff to do their cooking for them, and they don't want the staff out in the open.

There's a long booth seat in the opposite corner, with a little breakfast nook boasting a single carnation in an elegant vase.

The island is topped with a huge slab of marble, with a chandelier glittering above. Velvet-upholstered seats line the island's overhang, with neatly folded newspapers set on a silver tray. Literal newspapers on a literal silver tray. Wow.

Arlo is seated at one of those seats, and he looks up when I enter. His dark gaze hits me like a rocket right between the legs, so I erect my best rocket-blocking shields and give him a slight nod.

"Alex said there was coffee," I explain.

"You sure you can handle it?" The words are a low growl that rumbles over my skin. They sound dirty, and they totally shouldn't.

I'm blushing already. Dang it. "I sure can," I answer brightly.

He leans back on his tall chair, stretching an arm across the top of the next seat over. He did that when we met at the bar. The stools had these little curved backs, and he stretched his arm out toward me, his hand dangling in space between us. I stared at his hand that night. Big, rugged knuckles. Broad palm. Long fingers.

But not anymore! I'm a new woman. I have shields. I don't get turned on by hands like some depraved, wanton, desperate ninny.

I pour coffee into a mug I find above the coffee machine, then turn while lifting the carafe. "Top-up?"

He dips his chin, a silent nod. Because billionaire bosses don't need to use words to make their desires known.

Maybe the more time I spend with him, the more my lust will fade. His whole arrogant, brooding schtick is kind of annoying.

I pour the coffee into his mug, feeling his gaze on my face, my neck. Beneath my shapeless sack of a dress, my body heats.

I'm going to need to work on that. Maybe I can hide ice packs down my underwear.

Pretending I'm utterly unaffected, I put the coffee pot back and head for the fridge. I find the half-and-half in the door and the honey beside the coffee pot, and I plonk the two containers down beside his mug.

Then I freeze.

He stares at the cream and honey, then lifts his gaze up to me. "You know how I take my coffee." It's not a question.

I bat my lashes and tilt my head, like I'm confused. Meanwhile, my mind whirls.

Because yes, I know how he takes his coffee. That night, after our first romp in his hotel room, he called room service and specifically asked for half-and-half and honey. They forgot the honey, bringing sugar instead, and when they finally returned with the right items, they knocked on the door right when I had my legs spread and his face was occupied with things other than drinking coffee.

Then we used up the entire little pot of honey, and only a tiny dollop of it made it into his mug.

"Sorry?" I say, blinking. Maybe I can blink my way out of this. Blink, blink, blink.

"You know how I take my coffee," he repeats. He leans forward, those long fingers wrapping around the honey pot. It has one of those wooden honey dippers with horizontal lines on it, fitted into a slot in the lid for that exact purpose. He takes the lid off and lifts the dripper out of the pot, then we both watch the honey run down in ribbons. "And don't say it was in my file, because I'll know that's a lie."

"How would you know it's a lie?" I ask to buy myself a few seconds.

He drizzles honey into his mug, and my heart thunders. I remember him drizzling honey onto my breasts. I remember it like it happened ten minutes ago. The rasp of his tongue. The possessiveness in his hands. Oh, no, no, no. I don't think I can do this for an entire month.

His eyes lift to mine. He's doing that non-speaking thing again, and I know it's to pressure me to fill the silence.

And damn him, because it works. I scrabble for an explanation that doesn't involve a night of wanton sex and my nipples in his mouth. "I saw the honey on the counter right beside the coffee machine, like it was there for that exact purpose," I explain in a rush. "And when I topped you up, I saw the color of what was left in your mug. It looked like milk or cream." I wave a hand, flicking away his concerns. "I used my amazing powers of deduction."

A hum vibrates through his throat. My hands tremble as I put a drop of cream in my coffee, then wait for him to do the same. I feel his eyes on me as I place it back in the refrigerator.

Clouds of cream drift through my mug, and I use a spoon to dispel them. Then I take a sip and give him a smile. "Alex needs me," I say, then I float through the kitchen door, like my heart isn't pounding so hard I can't even hear myself think.

As soon as I'm through the door, my floating turns to scurrying, and I head back to the living room without looking back.

THE DAY PASSES QUICKLY. Alex is an amazing nanny who obviously cares deeply for William. She tells me how excited she is for her own baby girl. We bond over working for the Delmar Agency, and I tell her about all the years I was a part-timer at the daycare Linda runs, and how I'd fill in while I was putting myself through college. She loves Linda—which, of course she does. Everyone loves Linda. Linda is the firm, loving mother who makes you feel like you can do anything.

I know, because she did that for me. She built me up so high, I thought I deserved all the success I had.

And now I'm here, at the bottom. Starting over. Floundering. Again.

At the end of the day, we get Will ready for bed together. He chooses his Batman pajamas and tells us a story involving a pigeon and an accordion player in the park, which makes no sense but is still very entertaining. Alex smiles as she sits on the bed beside him. I can tell she's exhausted. I can't believe she's still working when she's about to give birth. When Will's in bed and his father is reading him a bedtime story, Alex gives me a hug and a bright smile and leaves for the night.

Apparently, Arlo put her and her husband up in an apartment on the fifth floor of the building when she first started working for him. Perk of the job.

"He told me he tried to get another apartment in the building, but none were available. That's why you have to stay on the first floor."

I think about that gorgeous bedroom. "Could be worse."

She grins. "See you tomorrow!"

When she disappears behind the elevator doors, I wander to the staff kitchen. Steve, the chef, stocked it with the basics, and Laura showed me where the household's virtual grocery list is kept on the cloud, so I can add anything that might be missing.

With practically no expenses this month, I could really get my feet back under me. *And* I'm helping out my sister, who's always had my back. I really can't mess this up.

"I was going to ask you if you wanted me to order you something, but I see you have everything under control."

The knife I'd been using to slice half an onion freezes. I glance sideways and see Arlo leaning against the wall at the opening of the galley kitchen. He changed into a dark-green tee that makes his skin look very lickable. Or it would, if I were interested in licking him. Which I'm not.

"I'm making a stir-fry," I tell him, returning to the onion. "You want some?" The words slip out before I can stop them, and I cringe. I glance at him again. "But you can't judge my cooking. Those are the rules."

He pushes off the wall and comes closer, inspecting my knife skills. I can smell him under the bite of the onion tickling my nose. "Last I checked," he says in a low rumble, "this is my house. Who said you can make any rules?"

"This might be your house," I say, "but for the next half hour, this is my kitchen."

He grins, revealing long dimples on either cheek. I want to touch them with the tips of my fingers, feel the rasp of his stubble against my skin.

Heart fluttering, I turn back to the onion and shove it to the corner of the cutting board in a neat pile. I grab a mushroom and start slicing that under his watchful eye.

He backs away slightly, leaning against the counter on the opposite side of the stove. I can breathe again. His hands curl around the edge of the counter, long legs stretching out before him. "How did it go today? William seemed happy."

I can't help my smile. "He's a great kid." I finish the mushroom and make a neat pile of that too, and then I grab a few snow peas from the fridge. "I'm not just saying that because he's your son, either," I add, cutting the stems off the peas.

A huff from the other side of the stove. "Good to hear. Wouldn't want you to say anything nice about me."

"I'm doing you a service, really," I say, trying to hide my smile. "Flattery would only inflate your ego."

"And it's already so big."

"Exactly." I slice the last stem with a decisive chop, then make a neat stack of snow peas. Next is the red pepper.

Arlo pushes himself off the counter in a smooth, controlled move and heads to the wine rack on the opposite side of the galley kitchen. He pulls out one of the two bottles stacked in the grate, frowning at the label. Then he puts it back and stalks out of the kitchen.

Curious, I peek around the corner and see him disappear down the opposite end of the hallway from where the elevators are. He pokes at a little beeping control panel on the wall and disappears. I really shouldn't follow, and if I were a cat, I would be so dead right now. But I leave the knife on the counter and follow him down, coming to a stop in front of an enormous wine cellar. I lean on my good leg, because after so much time on my feet today, my ankle is starting to throb.

I knew I shouldn't have worn Nikki's heels last night.

I can see Arlo through the glass door, crouching down in front of a rack filled with bottles. He grabs a bottle of red and looks at the label. Then he touches his chest, and his head, like he's patting his pocket for something. I watch him shake his head slightly, then frown at the bottle. He stands.

It's too late to run away—he'll see me in the hallway before I get to the kitchen—so I just smile and wave like a dork when he meets my gaze through the glass. The door opens in a gust of cool air, then locks behind him. He lifts the bottle. "This is better than what you have in your kitchen."

"I'll have to take your word for it," I tell him, heading back to my abandoned stir-fry.

"Not a wine drinker?"

I glance over my shoulder, catching his gaze lifting from the general vicinity of my butt, which is crazy, because I'm wearing a sheath dress that reveals exactly zero curves. I give him a bright smile. "Let's just say I don't have a wine room with a keypad lock in my apartment."

I try to hide my limp, even though pain is pulsing up the side of my ankle. I should have just worn my sneakers last night. I don't usually dance that hard, but I was so strung out that I danced for hours. Now I'm paying the price—and it's reminding me of the very first time I lost everything and had to start back at zero. My life has been one long game of Snakes and Ladders. Just when I start to feel like my life is coming together, when I'm climbing the rungs and getting somewhere, I land on a snake and slide right down to the beginning again.

But I've done it twice, haven't I? I can do it again. Scratch that —I'm *doing* it again.

And an old college sports injury isn't going to stop me now. The memory of my failed finance career won't stop me either. I do my best to hide my limp, feeling Arlo's eyes on me the whole way.

He finds two glasses while I pull out a wok from one of the cupboards. I check the rice cooker and see there's still a few minutes before it's ready, so I don't start cooking just yet. Stir-fries come together really quickly.

I accept a glass from him and take a sip, knowing he's studying my reaction. "It's good," I say.

"You hate it."

I laugh, and he gives me a strange, scowly look. Does he remember my laugh from three years ago? How does he read me so easily? "I don't hate it. I'm just not much of a wine drinker."

"What do you drink?"

I can't tell him that I like Moscow mules best, because that's what I was drinking that night. We talked about the copper cup they were served in, about how the tradition of serving the drink in that vessel began as a marketing campaign. Two friends were trying to sell vodka and ginger beer, and the copper cup became the iconic receptacle to go with it. It was a memorable conversation—to me, at least. Everything about that night was memorable.

The fewer hints I give Arlo about myself, the better. We were only together for a night, but we talked. We screwed. We even cuddled. Sure, we were both tipsy. He even bumped into walls and a table, so I know he wasn't totally sober, but I can't take the risk of him remembering. I can't take the embarrassment.

"More of a beer girl," I tell him.

His scowl becomes scowlier. "I don't quite believe that either."

I click my tongue and roll my eyes, amping up the drama. "Of course you don't. Mr. Suspicious."

His lips kick, and he takes a sip of his wine. He holds the glass by the stem, a delicate touch from those powerful hands. I blink and check the rice cooker again. The timer's counting down, and I think I can start the stir-fry now.

While I throw it together, Arlo approaches, the heat of his chest an inferno next to my shoulder. He watches me, intent, then accepts a steaming bowl of food with a nod and a rumbled, "Thank you." We eat sitting on either side of the small peninsula at the other end of the kitchen, and Arlo points his fork at the food. "It's good," he says, which pleases me more than it should.

"Thanks."

"I'll have to cook for you next time." He takes another bite, and my stomach dances a little jig.

"You can cook?" I squeeze out between bites.

He blinks, lifting his gaze to mine. "You don't believe me?"

I point my fork at him, his body. "You're...you. Billionaires don't cook."

"What do you know about billionaires?"

"I know they have locked wine rooms and three-story penthouses."

He arches a brow and takes another bite. Swallows. "I can cook."

"I'll believe it when I see it." I'm being sassy. I'm being myself. I need to stop that. Bonnie the bland nanny isn't sassy. She's professional and aloof and a little bit boring. She's forgettable.

Then again, I'm forgettable too, aren't I?

But here I am, eating dinner with my boss, breaking my own rules, being myself, staring at my bowl of food while wanting to vault over the counter and land on his cock.

Maybe that's what makes me want to play with fire—the feeling that everything is spinning out of control and the question that comes out of my mouth is a natural response to this swirly, swooping feeling inside me. "Have you figured out what I'm hiding yet?"

He puts his bowl down. Our eyes meet. He stands.

My heart forgets how to do its job, then tries to make up for it by beating twice as hard. He circles the end of the peninsula, takes the bowl out of my hands, and spins me around so my back is to the counter. His hands land on the counter on either side of me, his face leaning in only inches from mine.

I'm trembling, I realize. Trembling with lust and nerves and danger. His face moves closer, the heat of him burning my cheek as his lips move closer to my temple.

"No, but I will," he says, breath ghosting over the shell of my ear. "Do you believe me?"

No part of him is touching any part of me, but I feel him everywhere. In my fingertips. My thighs. The backs of my knees.

I'm not even playing with fire right now; I'm reveling in it. Burning up all the way to my toes, laughing and dancing in the feeling. A little gasp escapes my lips, and I wonder if he can see the pulse pounding in my neck. I can sure feel it, thumping away, doing its best to help me pass out.

"Have you considered the possibility that I'm not hiding anything?" I whisper. It wasn't supposed to come out as a whisper, but it does. Breathy and raspy and totally transparent. He probably knows how wet my panties are.

Arlo straightens, taking his heat with him. He stands in front of me for a beat, watching me, then reaches over and grabs his bowl. He finishes his food, puts the bowl in the dishwasher, and wipes his hands on a tea towel. "Thanks for dinner, Bonnie," he says, and then he walks away and disappears into his upper-story lair.

I manage to finish my own dinner, and then I retreat to my bedroom. I stare at the ceiling, heart still not working right, wondering if I've misjudged how big a mistake it was to take this job.

Because this man couldn't just embarrass and mortify me. He could completely destroy me.

EIGHT
ARLO

IT WAS a mistake to go down there. My feet carried me to where I knew Bonnie was, as if I could tease the threads of my memory out of hiding. Watching her cook in that tiny kitchen didn't help. It made me ache for everything I thought I had with Alice but was only an illusion.

All the money in the world is at my fingertips, but something is always lacking. I'm closer to being whole when I spend time with my son, but I crave more meaning. Fulfillment. A humble meal at a kitchen counter settled my heart more than my last dozen dates and my last hundred business deals.

It's Bonnie. It's her sly gaze and the arch of her brows. It's the slope of her nose and the way she leans on one leg when she's standing in one spot. It's the feeling that I know her.

Maybe she's telling the truth, and she's not hiding anything from me. Maybe the feelings I'm experiencing are simple lust and loneliness. It wouldn't be the first time that I misinterpreted physical desire as something more.

Isn't that what happened with Alice? We were explosive together, and I thought it was love. I was wrong.

I wanted to kiss Bonnie. More than that, I wanted to swipe our bowls off the counter and grip her hair, then plant her pretty ass on the edge and fuck her until she forgot her own name. The feeling was a raging beast inside me, a need that welled up from some hidden corner of my heart.

But I can't touch her. Not when she works for me. Not when she's hiding something.

And what was up with that limp? I noticed it when we were walking back from the wine room. She was trying to hide it, but I could tell. Does she have an injury? Is it serious? Is it some sort of manipulation to make me feel protective of her? If it is, it's working.

The whirling thoughts make me restless and angry.

I head to the gym on the third floor and run on the treadmill until sweat drenches my shirt. Then I lift weights until my mind is blank and I feel almost sane again. I rub a towel over my face and drain a bottle of water, knowing it's not enough to clear my mind.

As soon as I head back down and check on my son, I smell the fading scent of sweet vanilla cupcakes in his room. I loved how Bonnie was with Will today, laughing as he chattered. He showed all his favorite toys off, studying her reactions intently. Will's already besotted with Bonnie, and I can't blame him. She listened to all his strong five-year-old opinions like they held weight with her. She treated him with respect while still being firm. He brushed his teeth without even a peep of protest, then looked at her with a big smile to gauge her approval.

I know the feeling. It's impossible to be in the same room as Bonnie and not have your gaze drawn to her. She tries to hide herself, but she's the center of the world. God—what am I even thinking? I'm as taken with Bonnie as my five-year-old son.

Will shifts in his bed, hand relaxing on his Batman bedspread. I touch a strand of his dark hair.

If I were thinking logically, I would take these feelings and read them through to their natural conclusion: disaster. I've been here before. Alice spun me around her little finger, then used our nearness to stab me in the back. It took me years to claw myself back from the brink of despair. If it weren't for Will, I'm not sure I would've been able to do it at all.

It's not going to happen again.

I pride myself on reading people, and I know I'm missing something with Bonnie. I can't let her leave until I know what she's hiding. It's like a splinter under my skin; until I dig it out, the scab won't heal.

My son's hands curl into fists, and I let my fingers brush his cheek. His skin is softer than anything I've felt before. When this little guy came into the world, it caused a seismic shift inside me—and when I found out how badly Alice was playing me, the fault line grew so deep I knew I'd never go back to the man I was before.

I would burn down the world for my son, including his pretty new nanny.

Stalking out of his room and gently closing the door, I head upstairs and into my office. There, I call my PI.

"What have you got for me?"

Greg is an old, grizzled ex-cop who is able to dig up dirt on anyone. He hums into the phone. "Something weird about her leaving her job. Happened over a year ago."

I pull up her file on my computer and see Greg has updated it. I frown. "She worked at Holt & Holt."

He hums. "Yep."

"The same hedge fund that's courting me. The ones who want me to transfer my investment portfolio into their capable hands for management."

"I did notice that, yes," Greg responds.

Looks like Nortley aren't my prime suspect anymore. I'll get Greg to research if they have anything to do with Bonnie, but her connection to the hedge fund is much more interesting.

Holt & Holt is a huge firm on Wall Street. The hedge fund has close to sixty billion dollars' worth of assets under management, and they've been courting me for months. For Bonnie to be hired by the firm—I check her file again—directly out of college means she's extremely bright. Then she quit a mere year before going back to work as a nanny—and coming to work for me.

I'm missing something. Why would she give up her career in finance to work for her sister? Is this about me? She's got to be making a pittance compared to what Holt & Holt were paying her.

I lean back, a sick feeling sluicing through my stomach. "Seems like a pretty big coincidence."

"I've been trying to find out what happened when she left the job. It was over a year ago, and so far I've heard that it wasn't on amicable terms. But that could be a rumor."

"And rumors can be planted."

"Exactly." A keyboard clacks on the other end of the line. "I'm talking to a woman who worked for Holt & Holt next week, so I'll know more then. An administrator. Seems she left shortly after Bonnie, so she might know what happened and she might be willing to talk."

"Okay," I answer, thoughts whirling.

"What's your take on her?" Greg asks. "Anything I can use in this interview?"

"She's hiding something from me," I respond, "but I don't know, Greg. Something tells me it isn't malicious. Her resume is pretty damning, though."

"You going to fire her?"

"Not until I know why she's here."

Greg hums. "I'll update you when I know more."

We hang up, and I lean back in my chair. A dark feeling grips my chest.

If Bonnie is here to feed information back to her ex-employers, I will tear that hedge fund to pieces.

Interrupting my thoughts of brimstone and destruction, my phone rattles on the desk, lighting up with my best friend's name.

"Hey, Rome."

"He's alive."

I snort, leaning back in my chair as I kick my feet up onto the desk. "What's up?"

"You and me in Ibiza is what's up. We leave in two hours. My crew is preparing the jet as we speak."

Rome is about ten years younger than me. He's an advertising executive who lives by the mantra of work hard, play harder. We've been friends for years. He donates generously to the Noble Foundation causes.

Huffing, I stare at the ceiling. "I have a son now, Rome. And I'm in my forties. I'm not going to Ibiza to party with a bunch of kids."

"Fine. We'll go to Mykonos. Bring the kid. Chicks love a single dad. He could be useful."

"You're such a dick."

Rome laughs. "Come on, Arlo. Live a little."

"You know I can't. I have this charity dinner to plan, and I'm working on the IPO."

"Three years ago, you would've brought your spawn to Mykonos with me. Now you hardly do anything but work."

"Work is what got me here." I look around my home office, perched on the top floor of one of Manhattan's highest skyscrapers.

"Work is going to put you in the ground if you don't loosen up a little."

"Yeah, well, I saw how that turned out last time I tried to loosen up."

"Your ex-wife was a shitty person, but she's gone now. You won. It's over."

I grunt. Rome saw what Alice did to me. He saw the betrayal, and he helped me pick up the pieces. He and my sister Beth are the only people who really know the hell I went through to keep my son by my side, to make sure that Alice couldn't slide another knife between my ribs.

He lets out a sigh. "Fine. I'll go to Ibiza by myself, and send you pictures of all the supermodels I meet."

"You do that."

I can hear the frown in his voice when he says, "What's gotten into you, man?"

If I can't confide in Rome, I can't confide in anyone. I run a hand through my hair. "My new nanny is hiding something from me. I'm working from home while I try to figure out what her deal is."

"So? Fire her and get a new one. Better yet, get Laura to do it. Keep your hands clean while you deal with real business."

"Not until I know what's going on."

A low hum turns into a chuckle. "Let me guess. She's pretty, and she makes you feel special little tingles below the belt."

"Screw you, Rome."

"You know, you haven't been the same since that chick in London."

I drop my feet to the ground, bristling. "You have no idea what you're talking about."

"A one-night stand with a woman you never even saw clearly messed you up, my man."

"I saw her."

"You saw pieces of her when your face was two inches from her body. Which, I'll be the first to admit, is a vantage point I enjoy as much as the next man, but it doesn't exactly give you the full picture."

Before I got my eyes fixed, I was severely nearsighted. That night in London shouldn't have affected me as deeply as it did. I never even knew the woman's name. I never saw her face clearly, because I'd lost my stupid glasses—again. Then she left before I woke up. When I told Rome about it, he didn't stop laughing for a week. He called me a blind old man for a full year.

"I saw her," I repeat, voice a low growl.

"If you walked by her on the street, you'd have no idea, Arlo. You couldn't even tell me what color her eyes were."

I huff. He's right. That night was a bright spot in my life after years of trudging through shit. She was the first woman I felt a connection to after the divorce. She made me feel alive.

And I didn't even know her name.

"She must have been a good lay to have this much of an effect on you, though. It's been years, man."

"Why are we even talking about her? I'm never going to meet her again. This is about my nanny hiding something from me. I'll find out what it is, then I'll fire her."

"Right."

"Enjoy Ibiza, or Mykonos, or wherever else you end up."

"I will. You sure you don't want to come?"

"I'm sure." I hang up the phone, jittery and frustrated. Why did he have to bring that woman up? It was nothing. It was one night. I was half-drunk and mostly blind. We had sex. She left. End of story.

Ignoring the wisps of anger poisoning my veins, I stalk out of my office and head to my bedroom. This has nothing to do with my ex-wife or the stranger in London. It barely has anything to do with me.

I just want to know what my new nanny is hiding, and then I can fire her. The sooner I can get Bonnie out of my life, the better.

NINE
BONNIE

IT'S SATURDAY MORNING. Today and tomorrow will be full days with William and Alex, and then he'll be off in kindergarten from Monday to Thursday next week. Since I'm only working for one month, I agreed to only have every second Sunday off work. That means I have a week and a day before I get any respite from Arlo's brooding, intense presence.

Yesterday, Alex told me he had a night nanny when Will was very young, but when Will started sleeping through the night, Arlo took over the night duties.

It surprised me. I would have expected a man in his position to pawn off childcare to a staff member while he did important, billionaire businessy things. Most of my bosses and coworkers on Wall Street were like that. They didn't give two shakes about their kids.

Last night, when I got tired of staring at the ceiling, I started a deep dive into everything I could find about Arlo Noble in all the far reaches of the internet. I found a ton of photos of him at galas and charity events. He's usually serious and scowly in the photos, surrounded by his glittering peers. I found a high school yearbook photo of him in his junior year, which was taken the year I was born.

The age difference isn't something I really thought of before I saw that photo. He's a little over sixteen years older than me, but I didn't realize it when we had our night together. He sold his first company when I was in pigtails. He made his first billion when I was wearing berry-flavored lip gloss to high school math class and mooning over my crush, the floppy-haired, gangly-limbed Ben Chalmers.

He looks younger than forty-nine. Or maybe he just has that aura of agelessness, that pulsing power and energy that makes him seem like more than a mere mortal.

There's a baby monitor app linked to my phone, which alerts me that William is up at five forty-five. I make my way upstairs and find William cross-legged in his playroom, reenacting our epic battle of Mr. Freeze vs. Batman for the six-hundredth time.

He grins at me. "Hi."

"Morning, Will," I say, leaning against the door. "You want some breakfast?"

"Can I have pancakes?"

"Sure," I answer.

Alex appears in the doorway, pleasantly surprised that I'm already slipping into the role. "Sorry I'm late," she says, bleary-eyed. Her hand smooths over her bump. "This little girl wouldn't stop kicking my ribs last night. I finally fell asleep around five o'clock, and I missed my alarm."

"You can start later tomorrow if you want," I tell her. "I don't mind doing the morning on my own."

She gives me a grateful smile. "I might take you up on that."

We head to the kitchen, William tearing down the hallway in

front of us. He slides into the corner booth seat and plants Mr. Freeze and Batman on the table. Alex gets him a glass of orange juice.

The chef, Steve, comes in every three days to stock the fridge with ready-made meals and snacks. I spy some frozen breakfast burritos in the freezer that look *very* intriguing, so I take one out and put it on the counter for myself. Then I find the fixings for pancakes and mix up the batter, humming.

I feel the instant Arlo walks in. His presence shivers over my skin, bringing awareness to every hair follicle, every place where even a single stitch of fabric rubs on my skin. I straighten and turn to face him where he stands in the doorway. "Good morning," I say, arranging my face into a pleasant smile, even though the darkness in his gaze makes my insides clench.

His gaze skips over me and goes straight to Alex. "My sister just called. She'd like to see William, so Bonnie and I will take him over. You can have the morning off."

She straightens. "Oh. We were going to go over his playdate schedule for the next month, but I guess..." She looks at me. "That can wait."

I nod. "Uh-huh."

"We'll leave in twenty," Arlo says. He crosses to his son and ruffles his hair.

Will smiles. "Hi, Dad."

"Hey." The harsh lines of his face soften. "We're going to go see your aunt Beth at her café this morning."

"Can I have a hot chocolate?"

Arlo grins. "Sure." He kisses Will's head, then straightens, spins on his heels, and disappears through the door.

Alex glances at me, wide-eyed.

"What?" I ask.

"Nothing!" She smiles. "You'll do great."

I frown. "What do you mean? What's his sister like?"

"Oh, his sister is amazing. It's just..." She leans in. "Arlo sometimes gets in one of those moods." Her eyes widen, glancing at the door. "But he'll be fine. He probably just got some bad news about work or something."

I nod, not wanting to admit that Arlo seems to be in "one of those moods" anytime he's in the same room as me.

A short while later, we've got William's bag packed with everything I might need, and I have my crossbody purse slung over my shoulder. William is doing a goofy walk, swinging his arms all over the place to make me laugh. When I do, he gives me the cutest, most impish grin I've ever seen. The knot in my stomach relaxes. Cute kid.

The second level of Arlo's residence has a much grander elevator lobby than the bottom level. Rich marble covers the floor, and a ginormous vase bursting with fresh flowers towers in the corner. It's taller than I am. Interesting, abstract artwork takes up a place of honor directly across from the elevator, an angry, chaotic mess of color and energy. It reminds me of Arlo.

My boss has a dark look painted on his brow as he waits for Alex, Will, and me next to the open elevator. For once, it's not pointed at me; he's frowning at his phone. He looks up when the three of us approach, nodding as he enters the elevator. We follow him in, stopping off at Alex's floor before heading down to the lobby.

A limo is waiting for us outside, parked next to the curb directly in front of the door. The driver hustles out and opens the back door for us, and I see a booster seat on the back bench. Arlo enters first, and the driver—Fernando, I remember—grabs my bag of snacks and toys and slides it into the trunk.

Will climbs into his booster seat and grabs the seatbelt, holding it out to me. I clip it in and wink at him, then turn to survey the rest of the limo.

There's a seat next to Arlo on one of the side-facing benches, but I choose instead to sit across from him. He reaches down to the slim console between us and pops it open, handing me a bottle of water. I take it, and our fingers brush. That touch really shouldn't send a jolt through me. It really, really shouldn't. But it does.

"Thanks," I croak, then twist off the top of the bottle.

William suddenly flings his Batman figurine across the limo and yells, "Noooooo!" then laughs maniacally, brandishing Mr. Freeze.

"Not in the car, Will," Arlo says sternly.

Will ducks his chin, cowed.

I stretch across the console to retrieve the figurine, and the limo happens to lurch into traffic when I'm at full stretch. All my weight lands on my injured ankle, and I let out a little whimper as I fall sideways. The joint does that sometimes; it just gives out under my weight. That's why I rarely wear heels anymore, unless I'm dancing salsa. Even then, I usually go with something sturdier than the ones Nikki lent me.

As I wobble, Arlo steadies me with broad, warm hands on my shoulders, then scowls at me when I sit back down in my seat.

"Seatbelt," he barks.

That tone is seriously unnecessary. It's my turn to scowl at him, but I do up my seatbelt before giving William his toy back. He crashes the two figurines into each other, and Mr. Freeze dies a dramatic death. He doesn't throw the toys again, but he does peek at his father with a mischievous expression on his face like he might be considering it.

When I'm settled with my seatbelt clicked, I realize that it's actually really hard to sit across from someone and not look at them. But when I lift my gaze to Arlo's eyes, I find him staring right back at me, fire burning in his gaze. He looks angry. I glance away and smile at William, who's busy with his action figures.

"Your sister's name is Beth, right?" I ask, going for casual curiosity.

"Been doing your homework beyond just hunting for shirtless paparazzi photos of me?"

I give him a dark look, which, judging by the infinitesimally small, wry twist in his lips, seems to amuse him. "You are so arrogant."

His eyebrows slash down over his eyes, which pleases me. I really shouldn't needle him like that, being that I'm supposed to be the bland professional nanny and all, but I can't help it.

"Yes, her name is Beth." His gaze shifts to my leg. "What's wrong with your ankle?"

I startle. "What?"

"Your ankle. What's wrong with it." He doesn't say it like a question. He says it like he's frustrated that he had to repeat himself.

"It's just an old injury," I say, waving a hand. "Happened in college. Flares up sometimes."

"Why is it flaring up now?"

I readjust my seatbelt over my chest, trying to ignore the sparking frustration in my veins. "What makes you think you have a right to know?"

"If you're going to be injured while you take care of my son, I want to know about it."

Thank goodness I have years of experience working in a male-dominated field, because I'm able to keep my instinctive reaction—which is an eye roll and a snarky response—to myself. He's exactly like the men I used to work with. He thinks I'm silly and stupid, and he doesn't respect me. He's big and domineering and he thinks he can push me around. I straighten and look him dead in the eyes. "It's none of your business, okay? It happened a long time ago. I just fell on it wrong when the car lurched. It's fine."

His lips thin. He's not happy with that answer. His gaze drops to my shoes—flat, sensible sneakers that cover the worst of the scar under my ankle bone. "You were limping yesterday," he says, and I startle.

He noticed that? I meet his gaze with wide eyes. "What?"

Arlo says nothing, just frowns harder at my shoe, like he'll be able to spontaneously develop X-ray vision and see the screws and pins keeping my foot attached to my leg.

"I went out dancing the other night," I finally admit. "I wore my friend's heels, and now my ankle is sore. It'll be fine by tomorrow."

"What kind of dancing? With who?"

I stare at him, incredulous. "What does that have to do with anything?"

"Who were you dancing with," he grates out, jaw hard.

A small, illicit thrill zips through my stomach, like I'm sticking my hand through the bars of a cage just to see what the growling lion on the other side will do. I lean back and cross my arms. "I don't think I want to tell you."

His nostrils flare. A little bolt of heat darts down to my belly in response. "You're being a brat, Bonnie."

My jaw drops. "Ex-*cuse* me?"

"You heard me," he says through clenched teeth. Then he says it again: "Brat."

My thighs squeeze involuntarily. Heat snakes in my belly as my heart picks up speed. His eyes are so dark. His hands are so broad, resting on his thighs.

I snort, lifting my chin. "You are asking completely inappropri-ate, irrelevant questions about my personal life. I am upholding a completely reasonable boundary by not telling you. And by the way, I'm thirty-three years old. So spare me the brat nonsense."

"*Brat*," William whispers under his breath, and I give Arlo a death glare. If his five-year-old starts calling me that, I *will* throw myself out the windows of his fancy penthouse.

Arlo has the decency to look like he regrets his words. Sort of.

Honks sound from very far away. I barely hear them past the thumping in my ears. We get stuck in gridlock traffic, and the air in the limo becomes so thick, it's unbearable.

Finally, I crack under the pressure. "I was dancing salsa with my girlfriend, Nikki. Is that allowed when one is employed by the great Arlo Noble?" I sass him extra hard, tilting my head, challenging him.

He grunts, then pulls out his phone and stares at it. "Not if it ends up with you injured."

I clench my hands into fists and stare out the window at the passing buildings.

After a while, Arlo puts his phone down on the seat beside him. "Did you ice it? Your ankle? After you went dancing?"

"Why are we still talking about an injury I got fourteen years ago?"

"Answer the question, Bonnie."

"Yes. Okay?"

"And it's still sore? Did you go to a physical therapist? Have you asked a doctor about it?"

I just gape at him. "It won't impact my job. I promise."

My boss's jaw hardens. The limo turns, and Arlo glances out the windows. He slips his phone into his pocket, and I sense that we're almost at our destination. I feel strung out and on edge, and I don't like it.

A minute later, we stop in front of a café, and Fernando comes to open the door before jumping to grab the bag from the trunk. I get William out of his car seat without looking at Arlo even once, which is a success in my books. When I've got William's hand in mine and I'm facing the building, Arlo grabs the coffee shop door and holds it open for me.

I don't say thank you, which feels like a much bigger rebellion than it actually is.

We step inside an eclectic, boho space that's furnished with lots of soft fabrics and mismatched chairs. It's very cool. The espresso machine hisses while a woman directs two workers to straighten out a canvas on the wall. She turns when we enter, and a gigantic smile spreads across her face.

She's wearing a bright-pink cable knit sweater and tight pants tucked into black booties. Her earrings are ginormous and funky splashes of neon yellow. Her hair is a big poof of a messy bun on top of her head, and she has pink-framed glasses on her face. "You're here!"

This is Arlo Noble's sister? She's so...happy. And colorful.

I frown at Arlo and catch a fleeting softening in his face. "Hey, Beth."

"Move over," she tells him playfully before bending at the waist to greet William. "There's a more important man in my life now. Hi, buddy."

William grins. "Hi. Can I have a hot chocolate?"

She laughs. "Of course!" Then she wraps her arms around him and dips him like they're ballroom dancing, blowing a raspberry on his neck. William laughs and squirms, and I find myself smiling along with him.

When William is back on his feet and claiming one of the nearby tables, she turns to me. "I'm Beth," she says, sticking out her hand. We shake.

"Bonnie," I reply, slightly surprised that she even acknowledged my existence. When I worked for Linda in college, I was mostly overlooked by clients and their peers. I was just the help, and I mostly stayed invisible.

"Nice to meet you, Bonnie. My brother tells me that you'll be taking care of Will for the month, until Sofia starts full-time."

"That's right," I answer, surprise deepening.

She smiles at her nephew, who's adjusting one of the pillows lining the bench behind him. "Lucky you," she tells him. "All these pretty girls all to yourself."

"Did you buy the piece you wanted?" Arlo asks, gruff.

Beth walks over to the canvas the two men had been straightening on the wall. Her gait is less of a walk and more of a stomp, like every movement is bigger and bolder than is strictly required. She flings her arms out to the sides. "Behold," Beth says, "my latest gem."

An oil painting with hyper-realistic details stares back at us. It's an old woman scowling at her snarled knitting project, a cat curled at her feet reaching for the skein next to her toes.

I can't help the smile that steals over my lips.

"Right?" Beth says, seeing my reaction. "Same here. I saw it and couldn't stop grinning."

Arlo glances between us, a line between his brows.

"He doesn't get it," Beth says to me. "He never does."

"I get art," Arlo protests.

The coffee shop has dramatic wooden arches that line the walls and ceiling. In the space between each arch is a painting. I look at the one next to the oil painting, tilting my head. It's the same artist as the elevator lobby piece in Arlo's house, I can tell. Abstract, dramatic, bold. This one is monochromatic, slashes of black and white and gray that make me feel lighter inside.

"That's one of mine," Beth says.

I look at his sister. "You painted that piece in front of the elevator, didn't you?"

She beams at me. "Did you like it?"

"It reminds me of Arlo."

Her laugh is as big and bold as the rest of her. "You're the first person who's said that to me. And that's exactly who I was thinking of when I created it."

The line between Arlo's brows deepens. "That painting is about me?"

"Your energy," I say.

"Exactly," Beth says. She looks at William. "Isn't that right? Your dad doesn't even understand art when it's like staring at a mirror."

William is busy staring at the cup of hot chocolate that the barista dropped in front of him. He takes a sip and gets a whipped cream mustache. I grin, then turn to Arlo to catch his reaction.

"Yeah, yeah," Arlo says, the corner of his lip twitching. He glances down at my foot and the half-smile fades. "Sit down. I'll get us some coffees."

"Yes sir," I say obediently.

His eyes narrow. "Careful."

I blink innocently, then take a seat under the old woman knitting. That's when I see the look on Beth's face. She's looking at her brother as he walks to the counter like she's just seen something shocking. Then her expression clears, and she plops down beside me. "So," she says, "how are things in the eagle's nest?"

"Your brother's penthouse?"

She nods.

"Good. Just getting the lay of the land. Alex is finishing up this week, but it helps to have her show me the ropes."

More nodding, but her eyes are full of far-too-perceptive light.

Then her brother comes stomping back to the table. He glares at me. "What are you having?"

Something about his tone of voice makes everything tighten

inside me. I don't know if it's frustration or anger or pettiness or what, but all I want to do is sass him. Instead, I blink.

That seems to enrage him, which is oddly satisfying. "You know how I drink my coffee," he says, "so tell me how you'll drink yours. Unless you already had one today? I don't want you jittery if you're taking care of Will."

Drat. I'd kill for another coffee, but I've painted myself as a jittery caffeine mess. "Green tea would be great."

He turns back to the counter and stomps away.

"Someone's got a bee in his bonnet today," Beth mock-whispers, which makes Arlo turn around again, sending Beth into a fit of cackles. She glances at Will. "When are we having our next painting session, buddy? You want to see how good your last piece came out?"

Will brightens. "I can paint again?"

"You sure can."

"With my hands like I did last time?"

Beth laughs. She glances at me. "We had to hose him down from head to toe when he was done. Paint *everywhere*."

"It was fun," William proclaims.

Arlo comes back, placing coffees on the table in front of them and a green tea in front of me. The barista comes over with a little mini pot of honey on a plate.

I find out that Beth owns this café, which she mostly uses to display pieces from up-and-coming artists. It's open late most nights, and she tells me the poetry slam is always a blast. That earns her a grumble from Arlo about poetry making no sense. I laugh, which makes his scowl deepen. The entire exchange is deeply pleasing to me.

Beth's eyes sparkle the whole time.

Finally, when William says he needs to pee, I walk him to the bathroom. While we're there, I stare at myself in the mirror and shake my head.

The more time I spend with Arlo, the more I like him. It's the opposite of what should be happening—the opposite of what I need to happen.

If I'm going to survive this month, the distance between my boss and me needs to remain vast. Unfortunately, that doesn't seem to be what's happening.

TEN
ARLO

WHEN BONNIE DISAPPEARS, Beth gives me a *look*. It's a raised-eyebrow, what's-going-on-there look.

My brows lower. "What?"

"Nothing," she says, taking a sip of her coffee. "Nothing at all."

"Do you recognize her?"

That seems to surprise my sister. She tips her head toward the washrooms. "Your new nanny?"

I nod. "Yeah. Does she seem familiar to you?"

Beth hums. "Not really."

I lean forward. "Are you sure?"

Beth has an artist's eye. She hasn't drawn portraits since she was in art school, but she notices features and knows faces. If she'd met Bonnie, she would remember. So, when she shakes her head, I let out a frustrated huff.

"Why?" Beth asks.

"I think she's hiding something from me," I admit.

Beth's brows climb. "Hiding something? Like what?"

"I don't know. I feel like I've met her before, and last night I found out she used to work for the hedge fund that's been trying to court me for months."

"You think you met her at their offices?"

"No," I answer, frustrated. "I would've remembered her."

Beth snorts.

"What?"

"Nothing," she repeats, angelic.

I growl, which makes my sister laugh.

She pats my hand. "Don't shit where you eat, Arlo."

"I'm not an idiot," I answer. I glance at the narrow hallway leading to the washrooms and scowl. Then I turn to Beth again and ask, "Have you sourced all the art for the auction?"

As part of the Noble Foundation gala, I'll be throwing a silent auction with proceeds going to the children's hospital. My sister is in charge of procuring art to be auctioned, along with choosing one piece of hers to donate. The event is happening in six weeks.

"Not yet," she says, "but I've been talking to a few artists from Heart's Cove that are interested in participating. A potter has already confirmed he can donate a piece."

"A potter?"

"Mac Blair," she answers, pulling out her phone. She taps on it and spins the screen, showing me a dramatic glazed vase of glossy black, speckled with white.

"Nice," I answer.

Beth snorts. "Not that you'd know the difference, but yes, it is nice." She slips her phone away, and we both look over as Bonnie reappears with Will. She's laughing at something my son says, and I can't help but stare at the way her face moves. The gentle slope of her nose draws my eyes all the way down to her full lips. I wonder how it would feel to run my thumb over her lower lip, to feel the pillowy softness depress under the pressure of my finger.

Her body is gently curved, her breasts teasing through the

fabric of her tee. Her jeans hug her hips like they were made for her, and I can't help but watch the way she walks, all elegant grace and catlike movements.

She's hiding her limp better today, even after her wince in the limo, and I wonder if she's doing it to conceal it from me. The thought bothers me, and I'm not sure why.

Then the door opens on the other end of the café. Bonnie looks up, and her face breaks into a smile. "Teddy!"

I follow her gaze to see a huge beast of a man standing there, arms spread at his sides. "Bonnie? Bonnie Delmar? In the flesh?"

She laughs, a beautiful, musical sound that tugs at something in my gut—but she's doing it for another man.

It shouldn't bother me. Bonnie is my nanny, nothing more. But to see her face light up at the sight of this meathead makes me want to flip the table and watch our mugs shatter against the floor.

The huge man puts up his index finger and moves to the iPhone plugged into the wall. He taps on it, and the quick rhythm of Latin music starts playing through the speakers. He arches a brow at Bonnie, then crooks a finger at her.

Crooks a fucking finger at her.

"Easy, tiger," Beth whispers, eyes dancing. "You look like you're about to snap."

"What?" I hiss, then inhale to control myself. "I'm fine."

Well, I would be fine if Bonnie didn't sway her mesmerizing hips toward another man. She dances right into his arms, and his hand splays over her mid back. I want to rip his arm off.

What the hell is wrong with me? I'm losing my mind.

Bonnie moves beautifully, and for a moment, I'm entranced by the motion of her hips. She tips her head back and laughs, the end of her ponytail swinging back and forth. Her dance partner spins her out, grinning, then brings her back into his arms.

Bonnie shouldn't be dancing on that ankle of hers. I saw her wince in the limo, and there was no missing her limp last night. She's injured, and the last thing she should be doing is letting this asshole twirl her around like a prop.

That's why I'm crumpling my napkin up so tight it's about to turn into a semiprecious stone from the pressure. Not because the sight of some guy's hands on Bonnie's back and hips makes me want to punch a hole through the wall.

Beth is laughing, hauling my son up onto her lap so they can both watch the show. Will's eyes are huge as he watches, his feet bouncing to the beat.

My gaze cuts to the phone connected to the speakers, and I wonder if I can walk over there and rip it out of the wall. Then, like I have no other choice in the matter, my eyes are drawn to Bonnie once more.

Her loose tee slips over her shoulder so I can see her collarbone when the dancing dickhead twirls her around. I want to brush my lips over her collarbone, follow the line of it to that hollow depression at the base of her throat.

She's giggling, and I hate that she's giving that to him and not me. I hate everything about this. I hate that her hips are moving like that and it isn't my hands that get to slide over them.

"You okay over there?" Beth asks, eyes twinkling.

I slam back the rest of my coffee. "I need to go. I have work to do."

"Already? But I hardly got any time with my little man here." She smiles at William, who's still busy staring at the dancers. "And it's Saturday. Can't you take a day off? What's the point of being mega-rich if you can't have time to yourself?"

Bonnie breaks away from her dance partner and comes wiggling toward William. She picks him up and twirls him around, dancing along to the beat as my son bounces in her arms.

Then she places him down and tries to teach him a few steps. His face is red, and he's smiling so wide I can see nearly all his teeth.

I grab the bag Bonnie brought for him and stand, nodding to my sister. "I'll call you about the auction. Buy the vase."

"Fine," she grumbles, but there's a smile on her lips and a twinkle in her eyes. Whatever that means. I've given up trying to understand women in general, and my sister in particular.

I head for Bonnie, placing my palm on her back. She turns to face me, eyes wide, and my hand slides to the curve of her waist like that little hollow was crafted exactly for my fingers to fit into. Her lips part in surprise, a small intake of breath.

The beast inside me settles, because she reacted that way to *my* touch. "We're leaving," I growl.

"Already?"

Hand still on her waist, I exert a small amount of pressure on the point of contact to usher her toward the door. Her chest rises as she inhales once, even more sharply. She glances over my shoulder. "Nice to meet you, Beth."

"You too!" my sister yells over the music.

"Bye, Teddy!"

"See you at Iguana on Wednesday?" he calls out, lowering the volume on the speakers.

"Can't," she says, dipping her head toward me. "Working. Maybe next month."

He winks at her. *Winks* at her.

We head outside and into the waiting car as Fernando deals with the bag and Bonnie deals with the car seat. I throw myself into the same bench seat I was in before, watching Bonnie straighten the straps of the car seat harness.

Then she takes her own seat and clips herself in without a word.

"Who was that?"

Her blue eyes meet mine, a spark flaring in them. There's red on her cheeks, and I know she's angry. "Who?"

"That guy who just manhandled you in there."

"Someone manhandled me, but it wasn't Teddy."

"Who calls their kid Teddy? Is that some sort of joke?" I sound like a jealous asshole, because that's what I am. I've lost my mind.

She crosses her arms, which pushes her tits up and gives me a view of the delicious space where they meet. I shift in my seat and stare at the privacy screen separating us from the driver's seat. Then I turn back and look at her foot. "You shouldn't be dancing on your ankle if it's sore."

"I'm sorry, what was that? Are you trying to control how I manage my own injuries? That's a bit much, don't you think?"

"Is he your boyfriend?"

She arches a brow. "And how is *that* relevant?"

"Answer the question, Bonnie."

"No. I don't think I will." She turns her head away from me, staring out through the back window.

I shouldn't push this. I know I shouldn't. But I can still see his hands on her back, sliding over her hips, touching her hands and arms... "I deserve to know who my employees are associating with."

Her head turns slowly, eyes shooting flames across the limo at me. "He's not my boyfriend. And neither are you."

I clench my jaw. Will is quiet in his seat, watching us.

With a deep breath, I try to gain control over myself again. Bonnie is nothing but an employee, and as soon as I find out what she's hiding—as soon as I have whatever evidence I need to protect myself and my son—she'll be gone from my life for good.

ARLO DISAPPEARS INTO HIS OFFICE, and I spend the rest of the day with William. He's a good kid, but like all kids, he picked up on whatever weird energy happened after the café. For the rest of the day, he's fussy and difficult. By the time bedtime rolls around, I'm dead on my feet.

As soon as Will is in bed, I make my way downstairs, bypass the kitchen, and collapse onto my bed. Throwing an arm over my face, I lie there for an indeterminate amount of time, trying to gather the energy to get up, feed myself, and get ready for bed.

Then there's a knock on the door. I sigh, then haul myself to my feet and pull it open.

Arlo looms on the other side, his dark brows low over his eyes.

"Yes?" I ask, not having the energy to be sassy with him. I just want to sleep.

"Have you eaten?"

I blink, then straighten. "Um. No."

"I ordered Thai. There's more than enough for both of us if you're hungry."

I'm about to refuse when my stomach growls. Arlo's lips kick, and he takes a step back to gesture down the hall. We make it all the way upstairs and into the kitchen without speaking. Takeout containers are strewn over the island, and there are two plates set out in front of the tall velvet stools.

Arlo pulls one out for me.

"Thanks," I say, and take a seat. "It smells amazing."

"Call it an olive branch," Arlo says, opening a container of pad Thai and another of green curry. "I know I acted like an ass today."

"That's remarkably self-aware of you."

He gives me a sideways glare, and I laugh. We pile our plates with food and eat in silence for a while, until Arlo turns to me again.

"You studied finance," he says.

"Looks like I'm not the only one who did my research." I twirl the last of my pad Thai around my fork and stuff it in my mouth. It tastes divine.

"Why did you quit your job to come back and work for your sister?"

I chew and swallow, then stare at my plate for a while. "I had no choice," I say. The last thing I want to do is tell my boss—who happens to be the hottest man alive—about the night that ruined my career. I had my reputation destroyed, my credibility stripped from me.

"Why not?"

Knowing I have to give him some truth, I push my empty plate back and take a sip from my glass of water. "Someone I trusted started rumors about me," I tell Arlo, not looking at him. "The rumors spread, and it undermined the respect I'd spent years building. My performance dropped as a result, and it was either quit or be fired and have all my dirty laundry aired. I chose to quit."

He watches me, and I gather my courage to meet his gaze. His eyes are dark, somber. There's one seat separating us, but it still feels too close. It's his presence, his energy. He takes up more space than his physical body. I feel a tingle wash over my skin whenever he's near.

And right now, with those dark eyes sweeping over my face, the tingles intensify.

His hand lifts up toward me, and I freeze. Then his fingers move softly over my temple, tucking a strand of hair behind my ear. I can't breathe. I can't think.

"Do you miss it?" He asks the question like he cares about the response.

I snort. "Nope. I never wanted to work in finance. I wanted to run track. I had dreams of being in the Olympics." I swing my ankle out. "Then that happened."

His eyes coast down my leg and back up to my face. "You've been through a lot."

My smile is more of a grimace. "Could be worse." I push myself off my seat and grab my plate, needing to do something with my hands. Once it's in the dishwasher, I busy myself packing up the takeout containers. Arlo puts his own plate in the dishwasher, then comes beside me to help me stack things into the fridge.

That's how we end up next to the fridge, standing beside the counter, when he faces me. His chest is only inches from mine, crowding me against the cabinets. "You're not here to spy on me on behalf of my ex-wife, are you?"

I jerk back. "What? Is that what you think? No!"

He nods, just a slight dip of his chin. "And you're not here as part of a corporate espionage plot either."

I—excuse me? What did he just say? Oh my word. Is *that* what he thinks I'm hiding? I stare at him, mouth hanging open. "No," I tell him. "Of course not."

He nods, and for a brief moment, I consider coming clean. I could just tell him that I'm acting like a dolt because we slept together three years ago. I mean, really, it's not so bad. Maybe if it's out in the open, we can move on. Get through the month and then go our separate ways.

But then his fingers ghost over my cheek again, and he's tracing the shell of my ear. A shiver runs through me.

"It drove me crazy seeing you in another man's arms," he says in a low, rumbly voice. "Tell me why I feel that way."

"Um," I answer, gripping the counter behind me to stop myself from twisting my hands into his shirt. "Because you're really, super, inappropriately arrogant and possessive?"

His fingers slide down to my jaw, tracing the line from my ear to my chin. Then his thumb slides over my lower lip, pressing gently. Heat blooms low in my stomach, and I part my lips in response. My head is full of noise. My entire existence narrows to his thumb on my lip.

"You feel it too," he says, almost like it's an accusation. His thumb slides off my lip, and the tips of his fingers trace a line down the side of my throat and over my shoulder where my top has gaped slightly. My skin tingles as his fingers stroke back along my collarbone, his eyes following the movement like it's all that matters in the world.

It would be a really, really bad idea to sleep with my boss. Reminding myself of that fact doesn't make it sound any less enticing, though.

"The last time I was this attracted to a woman, she ruined my life," Arlo says, almost to himself.

"Oh," I whisper. "I'm sorry about that."

His lips curl at the corners, eyes climbing up to meet mine. His fingers move back over my collarbone toward my shoulder, a slow, torturous, sensual movement. He crowds closer, his chest pressing mine. The edge of the counter digs into my lower back, and then I realize my hands are on his stomach. When did that happen?

I can feel the heat of him through the fabric of his shirt, the solid pack of his muscle as bulky and firm as I remember. I close my eyes and inhale, but the scent of him makes me dizzier.

His hand slips from my collarbone, drifting over my shirt, following the slope of my breast. My whole body trembles at the touch. He strokes the side of my breast, feather-light, then moves the backs of his fingers over my nipple. Even through my padded bra, the touch feels intense. I look down at that big, rugged hand on my body, and I feel my resolve crack.

It would be so easy to tell him how we met. To admit that I've dreamed of it ever since. If I spoke the words and told him the truth, what would he do? Would he keep touching me with those gentle, torturous fingers, or would he grip me harder? Would I get to feel those possessive hands on my bare skin once more, or would responsibility and propriety take over?

He slides the back of his fingers back and forth over my nipple as I watch, my chest heaving with every breath. His other hand moves to my hip, a single finger dipping below my shirt to find the bare skin just above the waistband of my jeans.

I close my eyes.

Turning his hand, Arlo uses his thumb to make slow, steady circles over my nipple. Even through all my layers of clothing, I can feel his touch sparking lightning in my veins. Every brush of his thumb against my furled breast makes lust dart down between my legs. And when he pinches, I clamp down on the whimper that threatens to escape my throat, my hands curling into the fabric of his shirt. He's everywhere, the warmth of him pressed up against my legs, my hips, my chest.

His thigh shifts to press between my legs, drawing a gasp from my lips. With the slightest touch on my hip, he draws me closer, pressing me against his leg where I need him most. He lets out a low, deep rumble from somewhere in his chest. I drop my chin to my chest, breathing heavily.

This shouldn't be affecting me this much. We're fully clothed. We're moving so slowly, I could stop him at any time. But the intensity of every touch has me reeling.

His hand leaves my breast, and two fingers touch my chin, tilting it up. His warm breath coasts over my lips, my cheek. With my lids closed, the sensation feels so intense I can barely breathe.

Is this where he kisses me? Is this where we ignore any pretense of boss-employee relationships and give in to temptation?

I know one thing: If Arlo kisses me right now, I'll have sex with him. If I feel his tongue sweeping over mine, my clothes will disintegrate, and I will fuck this man right here on the kitchen counter. His thumb on my chin is like a brand, like a promise of everything to come.

I feel him shift closer. My stomach trembles as my hips buck, giving me sweet, delicious pressure against his thigh.

Then his lips slide over the corner of mine and over my cheek. His breath is gentle against my ear, and he says, "What are you hiding from me, Bonnie?"

Ice water jets through my veins, and I freeze. From one heartbeat to the next, sanity returns.

What am I *doing*? What is *wrong* with me?

I use the hands that are still propped against his stomach to push him away. Cold air rushes in, clearing the fog of lust from my vision, from my thoughts. "What?" I shout. Embarrassment rushes in like a wave.

I can't believe I let my boss touch me like that. Have I not learned my lesson about workplace romances? Not to mention this guy is my *boss*, which is even worse than what happened before. I am such an *idiot*.

He's breathing heavily, like he wasn't just trying to use sex to manipulate me.

Glaring, I slide away from him and put three big steps between us. "I can't believe you just touched me. I can't believe I let you."

"Bonnie, just tell me what you're hiding."

"Who says I'm hiding anything? You've got it in your head that you recognize me, but *we don't know each other*. I'm not some spy for your ex-wife or an evil corporation. I'm your *nanny*. I'm here for a month, and then I'll be out of your life." I heave a breath, glaring at him. "Don't you dare try to use sex to manipulate me again."

"I wasn't manipulating you."

I scoff. "Right. What was that, then? Why touch me like that until I'm soft and pliant, then try to ask me a stupid question that you already know the answer to?"

His jaw is diamond hard. He shoves a hand through his hair, trying to burn a hole through the kitchen cabinets with his gaze. "It wasn't like that."

"Uh-huh. I'm going to bed."

"Bonnie, wait—"

"Goodnight." I shove through the door to the kitchen and run downstairs, locking myself in my bedroom. Then I turn the shower on full blast and wash the last hour of my life off my skin.

But I don't cry. I've cried enough about men like Arlo Noble. I have no more tears left for him.

TWELVE
BONNIE

THE NEXT DAY, I'm happy to see that Arlo isn't in the kitchen when Alex and I make breakfast for Will. Then we have a play-date set up with one of his friends, so I get to take the limo across town and spend a few hours with William and another five-year-old boy named Vance.

I'm grateful for the distance from my boss, even if the two boys are terrors together. The sting of Arlo's manipulation still feels too intense to deal with. I thought the sizzle between us was mutual, but he used it to play his stupid mind games.

Well. Maybe Nikki was right. The reality of him is nowhere near the fantasy I've built up. He's a colossal asshole, and no amount of good sex can ever make up for it. Mr. Sexalicious only existed in my mind. Nikki will enjoy saying "I told you so."

Alex gives me the rundown on the schedule for the month and shows me how the rest of the household systems work. There are group chats with other staff members and a household schedule that we can all access and edit. I already know about the grocery list, and she also gives me access to the maintenance request portal. I throw myself into work, resolving to be nothing but professional from now on.

Even if I can feel the memory of Arlo's hands on my body, I tell myself it was all a lie. I shore up my defenses enough that when I walk into the apartment that afternoon, with Alex and Will in tow, I'm ready for the sight of him.

One thing I'm not ready for?

Hearing the voice of the man who ruined my career.

I freeze outside the elevator in front of Beth's painting, listening to the laugh that I used to find so charming.

"So," Galen says, the smile evident in his voice, "are we on for lunch next week?"

"Galen knows all the best spots," another voice says, and I recognize Chester Holt. The director of the hedge fund is a powerful, white-haired man, and I remember the way his attitude toward me flipped after the holiday party and the rumors that followed.

They're both here.

"Looking forward to it," Arlo replies, voice warm.

Panic is almost painful as it overwhelms me, rooting my feet to the floor. Alex heads for the living room and pauses when she sees me standing in the same spot in the elevator lobby. She arches her brows. "You okay?"

"Um, bathroom," I mumble, unable to make complete sentences in my panic. The only thought in my head is blaring, *GET AWAY, GET AWAY, GET AWAY!*

Footsteps approach. I dart down the hallway and lunge into the powder room that's already saved me once before and lean against the door, heart pounding, mind reeling.

Galen was a coworker of mine at Holt & Holt. I was the better performer, and when we began our illicit office romance, I started giving him pointers. I walked him through my systems for identifying equities that were undervalued, and I even shared my own spreadsheets with him. I handed him all my work on a silver platter in exchange for nothing more than a few mediocre orgasms in the office supply closet.

I was so, so stupid.

He'd smile at me and kiss me and tell me I was amazing—until he got the promotion that was meant for me. Then everything fell apart.

Why is he here? Is this some power play from Arlo? Is he trying to see my reaction to my ex-coworker to try to ferret out what I'm hiding? He thinks I'm a corporate spy, apparently, which would be funny if it weren't so ridiculous. If I'd just admitted that I was the woman from London he may or may not remember, I wouldn't be in this situation.

Taking a deep breath, I pull out my phone.

It's the second time I've had to hide in this bathroom, and this time I will call my sister. She answers on the third ring.

"Bonnie? Is everything okay?"

"No," I answer. "I can't do it, Linda."

My sister is seven years older than me. When my ankle injury happened and I lost everything the first time, she took me in when our parents wouldn't. They were disappointed in me. They told me I deserved to lose it all, but Linda housed me and built me back up to a point where I got accepted to a finance degree. She helped me fill out all the paperwork I needed to transfer colleges and even co-signed my student loans. She was more of a mother to me than our parents ever were.

Her voice is steady when she asks, "What's going on?"

And it's so Linda, it makes me want to cry. There's no emotion, no blame, no defensiveness. She's so used to me being a mess that she isn't even surprised. She's just standing with the safety net stretched below me, ready to catch my inevitable fall.

I'm so sick of letting her down.

But staying in this house might be a step too far. "He's here, Linda."

"Who?"

"Galen. Him and Mr. Holt."

There's a short pause that says more than any words. "They're in Mr. Noble's house?"

"Galen and Arlo are going to lunch next week. I heard his voice and now I'm hiding in the bathroom."

My sister's exhaled breath ruffles through the phone. "Okay," she says. "Okay. Let me look at my roster and see if I can get anyone else to take over from you. I can shuffle some things around, and worst case..."

I close my eyes. Failure is so familiar, it's almost comfortable. But I'm so ashamed to be here again, to be asking Linda for another bailout, that I find myself sliding down the door so I'm sitting on the floor. "Wait, Linda. Don't."

She pauses. "You don't want me to find a replacement?"

I think of Arlo's words last night, his touch, the way he used my weakness against me. I'm so sick of feeling like this—powerless. Alone. Pathetic.

When I hurt my ankle, I lost my scholarship and had to pull out of college. My boyfriend broke up with me and my parents refused to help. Linda took me in.

Then I rebuilt my life to a point where I had a beautiful apartment and a healthy savings account, and Galen took it away from me. I burned through my savings and lost my home. Linda found me when I was crawling around rock bottom and pulled me back up into the light. She put me here, in this house, so I could do this job.

Twice, my life has been knocked off course and my sister has been there to pick up the pieces. Can I do that to her again?

No, I decide. I can't. It's only a month—less than a month now. I can do it.

"I'll see it through," I tell her.

"Are you sure?"

"Yes. I probably won't see Galen at all. It's not like Arlo's going to bring his son's nanny to a business lunch. I can avoid him."

"Right."

The elevator dings, and I know Galen will be gone in moments. A weight lifts from my shoulders. I can't keep hiding in bathrooms when I get a shock. I can't keep running away when life knocks me off-course. I've started over twice in my adult life, and I can do it again.

I'll work for a month, get a healthy payout, then go to our family vacation home in Vermont to recover. From there, I'll have time and money and space to figure out my next steps. If I don't have the money from this job to bolster me, I won't even have a solid base to restart. I'll have to rely on Linda's generosity—again.

"I can do it, Linda. Galen's only my ex-boyfriend. Or ex-lover. Ex-fling." I huff. "Whatever. He's just an ex, and he was probably here on business. He and Mr. Holt didn't even see me, so it's no big deal. I can do this job. You don't have to find anyone else."

Linda lets out a long breath. "I'm glad, Bonnie, because I don't have anyone else who can step in until Sofia comes back from her vacation." The relief is clear in her voice, and guilt smashes my heart into a tiny ball.

I almost made Linda's life more difficult than it had to be—and she would have done it. For me.

I climb back up to my feet and say goodbye to my sister. Then I square my shoulders and stare at myself in the mirror. The woman who stares back looks frazzled and afraid, but as the seconds tick by, I watch the resolve settle into her pores.

I'm not going to fall apart at the sight of my ex, no matter how badly he used me. I'm not going to rely on anyone else to fix my life anymore. I'm not going to let Arlo Noble push me around.

So, when I grip the doorknob and exit the bathroom, I'm able to keep my spine straight and my head held high as I head to the living room. I'm able to paint a bright smile on my face when I see Alex, William, and Arlo sitting on one of the luxurious sofas. I'm even able to greet Arlo with a polite, "Hello," like we didn't have an interlude in the kitchen last night.

And when his brows lower, eyes dark as pitch, it doesn't even bother me.

I'm bulletproof. I'm standing tall on my own two feet. If I can make it through the past year, I can make it through anything.

Still, when it's time for me to retreat to my bedroom downstairs, I let out a long breath and let my shoulders drop.

Three and a half more weeks.

As night falls, doubt creeps in. For all my bravado on the phone to Linda, I don't know if I can do it.

THIRTEEN
ARLO

I MESSED UP. Bonnie's familiarity has been niggling at me so badly, and when Beth didn't recognize her, I thought I could get Bonnie to admit who she was.

But it all went wrong.

Now it's been a day and a half, and she won't look at me except when it's directly related to William. It's a perfectly adequate professional relationship. She hasn't done anything wrong.

Still.

I miss the spark in her eyes when she said something snarky. I catch myself staring at her chest, the dip of her waist. I hear her laugh and play with Will while she wraps him around and around her little finger, and I feel jealous of my own kid.

Today is Monday, and Will is off to kindergarten. He's excited, as he always is, running around like he's got batteries that never run out built into his feet. Bonnie laughs at his antics and somehow gets him fed, dressed, and ready to go with time to spare.

That's the worst part of all this—she's good with my son. I like seeing them together. I love hearing him cackle and play. Yesterday, I watched her teach Will how to write "Batman" in his clumsy handwriting, which put a smile on Will's face until he fell asleep.

I can't reproach her or complain to the Delmar Agency, because Bonnie might be the best nanny my son has had. Replacing her would be the wrong move, because Will deserves the best.

So, I watch Bonnie and Alex herd my son toward the elevator while I pretend to flick through emails on my tablet. William is beaming, strutting around with his Batman backpack like he's the coolest kid in the world.

Bonnie laughs, her smile so beautiful it sends lightning through my chest. She's wearing that silky skirt and a black tank top covered with a jean jacket. Her hair is in a high ballerina bun, held together with a black scrunchie. She looks elegant and stylish, and I want to fuck her so badly I can't think straight. The woman has driven me mad.

I don't even care that she might be a corporate spy. I don't care that she's hiding something from me. The distance she's put between us since I was such an ass in the kitchen has only made me want her more.

It's been a few days. Less than a week. Can I really stand this for much longer?

Bonnie kneels in front of my son. "What kind of backpack does Vance have?"

"He has a boring blue one," Will says, grinning. "He's gonna be sooooo jealous of mine."

"Yours is really cool."

"I know! And look!"

I glance up and see my son bent at the waist, pulling his pants up to show off his socks. They're Batman themed, of course. My son is at that age where an interest becomes an obsession. The yellow Batman symbol is dotted over his black socks all the way up his little calves.

"They're awesome," Bonnie says, smiling. "I like a man who's not afraid to take a risk with his socks."

I look up in time to see Bonnie freeze. With her whole body still, she lifts her gaze and meets mine. Her eyes are wide, something like panic flitting across her face. A memory clicks in my brain like a tumbler sliding in a lock.

And I know why Bonnie seems so familiar.

Rome was right to make the connection. I was a fool not to see it earlier.

It's *her*.

"Me too," Will answers with a nod, oblivious to what's going on over his head. "I'm going to wear these every day."

"Alex," I say, setting my tablet aside while I stand, "you go ahead with Will. I have to talk to Bonnie about something."

"Alex was going to show me how kindergarten drop-off works," Bonnie says, eyes still wide, hands clenched at her sides.

"Alex can show you tomorrow," I answer, approaching slowly.

Bonnie tears her gaze away from me and turns to look at Alex.

The other nanny shrugs and smiles. "We'll do it tomorrow. Say goodbye to Bonnie, Will!"

"Bye!" he says, stomping into the elevator. Alex smiles and presses the button, and the doors start to slide shut.

When both sides of the doors meet, Bonnie tries to sidestep around me. I catch her around the waist and walk her backward to the wall. Her hands splay near her hips against the cool marble, while mine are planted near her head.

"London," I growl, my body on fire.

This is the woman who drove me wild and then left before I woke up. She slipped through my fingers before I even learned her name.

Her eyes close. The pulse jumps in her neck. "Let's just pretend it never happened," she whispers. Caged in my arms against the wall, she lifts her chin and opens her eyes again to gaze at me, defiant. "You're my boss now. It's better to forget about the past, you know, considering."

I take a step forward so my chest is an inch from hers. "Considering what?"

"Considering you didn't even recognize me." Bright eyes. A sassy tilt of the head. I want to take this woman right here against the wall, just like I did in my hotel room three years ago.

"This is what you've been hiding," I say, realization hitting. "You recognized me when you walked into the room."

She pushes against my shoulder, and I rock back a step, my hands sliding off the wall to hang by my sides. My blood is like fire in my veins. I can't stop staring at her eyes, the line of her jaw, her lips.

I want to consume this woman. I want to drink her down until the taste of her is embedded inside me.

A night with her was a night like no other. I met her at a hotel bar and never looked back. We fucked like we were meant for each other. She turned me inside out.

And then she left when I was asleep, slinking off in the early morning hours like she was embarrassed of what she'd done with me.

"Look, Arlo," she says, smoothing her hands down her thighs, "this doesn't have to change anything. I'm willing to ignore that night for the sake of this job, and I hope you're willing to do the same. I spoke to my sister, and I don't think she has a replacement available for the next four weeks—"

"You tried to leave? Again?"

Sweet, hot anger floods her expression. Her cheeks go pink.

"Excuse me? What do you mean, again? You didn't even recognize me!"

"I never *saw* you that night, Bonnie. I didn't know your name. How was I supposed to recognize you from across the room?"

Confusion and outrage war in her expression. Her lips fall open, and I want to take them in mine. Now that I know who she is—now that I know why my body has been so keyed up around her since the moment she walked into my house—I'm not sure I'll be able to resist the temptation of her.

"What," she says, chest heaving, "are you talking about?"

"I... Look, I lost my glasses that night. I was half-blind when I sat down at the bar."

Her mouth falls open, anger like lightning bolts in her eyes. "You lost your *glasses*? What kind of excuse is that?"

"It's not an excuse. It's the truth. I was severely nearsighted. I couldn't see a thing unless it was a couple of inches from my face. I saw parts of you—"

She scoffs.

"—but I don't know. I guess my brain never put them together into a whole."

"And you didn't mention this, why?"

"Because a beautiful woman was talking to me, and I didn't want to ruin the mood."

"You didn't want to ruin the mood. Oh my God. That's the most ridiculous thing I've ever heard." She is unbelievably gorgeous when she's angry. Her eyes are bright, her cheeks red. I'm hard as stone just standing here. "And how the heck would you know I'm beautiful if *you couldn't even see me?*"

I need her. Badly. I reach an arm toward her. "Bonnie..."

Her anger reaches new heights as she glares. "So, wait. You saw parts of me, but not well enough that you'd recognize me. And you slept with me?" She crosses her arms. Uncrosses them. "So you stumbling and bumping into stuff when we went up to your room...you weren't that drunk, were you?"

I tilt my head back and let out a bitter laugh. "No. I'd lost my glasses somewhere between the restaurant and the bar. One of the workers was checking the table and the lost-and-found at the hotel, and I said I'd wait at the bar. Then you and I started talking, and..."

She wraps her arms around herself. "God. I feel...dirty."

I frown. "Why?"

"You didn't even see my face! I was just some...*body* to you. A hole to fuck." Her face scrunches, and I hate that I put that expression on her face.

That night was the first good night I'd had since Alice betrayed me. Bonnie appeared in my life like a brilliant flare, illuminating the world in a way that was as unfamiliar as it was beautiful. And it wasn't just sex. The sex was hot as hell. But we talked. We laughed. I touched her body and *felt* something.

She wasn't just a body. She was the first good thing I'd experienced in two years. She was a balm to my aching heart. When I woke up in that bed, alone, reality rushed in hard and fast, and I almost thought I'd dreamed the whole thing.

And now she thinks that it meant nothing to me. She thinks I just happened to sit beside her and took advantage of it. Yes, I happened to sit beside her. I was horribly nearsighted so I didn't see her face until I was practically kissing her in my room, arms wrapped around her while I pushed her up against the door. Then we were frantic, and it didn't matter. Her body was in focus. Her lips. The noises she made. But it was so much more than that.

There was her wit, her laughter, her self-deprecating humor. I could tell she was beautiful without having to see her with crystal clarity. If I'd known she looked like *this* though, I probably would have tried harder to learn her name and keep her by my side.

I crowd closer. "It wasn't like that. You were more than a body, Bonnie."

"Oh, right." She scowls at me. "You waxed poetic about how beautiful I was, and you couldn't even see me clearly. Do you know how embarrassing that is? I *believed* you. You made me feel... You..." She turns her head to the side, tears welling on her lower lashes.

I want to tear the world apart. The sight of her almost crying because of *me*—that's unacceptable. "I knew you were beautiful, Bonnie."

She snorts. "Right."

"You made me laugh when we sat at the bar," I say, hoping she hears the sincerity in my voice. "Your voice turned me on from the first time I heard it. And you were so quick with that sharp tongue of yours. Sitting there next to you was foreplay. I'd never experienced anything like it. You *are* beautiful. I didn't have to see your face clearly to know it. But then I came closer and I saw your lips." My gaze drops to them, and they part on an inhale. "I saw your skin. I was drunk on you, Bonnie."

Her bottom lip trembles. I need to fix this.

"Bonnie," I coax. "Look at me."

She does. Her glare burns a hole right through me. "What about now? Why haven't I seen you in glasses? This is crazy. Just tell me you didn't recognize me, Arlo. I'd rather not be lied to again."

Again? What does that mean?

"I got laser eye surgery. I don't need glasses anymore." I step closer, sliding a hand over her hip. "You weren't just a body, Bonnie."

She huffs, turning her face away from me. Slight tremors pass through her body; I wouldn't notice them if I didn't have my hand on her. She holds herself so tight, so closed off.

It's a damn shame, is what it is. The Bonnie from three years ago was open and light and free. Something happened to her since then.

My hand slides up to her waist, thumb stroking along her ribs. "It killed me that you left before I woke up."

"Don't try to turn around and blame *me* for anything."

"I'm not." I stroke my thumb over and back once more. Another tremor passes through her body, stronger this time, like my touch is affecting her as much as it is me. Now I know why Saturday night in the kitchen felt like coming home. Now I know why I've been driven mad with fuzzy memories just beyond my grasp.

Because it's *her*. She's the one who slipped away. She's the one I wanted to keep.

And she's furious. Her eyes are bright, brilliant blue, and her fists are clenched. She crosses her arms, like she's doing her best to keep her hands off of me. "I can't believe you never even saw me clearly. It makes me feel like the whole night was a lie."

There's hurt in her gaze along with the anger, and the sight of it makes my soul sing, because that hurt tells me our night together meant something to her, just as it did for me.

I slide my hand from her waist to her back, then use my other hand to touch her jaw. "You left without saying goodbye," I say softly, tracing her lips with my gaze. "I hated that."

"We agreed it was just a night of fun," she whispers.

"That was before we even kissed," I say, letting my hand slide into the hair at the nape of her neck.

Bonnie's eyes droop halfway closed, like my touch is a drug. "It didn't mean anything."

I bring my lips closer to hers. "Liar."

Her chest rises and falls with shallow, quick breaths. "You are so arrogant."

Relishing the softness of her skin beneath my fingers, I meet her gaze. "I'm sorry about Saturday night. The kitchen. I wasn't trying to manipulate you."

"You thought I was a corporate spy or a friend of your ex-wife's." Hurt splashes across her face, quickly erased. "But I'm just some girl you screwed on a one-night stand."

I tighten my hands on her, bringing her flush against my chest. She fits like she was made for me. Of course she does. She's the one. She's the one who slipped through my fingers.

How did I miss it?

Maybe it's because this time, we met under such different circumstances. We're not at a luxury hotel bar. She wasn't wearing a hot little pencil skirt like the night I first met her. Context matters, but I still missed what was right in front of me.

She could still be here for Holt & Holt. It's a pretty big coincidence that she started working here after leaving their employ while they're trying to woo me. But all my blood must be occupied somewhere other than my brain, because I can't seem to find the will to care. She's here, and she's beautiful, and I want her so badly I can't think of anything else.

"We can't do this." Her body is soft against mine. Her lips are so kissable, it takes all my self-control to keep from taking them in mine.

"Why not?"

Her shimmery silk skirt moves like water over her legs. It tangles in my calves, and all I want to do is pull it up over her waist, hike her up against this wall, and take her right here. My cock is an iron bar between us, and I'm sure she can feel it. I *want* her to feel it. I want her to know what she does to me.

"You're my boss," she whispers. "I can't sleep with you." Her eyes flick from my lips to my eyes. "And you're such a huge asshole, I'd never be able to live with myself if I gave in to temptation."

My smile comes unbidden, just like it did that night three years ago. She has this uncanny ability to draw real emotion from me. Anger. Frustration. Joy. Lust.

"Don't you want to know?" I say, eyes on her mouth. Her sweet, dirty mouth. The mouth that drove me insane that night. The mouth I dreamed about for two months straight after our encounter.

"Know what?" It comes out as a breathy whisper.

"If the reality lives up to the fantasy?"

She lets out a derisive little snort. "You didn't fantasize about me."

"Oh?" I tug on her hair, just to see if she still likes it a little rough. Her sleek ballerina bun comes apart in my hand, hair falling around her face.

The hitch in her breath tells me she does like it. "No. You probably didn't even think about me after I walked out the door."

She doesn't know how wrong she is. This little vixen drove me nuts with what she did to me. "I looked for you," I growl. "I asked the front desk, but they wouldn't release your name. I scoured the brochures from the conference you attended to see if you were a speaker. I went through the websites of every company I saw listed to try to find your name." I tighten my hold on her hair. "I looked for you, Bonnie. Harder than I've ever looked for anyone before. But you were a ghost. I thought I'd made you up."

Her gaze takes on a dangerous light. "Now who's the cyber-stalker?"

"That mouth of yours is going to get you in trouble," I warn.

"At least I know that if everything goes wrong, you won't recognize me after I leave."

I let out a low growl—and then, unable to wait a second longer —I kiss her. Her lips are as sweet as I remember, pillowy and soft and perfect. I groan into her mouth, nipping at her bottom lip. She parts for me, and I slide my tongue against hers.

Bonnie's body melts, her hands coming up to cling to my shoulders. I love the feel of her against me. I love the way she rolls her hips like it's instinct, like she can't help herself from wanting me as badly as I want her.

In the kitchen, I was slow. I enjoyed teasing and torturing. Today, I'm not wasting any time. My need is too overwhelming.

Gripping her hair in a tight fist, I pull her head back and run my hungry lips down her throat. My other hand slides up her ribcage and cups her breast, fingers tugging at the neckline of her tank. I bare her breast to me, taking that soft, giving flesh in my palm. Skin against skin, we moan in unison.

Bonnie's chest heaves violently as I knead her breast, my lips finding hers once more. I kiss her like I've been waiting for her for three years. I kiss her like she's the only light in a dark, dark world. I kiss her like she's the missing piece.

And she lights up for me. Moaning as she kisses me back, Bonnie shoves her hands into my hair and gives as good as she gets. Sweet little points of pain in my scalp make our kiss that much hotter. I drop my hand from her breast and slide it up the inside of her thigh, beneath the shimmery fabric of her skirt. Her skin is like silk against the back of my hand, the soft give of her flesh an erotic temptation I can't—won't—resist.

Bonnie is mine. I'm not letting her go. Not again.

Lips against hers, I ask, "Are you wet for me, Bonnie?"

"You are such an ass," she pants.

My hand slides up to the gusset of her panties, feeling her warm wetness through the fabric. I groan as my cock throbs, my body remembering how incredible it felt to be sheathed inside her. Exactly where I'll be once more in about ten seconds.

Then the elevator bell dings, and we fly apart.

FOURTEEN
BONNIE

I'M A HOT, bothered mess, batting my hair back from my face as I scramble to put myself back in order. My scrunchie is on the floor. I pick it up and try to fix my hair while my breath saws in and out of my lungs.

A man steps out of the elevator, wearing a black suit with tiny charcoal pinstripes, a matching waistcoat, and a white shirt. His tie is skinny and black, and his shoes are very shiny.

He casts his eye over the two of us, a single dark brow arching. He takes in my messy, frazzled appearance, then flicks his gaze to Arlo, who looks remarkably put-together. He isn't even breathing heavily. The man jabs a thumb at the elevator. "I can come back when you're not...busy."

Arlo's voice is gruff when he says, "Go away."

The man's blue eyes twinkle with glee.

"Aren't you supposed to be in Ibiza?" Arlo growls.

The man spreads his arms. "Change of plans." His gaze shifts to meet mine. "You must be the new nanny."

I am *not* acknowledging that, because it means Arlo told this guy about me, and my brain is not running at full capacity right now. I can't process the implications. I fluff my skirt. "I was just leaving. Excuse me." I nod at the man, then at Arlo, and scurry away from the two of them, beelining toward the stairs. Taking them two at a time doesn't help slow my rioting heart, but somehow I manage to make it back to my room in one piece. I close the door and lock it, then drop my head in my hands.

What the hell am I *doing?*

I've made this mistake once before, with Galen. I had an affair at work, and it blew up in my face. I should have learned my lesson, but apparently I'm doomed to repeat the mistakes of my past. Except this time it's even worse, because Arlo isn't a coworker; he's my boss.

Linda is relying on me. Why couldn't I just tell her that Arlo and I slept together? She would have found someone else. I let my pride—or maybe my shame—get in the way.

The embarrassment is just too much. I hurry to the closet and grab one of my suitcases, tossing it onto the bed.

Linda will forgive me. I'll make it up to her.

But I can't do this. I can't spend the next three and a half weeks with this man when he knows who I am. When he says those sweet, beautiful things to me. When he touches me like he owns my body, like he craves me as much as I crave him.

I mean—lost glasses? Please. *Please.* I'm not a *complete* moron.

Well. That's probably debatable. But still—I know a line when I hear it. He could just admit that he didn't recognize me because I was one of many one-night stands and they all blur together for him. That, at least, would be more believable. It wouldn't make my heart ache with hope.

I toss things into my suitcase without folding them. Every ounce of my focus is trained on getting my things together and getting the hell out of here.

Then there's a knock on the door. "Bonnie." Arlo's voice sounds seductive, even through the locked door.

"I'm busy."

The doorknob rattles. "Open the door, Bonnie. We need to talk."

"I quit."

A pause, followed by a growl: "No."

"You don't get to say no to this, Arlo. You know as well as I do that this is a bad idea. I'll leave, and we'll both move on."

The knob rattles again, harder. "Bonnie, open the door."

I stand at the foot of the bed, holding a lacy camisole in my hands, and look at the closed door like it's a vicious beast about to attack me. Half of me wants to throw the door open. The other half wants to keep packing, call a cab, and get the heck out of here.

A slap on the door sounds, like Arlo just hit it with his open palm and left his hand there. "Please."

I hesitate.

His voice is cajoling now. "We need to talk about this, Bonnie. I was an ass to you since you started working here, and I'm sorry. We can figure this out."

"Figure what out?"

"Us."

I toss the camisole into my suitcase. "There is no us. There can't be an us. I work for you, Arlo. I'm your son's nanny. That's all."

"That's *not* all."

"It has to be all of it," I answer, grabbing a stack of T-shirts and tossing them into the suitcase. I'll re-fold them when I'm home—except then I remember I don't have a home. Panic wells in my chest, a hot, bubbling mess of emotion.

Where will I go? I can't stay here.

I'll call Nikki. She'll put me up until I can get a plane ticket to

Vermont. Yeah. That's what I'll do. What are credit cards for, right? I'll get a job somehow, and then I'll figure things out. On my own. No more relying on Linda to bail me out.

"That night *meant* something to me, Bonnie," Arlo says, his voice thick. "You have no idea. You were the first person to drag me out of the dark. You did it before we ever touched. Your voice did it to me. Your laughter. And then you left before I woke up, and it fucking killed me. Don't do it to me again."

I hesitate, heart pounding. On quiet feet, I walk to the door and lean my head against the frame. I should go back to the closet and keep packing, but his words are like sweet honey to me. My wildest fantasy was for that night to mean something to my mystery man the same way it did for me.

And now, Arlo is saying it did. It can't be true…can it? It's more silly lines, like the glasses.

But then I think of the way he patted his pocket in the wine cellar. I've seen Linda do that when she's looking for her glasses. She touches her head, then her pocket, then frowns when she realizes her glasses are on her face. Exactly what Arlo did.

Could it be true?

I hear myself ask quietly, "What do you mean, I pulled you out of the dark?"

His face is close to mine, just on the other side of the door. He's speaking quietly, but I can hear him clearly. "Our night together was two years after Alice and I decided to divorce. I'd fallen for her hard. We met, got together, and she got pregnant within six months. I was ecstatic. I married her within two months of finding out about the baby, like an idiot. I didn't realize she didn't care for me the way I did for her. I found her with another man."

I hear a rustle of fabric and another breath. I grip the door-jamb, frowning.

Then he says, "The divorce was messy and expensive. I thought she was upset about losing Will until she came out and asked me for money. And I realized she'd played me."

"You mean..."

"The guy she cheated on me with was her long-time boyfriend. Our entire relationship was a lie. I was just a meal ticket, and Will meant nothing to her."

Oh. Wow. "I'm so sorry."

He scoffs. There's a rustle of fabric, like he's shifting on the other side of the door. "I paid her to go away, and she did. I was ashamed and embarrassed and hurt and above all, worried for my son. I sank really deep, Bonnie. I couldn't see a way out. And then I went to London on a business trip, and I met you."

Oh, it's a tempting fantasy, isn't it? That I, in all my glory, could fix this big, wounded bear of a man. I lean my head against the door, not knowing what to say. What to think.

"You were this beautiful, light-filled fairy that flitted into my life, Bonnie. And I didn't even know what you looked like. I didn't know your name. You were this one bright moment in months and months of utter shit."

"I'm not a light-filled fairy, Arlo," I tell him quietly. "I'm just a woman." A broke, broken woman who's had to restart her life one too many times.

There's a pause, then Arlo continues in a low voice. "That night, you told me about your work. You said that you enjoyed the challenge but you hated the culture. You told me it wasn't something you'd ever seen yourself doing, but it provided you with a decent life, so you couldn't complain."

My throat closes up. He remembers all that? Maybe it wasn't just a night of debauchery for him. Maybe some of what he's saying about me—about us—is true.

"I remember you telling me about your sister. How she'd

started her own business, and how you'd always been a little envious of her. How did I not put it together? How did I not see that it was you?"

"You remember all that?" I ask softly.

"I remember every minute of that night, Bonnie."

Before I know what I'm doing, my fingers are turning the lock on the door. I pull it open and see him there, standing on the other side of the threshold with his heart in his eyes.

It terrifies me. I haven't felt this vulnerable since the holiday party at Holt & Holt, when I watched my reputation and career crumble before my eyes.

"What if we've created something out of that night that doesn't exist?" I ask softly. "What if I'm not as amazing as you remember, and it turns out I'm just the nanny who completely messes her life up every few years?"

He steps into the room and closes the door behind him. "What if I'm not what you remember? What if I'm just some arrogant rich guy who didn't even have the decency to recognize the woman who changed the course of his life?"

I roll my eyes. "Not only am I a fairy, but I also changed your life? Please."

"You made me believe in something better. I started the Noble Foundation after I met you because I couldn't stop thinking about what you said about meaning and fulfillment. I realized I felt the same way about my own work."

My heart thumps. Is it possible?

His hands slide over my hips, and he pulls me closer. He leans against the door and spreads his legs so I fit between them, my chest draped over his. I curl my fingers into his shirt and look up at his dark eyes, knowing I'm making a mistake.

I should pack my bags and run.

"You're my boss," I say weakly, trying to erect one last shield between us.

His hands coast down to my ass, squeezing gently. "Not right now, I'm not."

It's hard to think clearly when Mr. Sexalicious is here, in the flesh, kneading my butt. Arlo grips the elastic waistband of my skirt and gives it a little flick so it flutters to my feet. Then his hands slide to the skin he just bared, and I can't help but let out a shaky breath. His touch feels too good, like he's claiming what he's been owed all these years. Like I want him to claim more of me.

"Who was that guy?" I ask, trying to claw my sanity back.

"A friend. He's gone now." His hands slide up to my chest, pulling off my jean jacket. It falls to the floor in a heap. My T-shirt is next, the fabric shivering over my skin as he removes it. I stand in the vee of his legs as he leans against the door, wearing nothing but my underwear. Goosebumps rise over my skin as his hands coast up my thighs and down my back. He squeezes my butt, spreading my cheeks, then moves his hands up my back again. His fingers slide over my spine, then wrap around my ribs.

Over my bra, he touches my breasts. His thumbs brush over my nipples like they did in the kitchen, gently yet surely. I'm trembling, I realize, clinging to him with all my strength.

When I let my gaze climb up to his eyes, the desire written on his face makes my knees weak. He slides a hand up to my chest, placing his palm flat over my skin. His other hand curves around my back to hold me against him as he feels my heart pounding against his palm.

Only then does he drop his lips to my neck. Kisses rain down on me, up my neck and under my ear, across my jaw, on my temple. His hands glide and stroke, so softly, like he's memorizing the shape of me. It's a drugging feeling.

This big, powerful man is gentling me, coaxing me out of my fear and into his arms.

My own hands explore his shoulders, his chest. I tangle my fingers into the hair at his nape, then back over his shoulders. He's so broad, so strong, so incredibly perfect. I want all that bulk on top of me. Underneath me. I want him every which way, all day and all night. I want to forget my own name.

When he kisses my lips, it's with soft, gentle movements which are somehow more intense than the passion that exploded upstairs. He cups my cheek and systematically destroys every last wall I've built, so all that remains inside me is lust and need.

"Arlo," I manage to whisper when he moves his lips to kiss my neck.

Growling in response, he reaches behind me to unhook my bra. It falls on top of the heap of clothes at our feet—clothes that only belong to me. He's still fully clothed, the fabric of his shirt soft against my bare skin.

A big hand slides over my breast, sending darts of pleasure diving through my stomach. I arch into him, fusing my hips to his.

He's hard. I can feel his cock against my stomach. More pleasure arcs inside me at the feel of that steel between us, and I can't help but give in to the temptation to reach for it. But as soon as my palm touches his shaft through his pants, Arlo grips my wrist and pulls my hand away.

"No," he says.

"Let me touch you."

"Not yet."

"Please," I pant.

He smiles. It's an evil, delicious smile that sends another thunderbolt to the pit of my stomach. "As much as I love hearing that word on your lips, in that tone, the answer is no, Bonnie." He grabs both my wrists and walks me backward until I feel the edge of the bedpost behind me. The corner digs into my spine as Arlo lifts my arms up above my head. "Hold on, and don't let go until I say so."

"Okay, Mr. Domineering," I snark, gripping the post. "Happy?"

He steps back and looks at me, lids heavy. "Very."

With a single finger, Arlo draws a line from my shoulder, across my collarbone, down the center of my chest. Shivers erupt over my skin. That finger continues its path under my left breast and around the side, slowly spiraling toward my peaked nipple. My breaths become heavy and harsh. Every second is beautiful torture, every touch increasingly intense.

When his finger finally reaches my nipple, he tweaks it gently, then moves to the other breast and repeats.

This is madness. I should stop it. But my lids drop lower as desire wins over reason. I can't think of anything except that I want more.

Isn't this what I dreamed about for three whole years? Arlo is quite literally my most ardent fantasy come to life.

The outline of his cock is visible through his black pants, big and hard and ignored. Arlo continues his soft torture of my breasts, watching his fingers on my skin like it's the most fascinating thing he's ever seen.

"I could see your skin up close," he says softly. "That night. I remember this mole." He touches the beauty mark on the side of my right breast. "I saw your lips and your eyes clearly when we were face to face, but there's something incredible about seeing all of you. You're so beautiful, Bonnie."

Those words—so similar to the words he said to me that night. They send a wave of lust crashing through me. I want so badly to believe everything he says.

Arlo's finger continues its journey south, over the soft part of my lower belly. My stomach quivers at his touch, thighs clenching. He runs his fingertip along the waistband of my panties, from one hip to the other and back again. I whimper, wanting to touch him. Wanting him to touch me.

"Don't you dare drop your hands," he growls, like he can read my mind.

I grip the post harder, fingernails scraping the wood. My heart thunders. My knees are weak.

"Take your clothes off," I say, breathy and hoarse. "I want to see you too."

His gaze climbs all the way up to meet mine. That devilish smile graces his lips once more. "No."

"Arlo."

He slides his hand beneath my panties and groans at the wetness he finds there. "I like the way you say my name like that," he says, dragging his finger through my desire. "Say it again."

"Arlo," I repeat. "Stop torturing me."

A dark chuckle, and he's pushing my underwear down my thighs until it falls to the floor. He runs a broad palm from my knee to my hip then back down the inside, watching the movement of his hand with an intense, dark gaze. Slight pressure on the inside of my knee tells me he wants me to lift it, and I place my foot on the mattress.

He lets out a trembling exhale, his gaze on the exposed heart of me. Because that's what I am—exposed. Utterly naked to him, spread for his viewing pleasure.

It turns me on more than I can comprehend. I stand with my hands clinging to the post above my head, my legs spread, and I watch him watch me. I follow the movement of his hand as he squeezes his cock through his pants, like he's a moment away from losing control. His chest heaves.

"Touch yourself," he commands. "Show me how you make yourself come."

I inhale sharply. This is what I loved from that night. The growled commands. The edge of filthiness that somehow made me feel more beautiful. The way his hands and mouth and voice worshipped me from head to toe.

"Bonnie," he gentles, squeezing his cock once more. "Show me."

I lower my right hand and slide it up my inner thigh, then draw it through the wetness he's drawn from me. I'm flushed, trembling, and so turned on I can't think straight. I've never masturbated in front of anyone like this. Not when I'm utterly naked and he's fully clothed. Not when I know I shouldn't be letting myself be this vulnerable with a man. Not when I want his cock inside me so badly I can't even make words.

But I work my finger over my bud as he groans, watching me. Occasionally, his gaze lifts to my breasts, my lips, my eyes, then drops back down to what I'm doing between my legs. When I slide a finger inside myself, he lets out a heavy exhale and unzips his pants. I watch the movement of his fist beneath his boxer-briefs, pleasure arcing inside me at the sight of this man coming undone before me.

I know I'm close when my thighs start to tremble. The grip of my left hand on the post tightens, and my movements become jerkier, more frantic.

He urges me on with growled words and dark eyes. When I fall over the edge, I let out a cry, legs jerking. Arlo catches me when I fall forward, lifting me onto the bed. With a frustrated grunt, he knocks my suitcase off the bed.

"Hey," I protest weakly, but then he's tearing his shirt open and ripping his undershirt off. His chest is truly glorious. In the haze of my pleasure-drunk mind, it's all I can do to smile at the sight of it. I lift myself onto my elbow and reach up for him and run my fingers through the coarse hair I missed so much, and it feels like coming home.

"I dreamed of your chest," I admit, my eyes following the line of hair down to where it disappears beneath his open fly.

"Yeah?" He shucks his pants and underwear off, and I get my first look at his beautiful cock.

I lick my lips. "After that night, I compared every guy to you."

Arlo wraps a hand around his cock. "No one came close, did they?" He stands next to the bed above me as I run my hand from his chest, down his stomach, and over the fist that grips his shaft. I run a finger over every knuckle and onto the soft skin of his cock. He strokes himself. "Did they, Bonnie?"

"No," I whisper, knowing I'm telling him too much but unable to stop myself. "No one came close."

Then I bring my lips to lick the bead of moisture from his tip. His groan is like heroin to me; as soon as I hear the raw desire in his voice, I want more. I wrap my lips around his cock and suck him as deep as I can, loving the noises he makes. His fingers tunnel into my hair and hold me there while he swears a blue streak above me.

This shouldn't be happening. In some corner of my mind, I know that I'm making a mistake. He's my boss, for one, and no matter what he says about that night we had three years ago, there's no way it meant as much to him as it did to me.

Then there's Galen. Why was he here? How can I give Arlo even more power over me when he clearly doesn't trust me? He finally remembered me, but what about everything else? We can't possibly come at this as equals.

But oh, I want him. I want him so much I can't think straight. I've fantasized about having this man's cock in my mouth for three years. I've wanted him to push me down and fuck me senseless. I've dreamed of the orgasm he'd give me with his tongue.

And now he's here, and I'm here, and it's better than I remembered.

Those noises he's making drive me wild. The way he grips my hair and holds me where he wants me sends renewed desire dancing in my blood.

His fingers tighten on my hair, and then he's pulling me away. His eyes are completely black now, coasting over my body like he owns every inch of it. In this moment, he certainly does.

"Lie down," he says in that gruff, commanding voice, and I have no choice but to obey. I land on the heavenly pillows and spread my arms for him to join me. He kneels on the bed and spreads my knees apart, his breaths harsh in the silent room. His eyes are on my center again, and far from making me self-conscious, the lust in his gaze only heightens my pleasure.

A rough hand palms my breast as he leans over me. "I'm going to eat your pussy," he informs me as he drags his cock through my arousal. "You're going to come on my tongue while you scream my name." He rolls his hips, giving me the delicious contact of his steel-hard shaft against my clit.

I moan, arching into him. "Need you," I pant, and it's the truth. I'm an idiot for it, but it's the truth. I shouldn't admit how much I crave him.

"You'll get me," he says, grinding his cock against me. "But I want to taste you first."

It feels so good. So fucking good I can't think of anything else. I lift my hips, and his cock slides down toward my opening. "Please." I'm begging, and I don't care.

He lets out a low curse, his eyes on the space between us. I follow his gaze and see the tip of his cock fitted inside me. We both pause, wanting, watching.

"Please," I repeat, wiggling down onto his tip. Even the slightest stretch feels so good.

"Condom," he grunts. "You have one?"

"No," I whine. Why would I have a condom? I haven't had sex with anyone for over a year.

"Fuck." His hips move, almost involuntarily. He slides inside me another inch. "*Fuck.*"

He pulls out, but I'm so out of my mind that my legs wrap around his waist. "Bonnie," he growls dangerously. "We can't."

"I know," I agree, but my hips roll and take him inside me again. Just a bit. Just to ease the ache. *Need need need need...*

This is exactly why this is a bad idea. Arlo Noble has so much power over me, I forget myself. He did this to me three years ago too. Transported me to another world. Made me into a creature made of lust. It terrified me and turned me on. It left such an impression that I pined after him for three entire years.

He pulls out, and my legs fall open. We stay there—him kneeling between my spread legs, me prone on the bed—panting.

"You on the pill?" Arlo growls, hand on his cock again. His eyes are glued to my core as he fists himself. "Tell me you're on the pill."

"No," I whisper. "I went off it a few months ago. Wasn't having sex and I couldn't afford the prescription."

His fist pumps once, twice. He exhales, squeezing the root. It's so hot to see him this close to losing control. This big, powerful man is coming apart because of me.

"I got snipped after Will," he tells me. "But..."

"We should use a condom."

"Yeah."

I let my hand slide between my legs again and relish the groan that escapes his lips. He jerks himself off while I touch my oversensitive clit, and I want to cry because it's not enough. An orgasm shimmers in the distance, too far away. I growl in frustration.

Arlo exhales. His gaze meets mine. His jaw is so hard, a muscle jumps in his cheek. "I want you, Bonnie. I want you so bad I can't think straight."

At least it's not only me.

"I got tested after my ex," I pant, moving my hand away and spreading my legs wider. I'm wanton. I'm needy. I'm mindless with lust. It's hard to make words. "There hasn't been anyone since. I'm clean. Are you?"

"Yes." It comes out as a rasp, and his hands grip my thighs. He pushes them wider and shoves inside me.

We moan in unison. He grips my legs and pulls me toward him, holding me wide open while he works his hips in a steady, punishing rhythm.

Tears gather at the corners of my eyes. He fills me so perfectly that the only thing I can do is let my mouth fall open on a cry.

"My name," he says. "Say my name."

"Arlo," I moan, rolling my hips to meet his. This is insane. It feels too good. It can't be real.

"Who do you belong to?" He lifts one of my legs onto his shoulder and leans over me, his hand fisting into the pillow beside my head. "Say it, Bonnie."

He's so deep inside me, I've never felt anything like it. I reach up to touch his face, his shoulders, my nails digging into his hard muscle.

"Say it." His hips punch forward.

"You," I pant. "You."

A growl rides his voice. "Only me."

"Only you," I vow while alarms blare in some distant corner of my mind. This is too much, too soon. There's no trust between us. I can't make promises like that.

But his hands roam over my breasts, my sides, my face. His lips collide with mine, and he kisses me so hard I might bruise. Then his fingers tangle with mine and he slips my hand between our bodies. He levers himself up and places my hand where we're joined, groaning when I start rubbing my clit again.

"You like watching me touch myself," I pant, pleasure sparking in my thighs.

He sheathes himself to the hilt. "Fuck yes."

Arlo's face is so beautiful, drawn tight with pleasure and need. Redness sweeps over his chest and neck, darkening the gold of his skin. I want to feel him spill inside me. The thought of this big man coming apart like that, for me...

My orgasm is too intense for words. From a distance, I hear him growl with satisfaction as I clench around him. I leave this plane of existence for long moments as pleasure drenches me, arching my back and seizing my muscles.

Arlo's movements become rougher, his hands gripping my hips with bruising strength. With a roar, he pulls out of me and makes a dirty interlude even dirtier. I watch him orgasm over my core, my stomach, on my hand, across my thighs, and it's the most beautiful thing I've ever seen—which is really just more evidence that I've lost my mind for him.

It takes me a long while to catch my breath. Arlo recovers more quickly, disappearing into the bathroom for a moment. He comes back with a wet washcloth in his hands, then starts gently cleaning up the mess he made of me. His touch is gentle, reverent, and it makes my heart ache so much I can hardly breathe.

Then he collapses in bed beside me, wraps me in his arms, and places a tender kiss just below my right ear.

And I know, in that moment, that I'm in very big trouble.

FIFTEEN
BONNIE

AFTER ARLO LEAVES MY ROOM, I take my time as I put my clothes away and put myself together again. Then I head back upstairs and find Alex waiting for me in the playroom. We do the kindergarten pick-up together, then go through our afternoon and evening routine with Will. He's a great kid. While I spend time with him and Arlo, it makes me yearn for more of this—more family, more connection, more stability.

That evening, when Will is in bed, Alex is gone, and the rest of the staff have left for the night, I lie in bed and wonder what happens from here. What will I do when the month is up? What will I do with my life going forward in general?

Then the door opens, and Arlo stands in the opening with the top two buttons of his shirt undone, and at least I know what will happen for the next few hours.

THE REST of the week passes in a blur of five-year-old mania, kindergarten drop-offs and pick-ups, and last-minute preparations from Alex. Nights are another story. They're sinful, craven, and utterly secret.

Arlo and I act professional while the sun is out and people are around, and it only makes our illicit nights more exciting.

But that, in itself, scares me. Isn't this how it started with Galen? That secret, thrilling feeling of hiding what we felt for each other? Except it was only me who felt it. It was me who was the fool.

Still, when Thursday night rolls around and Alex says a teary-eyed goodbye for the final time as she leaves for her maternity leave, I watch the elevator doors close on her and know everything will be different now. And it is—as soon as Will is asleep, Arlo corners me outside the boy's bedroom.

"You're sleeping in my bed tonight," he informs me, his hands coasting down my sides.

"Am I?"

"Mm."

"That's very presumptuous of you."

He kisses my throat, a broad palm dropping between my legs. The seam of my jeans provides delicious friction as Arlo presses his hand where I need him most. "Yes," he agrees. "But it's still what's going to happen."

He unzips my pants and makes me come right there in the hallway, his big hand in my underwear, his dark eyes watching my expression. And I love it—the way he touches me, owns me. The way he watches me like he wants to commit every sigh to memory.

Eyes wide open, I walk into trouble. I follow him to his bedroom and enjoy every minute of what follows.

The next morning, I try to creep out of bed before the sun comes up. Arlo groans and hooks an arm around my waist, pulling me tight to his chest. "How many times do I have to tell you not to run away from me before dawn?"

"I have to go downstairs before Laura gets here," I protest, but Arlo is turning me onto my back and raining kisses down my body. He growls in response, pushing my thighs wide before licking me like he's starved for me. All the fight goes out of me, and I find myself burying my fingers in his hair and grinding my hips against his mouth.

He grips my ass and lifts me up to feast on me, using his lips and tongue to tear me apart. I come with a cry as he moans.

"I love the taste of you," he says, rising to his knees. He looks like a warrior god come to life, cock jutting out hard and proud as he lets his gaze take in my pleasure-sated state.

"I'm glad," I respond. "I love that you love the taste of me."

His lips curl. "Minx."

I stretch my arms overhead and luxuriate in the feeling of being watched by him. "I guess I should get up now. Thanks for that."

I make a move to get out of bed—and I don't make it very far. With a growl, Arlo grabs my hips and flips me over. I squeal, giggling, loving every second of being manhandled by him. His hands wrap around my waist as he pulls me up on my knees, keeping my chest and face mashed on the mattress. Then he enters me with a hard thrust.

"You know what to do, Bonnie," he says in a low voice, hands at my hips. He moves slowly and deliberately inside me, like he has all the time in the world.

I moan and reach down to touch myself. We fly apart together, and then he does let me get out of bed and sneak back to my room. Not a minute too soon, because I hear the elevator ding just as I close my bedroom door.

When I'm decent, I go wake Will up and pretend that my life is going according to plan. I see Laura in the kitchen and smile at her. "Morning."

She looks at me curiously. "You're in a good mood."

"It's a beautiful day," I say, hoping my blush isn't as obvious as it feels. This is all too familiar, but I can't stop myself. Now that I've had Arlo and he's made me hope for things I've wanted for three years...I'm not sure I can resist the temptation.

"On that note," Laura answers, "Mr. Noble wants you to put together a picnic basket for the three of you for today."

My brows jump. "Oh. Okay." I look at Will. "Any requests?"

"Ham sandwich." He stuffs a triangle of toast in his mouth. "I like ham."

"I can do that," I say with a smile. I pull out a picnic basket from a cabinet on the far wall and get to work putting the fixings together, trying to ignore the fluttering of my heart.

A short while later, Will, Arlo, and I are in the limo on our way to Fort Tryon park. Will chatters excitedly about his week at school.

"And Mrs. Hailey said I did a really good job writing Batman, but then she said I had to write my real name on my papers instead."

I laugh, glancing at Arlo. "Whoops." I arch my brows at Will. "Maybe I shouldn't have taught you that."

"How do you spell Mr. Freeze?" He pulls out the action figure he now carries most places and props it on his knee.

I spell it for him, feeling Arlo's eyes on me the whole time. We make it to the park, where Fernando walks with us and spreads a beautiful blanket on the grass. The air is cool but not cold, and the leaves are just starting to turn. It's one of those beautiful fall days that feel like the warmth will last forever.

The three of us sit, eat, and play together. Will becomes fascinated with a nearby group of pigeons, and I can't help but smile as I watch him.

"Your son is a great kid," I say, turning to look at Will's father.

Arlo is watching me. He reaches over and twists a strand of hair around his finger, feeling it between his thumb and forefinger. "You're good with him," he answers, then steals closer and places a kiss on my shoulder.

I glance at the car. "What if Fernando sees?"

"What if he does?"

I try to glare at him. "Arlo."

"What? Am I your dirty little secret?"

"You know we shouldn't be doing this," I whisper.

"Doing what?" Will asks, suddenly between us. He looks between me and his father with big, brown, all-seeing eyes. "Why are you whispering?"

Arlo drops my hair and grabs his son around the waist, throwing him up in the air. As a distraction tactic, it works wonders. Will starts squealing and laughing and crying, "Again!"

I grab a carrot stick from our picnic basket and munch on it, watching the two of them roughhouse. It does something strange to my chest. The laughter falling from Will's lips, the smile on Arlo's face.

I've always wanted this, in a secret corner of my heart. I pursued a career in a male-dominated field that demanded everything of me, and I was almost ashamed to admit that I craved the simple pleasures of having a partner, a family. Of course, I want to find my place in the world. I'd love to have a business like Linda does. But now that I've had time away from Wall Street, I know that life isn't for me. Maybe there's something else I can pursue, another way to feel like my life is complete. Maybe I can have this, right here. This quiet happiness. A picnic in a park with a laughing child and a beautiful man.

But as I watch Will and Arlo, I remind myself that this isn't my partner or my family. This is my wealthy boss and his son. I need to remember that; otherwise, I'll fall into the same traps I did with Galen. It was hard enough to survive a fall from grace the first time; I don't want to have to do it again.

SIXTEEN
ARLO

ON SUNDAY, I'm alarmed to hear Bonnie making plans over the phone to go dance with her friend, but it's her day off, and I know my jealous urges are just that—urges. She says she has errands to run and leaves for a few hours during the day, and I'm surprised at how much I miss her presence in my house.

It's been a week and a half since she moved in, and I'm already addicted to her presence. This is bad. This is exactly what happened with Alice: I got attached. I fell hard and fast, with no thought of the consequences.

Am I making the same mistakes all over again?

Will drags me over to play Batman and Mr. Freeze for the fortieth time this week, and I find myself loosening up with him. Even after the heartbreak and betrayal that Alice put me through, she still gave me the greatest gift a man could receive. My son is everything to me.

Will makes an explosive noise and tackles Mr. Freeze to the ground. "You lose," he proclaims. Then he stands. "I'm hungry."

I'm in the kitchen making him a snack when my sister appears.

She grins. "Look at you, all domesticated. Chopping veggies like us mere mortals." Her gaze shifts to my son. "Hey, kiddo."

Will jumps off his seat and comes barreling toward her legs.

She catches him and lifts him onto a hip with a grunt. "You're getting pretty heavy. Not sure how much longer I'll be able to lift you up."

"I'm getting strong!"

My sister laughs. "You sure are. Just like your daddy."

"Bonnie says I'm going to be tall when I grow up. Do you think so?"

"Well, I think there's a good chance, considering how tall your dad is."

"But my mom is short."

I glance over at Will, not liking the quietness in his tone. He stares at Beth's necklace, toying with it between his fingers.

"You'll just have to wait and find out," I say, then put a plate of veggies and dip on the table. "Have some food, Will."

He wriggles down and jumps back onto his seat, crunching down on a celery stick as his legs kick back and forth.

I lean against the counter and cross my arms, jerking a chin at Beth. "What brings you around?"

"I got confirmation from a few artists about donations, and I wanted to see this little guy." She winks at my son, then pulls out her phone and shows me pictures of the artworks she's procured for the charity dinner. "What do you think?"

"Very cool."

My sister huffs. "You have no idea if it's cool or not, do you?"

"Art isn't really my thing. I trust your judgment, though."

My sister rolls her eyes, then glances around. "Where's Bonnie?"

"Day off," I grunt.

"Ah. How are things going with her?"

My brows slam down. "What do you mean?" Does she somehow know that Bonnie and I have been hooking up? Is it that obvious?

Beth stares at me for a beat. "You were worried about her lying to you about something...?"

I relax, rubbing a hand against my jaw. "Oh. Right. No, that's fine."

"It's fine?" She frowns at me.

"Yeah, it's fine. I just recognized her from a business conference we were at a few years ago. No big deal."

My sister's eyes narrow. The problem with having an artist as a sister is that when she focuses on something—me, for example—she's remarkably observant. I don't want her to see the guilt written all over my face right now.

I scowl. "What?"

She throws her hands up. "Nothing. It's just not like you to do a one-eighty like this. Usually, when you have a thought in your head, you want to see it through all the way to the end. You were so sure she was hiding something. What changed?"

I got her naked, that's what changed. I let out a sigh and shake my head. "It's fine, Beth. Her background check came back clean. I was just being paranoid. You know how I get." I nod to my son.

Beth purses her lips and nods, relenting.

"Hey, are you free to babysit tonight?" I ask.

She arches a brow. "Why?"

I keep my face blank. "A few friends are going out dancing tonight, and I kind of wanted to head out with them."

Beth, who had been leaning sideways on the counter, turns to face me fully. She leans back, studying my face. "Who are you and what have you done with my brother?"

"Beth. Come on."

"I'm serious. *You* want to go out *dancing?*"

"No," I growl. "*I* don't want to dance. I just want to go out with people who do."

She shakes her head in wonderment, then lets out a short huff. "I mean...sure. Yes. I'll babysit. It's been a while since you've actually done something just for fun, and I don't want to be the one to stop you."

There's nothing like little sisters to needle a man about his shortcomings. "I have fun," I say, petulant.

"Your idea of fun is siccing your private investigator on unsuspecting nannies."

"I like dancing," Will cuts in, picking up a piece of cucumber. "Bonnie is teaching me how to salsa."

Understanding dawns for Beth, and then her gaze fills with warning. "Arlo..."

As if he could hear us talking about him a moment ago, Greg's name lights up my phone. Glad for the excuse to leave my sister's eagle-eyed stare, I answer the phone and step out of the kitchen. "Yeah?"

"I finally spoke to that administrator who worked at Holt & Holt," he says without preamble.

I duck into my second-floor office, where I interviewed Bonnie just over a week ago. "And?"

"There were some rumors about Bonnie having an affair with one of her coworkers. Or at least, she came onto him, and he rejected her."

I frown. "What happened?"

"The woman didn't know. She said something happened at a company holiday party, and Bonnie quit not long after. People were spreading all kinds of rumors about her cornering him at the party and trying to seduce him, but she didn't believe it. Said Bonnie wasn't the type."

"What's your read on the situation?"

As an ex-cop, Greg's usually got a pretty good nose for bull-shit. I know that I trust Bonnie, but I'm also desperate to have her in my bed. Even now, when she's been out of the house for a couple of hours, I have to hold back from calling her just to know where she is.

That's how I was with Alice—consumed with the thought of her. Desperate to possess what I could never have.

Greg hums. "She was sincere. Something happened at that holiday party, but she doesn't know what. She thinks Bonnie was pushed out of the company. Apparently Bonnie was a top performer, so it didn't make any sense for her to be fired, unless something happened that Holt & Holt wanted to cover up."

I don't like this. I frown as I stare at the window. "Okay. Thanks, Greg."

"I'm chasing up her financials, so that should tell me if anyone is putting any pressure on her. I'll let you know what I find."

"Thanks."

We hang up, and I don't like the sick, bubbling feeling in my gut. I don't like unanswered questions.

As I exit my office, I hear the distant ding of the elevator down-stairs. Bonnie's home.

SEVENTEEN

BONNIE

NIKITA WAS in good spirits today. We met for a coffee and then went window shopping, occasionally ducking into thrift stores while we gabbed. Despite being fired, she's optimistic. She has a lead on a temp job in an office building, which was surprising to me. She's not exactly the corporate type.

I didn't tell her what's been going on with Arlo, and I think she could tell that something was off. She kept prodding me about work, trying to figure out what I was hiding. I usually tell her everything, but I held back... I'm not sure why. Things with Arlo seem too surreal, too fast. Too good. I'm afraid if I talk about them, the bubble will pop.

Maybe I'm afraid that if I tell Nikki, she'll get that look in her eyes that tells me she thinks I'm making a huge mistake. I had a workplace romance with Galen, and that ruined my career.

Arlo is different, but there *are* similarities.

What if things with Arlo end as disastrously as things with Galen did? What if I end up in an even worse position after a month here than I did after my relationship with Galen crashed and burned?

I didn't tell Nikki about it because I already knew what she'd say: It's a bad idea to get involved with your boss.

The power imbalance alone is enough to make it inadvisable, even when the boss isn't a literal billionaire. Arlo could ruin my life with a snap of his fingers.

A knock on my door makes me turn in time to see Arlo slip inside my room. At the sight of his dark eyes, his full lips, and the tight, prowling way with which he moves, a knot tightens in my belly. All thoughts and worries flee from my mind.

It's easy to consider resisting the man when he isn't in front of me. As soon as he steps into my space, logic runs from me.

"Hey," I say.

He glances at the bed, where I've laid out an outfit for tonight. I'll be wearing tight pants and a loose lace camisole, which seems to make Arlo's eyes darken. His gaze skims back to me. "Going out tonight?"

I nod. "Yes. Going dancing with some friends."

He moves with the grace of a big cat, stalking closer. The backs of my knees hit the bed as he slides his hands around my waist, slipping them down to my hips and around to my ass. "You'll let another man put his hands all over you?"

"Arlo." I arch a brow. "Don't be a jealous jerk. It's not very attractive." Even though his hands on my body feel divine.

"I can't help it." He squeezes my butt, then pulls me tight to his hips. "The thought of some guy rubbing up against you tonight is driving me crazy, Bonnie."

"It's salsa dancing," I protest, but my voice comes out breathy and my lids start dropping. "There's no rubbing." Well. Mostly.

He shoves his thigh between my legs, his grip on my hips tightening. "There better not be. The only man you rub up against is me, you got it?" He punctuates his words by rocking my hips with his hands.

The center seam of my jeans is amazing. I hadn't realized *how* amazing until just now. I cling to Arlo's broad shoulders and let him guide my hips, grinding against him in steady, sharp movements. A gasp falls from my lips, which draws a growl from Arlo.

"Only me, Bonnie. I'm the only man who gets to hear you make sounds like that."

"Only you," I promise, right before a soft, keening noise escapes my lips. How does this man take me from zero to hot and bothered so quickly? His fingers dig into my hips, thumbs hard against my hipbones. He rocks my body, demanding that I move exactly how he wants. He watches me with dark, half-lidded eyes.

It's intoxicating having this big, powerful man so focused on me and my pleasure. I'm fully clothed, and the man is tearing me to shreds. My whole body begins to tremble as another rumble vibrates through his chest. Pleasure snakes through my thighs, my clothes too tight on my body.

With a grunt, Arlo wraps a hand around my waist and pulls me off his thigh. He flicks the button of my jeans open and unzips them with a hard tug, and then his hand is on me, skin to skin.

"No one else makes you this wet, do they?" He drags a finger along my seam for emphasis.

"No."

His thick fingers shove inside me, palm putting delicious pressure against my clit. "Nobody else makes you come the way I do."

"You know they don't, Arlo," I pant. My mind is unspooling. All I can do is cling to his broad body and hope I survive the detonation.

Arlo's grip on my waist is so tight, I wonder if I'll have bruises from his fingers. His other hand pumps in and out of me, the heel of his hand always providing mind-melting pressure where I need it most. My legs start to tremble, but he holds me up. I drop my head to his shoulder, clinging on for dear life.

"I want to be there," he says softly, lips brushing my ear. "I want to watch you dancing with all those guys, see them salivating over you. Then, after, I want you to crawl into my bed and spread those pretty legs for me. *My* bed, Bonnie. Where you belong."

An orgasm of an intensity I've never experienced washes over me. It's the possession of his words, his hands. It's the feeling of weightlessness in my body, like the only thing tethering me to the earth is Arlo himself. I cry out, shoving my face into the crook of his neck to muffle the noise.

He lets out a long sigh as he slides his fingers out of my pants. His eyes are so dark, they look completely black. I know, in that moment, that I'm in too deep. This will end badly for me...but I can't stop myself from welcoming disaster with open arms.

WE DRIVE to the bar in Arlo's limo, picking Nikki up along the way. She arches a brow at me in a way that says, *We will talk about this later*.

Once inside, Arlo commandeers one of the VIP tables and sets himself up with a view of the whole room. He buys a few bottles. When the three of us have a drink, Nikki leans over and says, "What's your deal, anyway?"

Arlo arches a brow. "My deal?"

"Why are you here?"

"I can't come dance?"

Her gaze narrows. "Do you always come out to dance with your employees?"

He sips his drink, shrugging. "No."

That's it. That's all he says. Nikki glares at me, then grabs my arm and drags me to the washroom. "What. Are. You. *Doing.*"

I reapply my lipstick and avoid her gaze. "So, um. He remembered me."

"Don't tell me you're sleeping with your boss, Bonnie."

"You go girl!" a drunk woman in one of the stalls calls out. "Is he hot?"

"Yes," I answer. "Very."

"It's a bad idea." Nikki shakes her head. "Come on, Bonnie. You know it is."

"Killjoy," the drunk woman grumbles.

"I know." I finally look my friend in the eyes and put a hand on her forearm. "I hear you, Nikki. I'll be careful."

She doesn't look convinced, but she lets out a sigh. "Let's just dance, okay?"

We go back out and find a group of friends on the dance floor. Teddy is already dancing with a partner, but another friend, Mark, sweeps me into his arms with a roguish smile. "You look beautiful, Bonnie."

I let the music infuse my movements and dance with Mark, spinning and swaying my hips over the dance floor. All the while, I feel Arlo's gaze on me. At one point, I look over my dance partner's shoulder and see him watching me, sipping his drink. The darkness in his eyes makes heat tighten low in my stomach, a promise of what's to come.

Another man I don't know cuts in, and I laugh as he twirls me. The music pulses around us as the club fills up, and I let the beat take me away.

This is how I used to feel when I ran track. It was almost like an out-of-body experience. It was something I was truly good at— good enough to get a full-ride scholarship to college. I mostly ran mid- and long-distances, when my body would take over and my mind would go quiet.

My ankle injury ended all that.

Tonight, I don't feel the throb in the joint as I dance. And whenever I feel Arlo's eyes on me, I might put an extra sway in my hips. I can't help it. He makes my blood heat with nothing but a look. It's always been that way between us.

A part of me feels vindicated, like the last three years weren't a lie. I pined over him, dreamed about him. I had half-convinced myself that I was making it up, that there was no way our connection was as electric as it was.

But I'm across a crowded club from him. He hasn't so much as touched me since he came to my room, other than a hand on my lower back, and I feel like I'm about to explode. That has to mean something, doesn't it?

Sweat dampens my skin as one song bleeds into another. I see Nikki flitting from partner to partner, her painted red lips split into a sensual smile. She meets my gaze and winks as Teddy dips her, wrapping her arms around his neck with a laugh.

Then, a hand on my back. Arlo appears behind me, pulling me from the partner who had claimed this dance. I face him, heart stuttering at the sinful look in his eyes.

"My turn," he says in my ear, "but you'll have to teach me."

Happiness blooms in my chest. "Really?"

"Did you enjoy driving me insane for the past two hours?" His voice is dark in my ear.

My lips curl. "Yes."

His grip on me tightens, pulling me close to his chest. Every point of contact between us feels too sensitive, too surtense. Voice weak, I cling to his shoulders and say, "Take your left foot and step forward, and transfer your weight..."

I show him the basic salsa step, our bodies close. It's stiff and clumsy, but it feels far more sensual than any other versions of the dance I've ever done. His hands skim down my sides possessively. We only do the most basic salsa step, but I get that same weightless, free feeling as when I'm deep in a dance.

Lust blooms between my thighs. We shift in a sea of twirling, sensual dancers, but the energy between us crackles more than I could have imagined. Arlo slides his hands to my hips, feeling the way my leather pants shape my curves. It's almost Pavlovian how that simple touch brings back memories of him urging my hips over and back on his thigh, how quickly it turns me on to feel his fingers sink into my flesh.

He must see the arousal written all over my face, because his lips lift into a dangerous smirk. "Time to go home, Bonnie."

I find Nikki and give her a quick hug, and she answers with a warning glare. "Be careful, Bonnie."

"I will."

"Call me if you need anything."

I hug her again, then follow Arlo out of the club. Cool air washes over my overheated skin, and I suck in a deep breath. The limo is waiting for us on the curb, and Fernando opens the door for us before disappearing into the driver's seat. The privacy partition is up.

I slide into my usual seat, directly across from Arlo. He watches me from the other bench seat as the limo starts moving, his arms propped over the top of the seat, his legs spread. I love the way he looks at me. I love knowing that he had his eyes on me the entire time I was out tonight. I love the possession and jealousy written all over his face.

"Slide your straps off your shoulders," he growls. "Show me your tits."

I tremble, desire arcing through me. This is exactly how it was during our night three years ago. He was filthy, commanding, and delicious. I loved doing what he told me to do. I loved feeling his touch, his possession. It felt like we forged a connection in those few hours, one that's survived the years that have passed since.

Slowly, I slide a strap off my shoulder. I'm not wearing a bra under the camisole; the straps would show, and my boobs are small enough not to need one. I let the silky fabric fall onto my bicep and expose one breast, then the other.

No other man has made me feel so desirable. I sit there, my top pooling around my waist, and I feel like a goddess. Arlo doesn't move. He keeps his hands stretched over the bench seat, tension keeping his body still even as a bulge grows in his pants.

I love the power he gives me in moments like these. I want to tease him a bit, torture him. I bring my hands to my breasts and start stroking, pinching, playing. His hands squeeze the top of the seat on either side of him. His breathing becomes jagged.

"I hated seeing you dance with those other guys," he says in a low voice. "Hated every second of it."

"Oh?" I pinch my nipples, then draw a circle around them with my index fingers, a reminder of what he did to me in my room.

His jaw clenches. "Every time one of them touched you, I wanted to rip their arms off. You drove me crazy. You've been driving me crazy since you walked into my house. Do you know what you do to me, Bonnie? Do you realize?"

"I liked feeling your gaze on me," I admit, sliding my hand down to stroke between my legs over my pants. "I liked knowing you were watching me. Wanting me."

My breathing is jagged. This is the most intense foreplay I've ever engaged in, and we haven't even touched each other since we got in the limo. But the whole night has been foreplay. Even the orgasm he gave me earlier only served to balance me onto a razor's edge.

No wonder Nikki is worried about me. If I were thinking clearly, I'd be worried about me too.

The limo slows to a stop, and Arlo tears his gaze away from me to look out the window. "We're here."

I cover myself up again, but I know I'm flushed and disheveled. A moment later, the door opens, and we exit the vehicle. Arlo's hand on my lower back is like a brand. He nods to the doorman, then to the man at the lobby desk, and I almost feel ashamed that they know what's going on between us. Almost. Mostly I feel turned on.

We enter the elevator. Arlo puts a fob up against the reader and hits the button for the 129th floor. As soon as the doors close, he crowds me up against the wall, puts a hand on my jaw, and kisses me—hard.

My hands have a mind of their own. They slide down his hard chest and fumble with his belt. I tug it loose with rough, jerky movements that draw hot, deep growls from Arlo's throat. Then my hand is in his pants and I'm stroking him over his boxers.

"I love your cock," I hear myself say, because apparently that's the type of thing I say to this man.

His lips curl. "I know you do, Bonnie."

His dark voice makes everything inside me go molten. I wrap my hand around him as far as the fabric will let me, stroking. He holds me against the elevator wall and kisses me, nipping at my lips, my jaw. We're feral, frantic.

As soon as the elevator doors open, I shove him up against the wall—exactly where he caged me when we first kissed. Then I free his cock from its fabric prison and drop to my knees.

"Bonnie—" A groan interrupts whatever he was going to say when I take his cock in my mouth. He drops his head back and it hits the marble wall behind him. His hand slides from my shoulder to my nape, then Arlo gathers my hair up in a messy ponytail with his fist.

I've never really enjoyed going down on guys. It always felt too transactional. But with every minute that passed in that club, every glance that told me Arlo was watching me with his dark, dangerous gaze, I found myself wanting to get on my knees in front of him.

He tightens his hold on my hair, gently guiding me to suck him off the way he likes—but I know the truth. I know that I'm in control here, that this big man is being torn apart where he stands. I can feel it in the tension of his thighs, in the trembling of his lower belly. I can taste it with every salty bead of liquid that escapes his tip. The little points of pain in my scalp where he tugs on my hair tell me just how close he is to losing control.

I want him to lose it. I want to be the one that drives him wild.

I use my hands and mouth, listening to his groans to learn what he likes. My nipples feel so sensitive against my silky top, and I know my panties are soaked. When I reach down to unzip my pants while I take him deeper in my mouth, he lets out the loudest groan of all.

He likes it when I play with myself in front of him, so I do. I slip my hand into my panties and bring us both to completion. I come first, too turned on by the situation to stop myself. When I moan on his cock, body jerking, his grip on my hair tightens.

"Bonnie, I'm going to—" He tries to pull me off, but he's not the one in control here. I keep my mouth on him until I taste his orgasm on my tongue, and another wave of pleasure washes through me. When I'm ready to collapse at his feet, Arlo grabs me and hauls me up to my feet, pushing me up against the wall and burying his face in the crook of my neck. He's breathing heavily, his hands holding my hips pinned to the solid surface behind me.

When he lifts his head, his eyes are wild, almost vulnerable.

He looks me in one eye and then the other, trying to read something in my expression. His hands come up to cup my cheeks, thumbs brushing my skin so tenderly it makes my heart ache.

"You..." He lets out a long breath, then kisses my forehead, my lids, my nose, and finally my mouth. He sighs, eyes closed as he leans his forehead against mine. "You're not real," he whispers, almost to himself. "You can't be."

WHEN MONDAY MORNING ROLLS AROUND, I have zero desire to go to work. I want to stay at home with my arms wrapped around Bonnie and my son and forget about my IPO, prowling hedge fund managers, and anything that exists outside my four walls.

Unfortunately, I have multiple businesses to run.

By the time I make it to my office, I have the sense that I'm emerging from a strange dream world. My assistant is at her desk, and all my other employees are nodding to me and tapping away at their computers. In the past ten days, life for everyone else went on while mine underwent a seismic shift.

I'm swept up in the tasks of the day, checking my phone intermittently to see notifications from Bonnie. She's sent me photos of her and Will doing arts and crafts after school with pipe cleaners and lots of glue. My son has that big, goofy smile on his face.

By the time six o'clock rolls around, my legal team is surprised to see me packing up to leave. I don't care—there's somewhere I'd rather be.

Will's getting ready for bed by the time I get home, but I manage to tuck him in, and then I'm cooking dinner for Bonnie. Filet mignon steaks with grilled asparagus and baby potatoes, with my special peppercorn sauce. The noises Bonnie makes when she takes her first bite make me not want to finish dinner at all.

"You weren't lying," she says, cutting a head off an asparagus spear. "You can cook."

"And don't ever doubt me again," I tease.

She laughs, and the sound settles over me like a balm. We eat, we drink wine, and then we use the kitchen counters for other activities. Then I take her back to my bed and hold her close until she's asleep.

As her breathing steadies, I watch the rise and fall of her chest and feel a niggle of worry in my own.

This is fast—even for me. Faster than Alice. Faster than any woman who came before.

In college, my friends used to tease me that I was a serial monogamist. That I fell hard in and even harder out of love. What if this is just me indulging in that same pattern? What if Bonnie isn't as special or perfect as she seems, and it's all going to blow up in my face? Can I really trust these feelings, when they've mushroomed in a little more than a week?

THE FEELINGS PERSIST the next day, and the one after. On Wednesday, I meet Galen Deely for lunch and listen to his pitch about the Holt & Holt qualifications. He promises me that my money will not only be safe, but it'll grow. He promises better-than-market returns, and he seems to actually believe what he's saying. I can tell it's a well-practiced pitch, because the man has an air of confidence about him.

"I've met one of your firm's old employees, actually," I say, leaning back in my seat as I dab my mouth with a cloth napkin. I watch him from across the table, trying to hide that I'm studying his reaction.

Galen is a man who looks at home in a place like this, a restaurant that caters to Manhattan's elite, where deals are made every hour of the day. He smooths down his tie and adjusts the jacket of his bespoke suit, waving to a waiter with a flick of his fingers. "Oh?" He turns to the waiter and asks for a bottle of sparkling water, his tone a touch condescending.

I nod. "Bonnie Delmar."

Galen's eyes snap to mine. "Oh," he repeats in a completely different way. This time, it sounds laden with hidden meaning and a touch of sourness.

"Her resume came across my desk," I say, not wanting to divulge too much. Let Galen wonder what business of mine she applied to—he doesn't need to know she's already part of my household. Maybe a part of me is still desperate to keep our budding romance safe and secret inside the walls of my penthouse.

I stare at the man across from me. "I figured since we were meeting, you could tell me if you ever worked with her." As the words leave my lips, a sick feeling slides through my gut. I don't like doing this. It feels dishonest. A week ago, I wouldn't have felt any guilt, because I thought Bonnie seemed familiar for nefarious reasons. Now I know why I recognized her, and it's not because she had a history with the hedge fund currently courting me.

But I still ask the question, because I'm the type of man who leaves no stone unturned. The connection to Holt & Holt seems like more than a coincidence, and I don't like unpleasant surprises. I don't trust my feelings for Bonnie when they've grown in only a matter of days.

I need outside information. I need to know if I should be worried.

"She left Holt & Holt over a year ago," Galen says, voice carefully modulated. The words sound bland, which sends alarm bells ringing in my mind.

"She left?"

"There were...personal issues. She wasn't a good fit for our company's culture. Very good at her job, but just couldn't hack it at the company."

I hum. "I see."

"I don't know what kind of position you're considering her for..." Galen lets the words drift off as he cuts into the tender chicken breast on his plate, and when I don't fill in the blanks for him, he continues: "But I'd be careful about giving her too much responsibility. Let's just say her moral fiber is a bit...weak."

Frowning, I nod to the waiter who arrives with a fresh bottle of sparkling water. We don't speak while our glasses are refilled.

"What kind of job did she apply for?" Galen asks casually. "Maybe I could give a better recommendation if I knew more specifics."

I know a fishing expedition when I see one. I wave off the question. "You've been more than helpful," I tell him, then divert the conversation back to Holt & Holt's position on derivatives and other risky investments.

From the sharpness in Galen's eyes, he knows I changed the subject on purpose, even though he obliges me and spends the next ten minutes telling me things I already know.

WHEN I GET HOME that night, Will's already in bed, asleep, which makes my dark mood blacker. I hate missing my kid, even for a day. When work is hectic, the only time I get to see him is in the evenings when I tuck him in. Only a bad father misses those moments with his son.

The rest of the house is silent. I find Bonnie in her room, reading a book with an arm curled around the back of her head. When she sees me, she sets the book down and sits up, leaning her back against the headboard. "Hey. How was your day?"

Despite everything—all my doubts, my fears, my worries that what's growing between us isn't real—her words loosen a tight knot in my chest.

"Long," I tell her. I sit down on the bed beside her, kicking my shoes off and loosening my tie.

She leans a head against my shoulder. "You want to talk about it?"

I hesitate for the barest of moments—and then decide to be a grown-up about this. "I met with an old coworker of yours. Galen Deely."

She freezes. I feel the tension steal over her body, then slowly drain away before she says, "Oh, Galen. Right."

"You worked for Holt & Holt for a few years, right?"

Bonnie lifts her head off my shoulder and lets out a long sigh. "From the time I got my MBA up until a little over a year ago, yes. It was the only big-girl job I had, actually."

"What's your take on Galen?"

A lift of her eyebrows tells me she's surprised by the question. To tell the truth, I'm surprised by the question too. I should be rooting around for her secrets, not Galen's.

"He's..." She drifts off, biting her soft lower lip. Meeting my gaze, Bonnie shrugs. "I don't feel like I can give you an impartial answer to that question, Arlo. He and I had a falling out, and he's not really my favorite person."

I grunt, adjusting the pillows so I can lean back more comfortably. I curl an arm around her shoulders and pull her into my chest, immediately feeling better. I place a soft kiss on the crown of her head and ask, "What happened?"

She traces small circles around the buttons of my shirt with her finger for a moment. "I'll tell you, but you can't judge me, okay?"

"Okay."

"He and I were coworkers. We were junior advisors, coming up in the company around the same time. He... We..." She huffs, like she's frustrated with herself. Then she blurts out, "We had an affair."

I freeze. "An affair?"

Pushing off my chest, Bonnie stares at me with big blue eyes. "I promise it's not something I do all the time. I never wanted it to happen again. When I saw you here on my first day, I totally panicked because I felt like it was yet another job that was going to blow up in my face because of my personal mistakes. And now I'm here, and we've...you know...and..."

Tugging her back down to my chest, I smooth a hand over her hair. "I believe you. This isn't something I do all the time either." Except...I kind of do, don't I? Fall hard and fast when I know better?

She sighs, relaxing against me. I like having her here on top of me. Her head fits perfectly in the crook of my shoulder. My arm feels like it's supposed to be around her back, fingers stroking the bottom of her ribs.

"Look, Galen is good at his job, but he's not what I'd call principled."

I frown. That's almost exactly what Galen said about her. So who's telling the truth?

"Why do you say that?" I hate that I'm asking these questions like this. I should just open up and tell her all the things that scare me. If I explained what happened with Alice, maybe she'd understand why our whirlwind romance—affair, whatever this is—terrifies me so much. Instead, I'm using vague questions to try to catch her in a lie. I'm ashamed of myself.

"I was good at my job," Bonnie tells me. "I'd developed this system to identify undervalued stocks. It was this complicated spreadsheet that used a bunch of macros to pull data from various sources... All you need to know is it was good. Okay? And I was doing really well. People were noticing—my bosses, my clients. Chester Holt."

"Galen Deely."

She hums, then pauses. "The first time Galen came into my office was after hours. He was...charming. He made me laugh. I felt, for the first time, like it was the two of us against the world. It sounds so silly, to have that feeling even for a few moments, but that's what it felt like. And I'd never really had that before. Not from a man."

Bonnie sits up again, her cheeks red. Bright eyes stare into mine, and I watch her make a decision as she reads whatever's written in my gaze. "Let me just start at the beginning." She gives me a sad smile, then stares at the wall across the room. "My parents were the 'get-out-of-our-house-at-eighteen' type of people. They probably should never have had kids, but they did. For as long as I can remember, I knew that when my eighteenth birthday hit, I'd be told to pack my bags and leave. It's what happened to Linda, and we both knew it would happen to me. Linda was my safety net, but I knew I couldn't rely on her forever either. She'd just moved into Manhattan and was starting her childcare agency, and she was pouring every penny into it. She didn't have money to support me. So I worked my little high school butt off to make some opportunities for myself, and I did it." Bonnie's smile is wistful. "I got a full-ride scholarship to the University of Florida for track and field. I was a good runner, Arlo. Really good. I lived and breathed it. I couldn't wait to be a college athlete, to get my degree and make something of myself. I met a boy who ran for the men's team, and I thought we'd get married after college and live happily ever after."

A silence settles between us, and I use a finger to tuck a strand of hair behind her ear. That seems to jar Bonnie out of a daze, and she turns to grimace at me. Then she tugs her pant leg up to reveal the scar on her ankle.

"This happened when I was a freshman in college. I was on a late-night run and got hit by a drunk driver. It was a low-speed collision, and I was lucky to get away with only a shattered leg and ankle. But I lost the scholarship and couldn't afford to pay for an out-of-state school, especially with a mountain of medical debt. When I was in the middle of talking to administrators and loan providers, panicking about my future, my boyfriend told me I could live with him until I figured it out. But then when I showed up at his door, he broke up with me on the doorstep. It felt like the end of the world."

If I could reach back in time and wring that little shit's neck, I would. I take my arm from around Bonnie's shoulders and place a hand on her thigh. I feel like an ass for questioning her.

Bonnie swallows thickly and lets her head fall back against the headboard. "Anyway, I moved back to New York and Linda took me in. I got accepted to a community college and eventually trans-ferred to a state school for business. Worked for Linda through college and did my MBA, then went to work for Holt & Holt. Life was good. Again. I'd survived the worst thing that ever happened to me. I wasn't having nightmares about car crashes anymore, I was making money, and I'd just bought a beautiful apartment for myself."

A bitter laugh falls from Bonnie's lips. It's a horrible sound, one I've never heard from her before. "And then Galen walked into my office and made me feel like the last puzzle piece was falling into place. I fell for his charm hook, line, and sinker. It was like the end of a long, long road. I'd survived the hardest thing I'd ever had to experience and come out on top. We kissed that night. The very first night he came to my office and tried it on with me. We'd hardly ever said hello before that."

It takes all my effort not to tighten my hold on her. Tension steals over me. I want to find Galen Deely and punch him in the face. I don't know exactly what he did, but I know he hurt Bonnie. I can taste it in the air between us.

"You don't have to tell me what happened," I say, praying she takes me up on the offer. I already feel ashamed of myself for asking these roundabout questions, for not being open about my continued suspicions about her.

"No, it's fine." She meets my gaze and lets out a long breath. "I'm embarrassed about the whole affair. I feel like an idiot—but I did it. I hooked up with him. I let him wriggle his way into my heart and I shared all my work with him. He used my systems to improve his performance and get a promotion, and then he broke up with me. Rumors of the affair got out, though, and you know how it is. The woman's reputation always gets tarnished more than the man's does. I ended up having to leave the company."

"And now you're here."

"Now I'm here," she says, voice falsely bright. "Sleeping with my boss. Funny how that works, huh? Some people just never learn."

"Don't paint me with the same brush as the other men who have let you down," I tell her, even though my motivation to start this conversation wasn't pure. Am I really any better than the others?

Bonnie won't meet my gaze, and I hate that she's ashamed of her past. I hate that she's been hurt, and there's nothing I can do about it. I especially hate that our relationship is calling up all those bad memories.

But that's exactly what's happening to me, isn't it? The speed that I'm falling for this woman makes me think of my ex-wife.

Are we both just trying to rewrite our pasts? Are we using this incandescent attraction between us to paper over old wounds, or are these feelings real?

Bonnie studies my face, then reaches up to touch my cheek. I turn my head and kiss her palm, leaning into her touch.

"Arlo," she says quietly.

"Yes?"

"Will you make love to me tonight?" Her fingers trace the line of my beard, eyes following the movement. Then her gaze lifts to mine, and I see real vulnerability there.

She's opened herself to me, handing me her biggest fears in her cupped palms. Now she's asking for reassurance, for connection.

My chest splinters. I've been an ass to this woman, and she's opening her heart to me despite it. I don't deserve her.

But she's here, and she's beautiful, and I feel things for her that don't make any sense.

"Of course I will," I answer, and I bring my lips to hers.

NINETEEN
BONNIE

A SHIFT HAPPENS after that conversation. Now Arlo and I aren't just having a torrid affair. It's not just blowjobs by the elevator and orgasms on the kitchen counter; it's deeper than sex. A thin bridge of trust reaches between the two of us, and I begin to hope.

For the first time since the disastrous end of my finance career, I'm hopeful for the future. It's terrifying to feel this way, because every time I've experienced hope of this kind, my plans and dreams have been ripped away. But with Arlo, I wonder if it could finally be real, if my life could really be looking up.

Our lives take on a steady rhythm. Arlo works long hours during the week and sometimes on the weekend too, and I build a relationship with his adorable son. I've been dropped into this beautiful life, and it's all too easy to forget that it isn't mine. Not really.

Which is why, when I've been living at Arlo's house for three incredible weeks, I decide to broach a difficult topic. It's Saturday, and Will, Arlo, and I are out for a walk in the park. Will is terrorizing packs of pigeons, laughing uproariously as they flap away from him. The air is crisp and cool, and the leaves are a thousand different shades of red, orange, yellow, and green. The crunch of their fallen brothers under my feet is as satisfying as it is loud.

Inhaling deeply, I find the courage to speak. "Arlo," I start. "What's going to happen next week?"

He frowns. "Next week?"

"When my contract is up."

His steps stutter. Will is busy splashing in a puddle in his rain boots, so we stand to the side of the path and watch him. Well, I watch him, and Arlo watches me. He vibrates with tension, so it takes me a few seconds to look up into his dark eyes.

"What do you mean?" His voice is a low growl. "Are you planning on ending things with me when your nannying contract is up?"

I stiffen. "Well, no, but... Arlo, you have to understand that we can't sneak around forever. And as soon as we are together publicly, everyone will know how it started between us. Am I just supposed to move my stuff from the downstairs bedroom to your room? What do we tell Will? What about Sofia? What about my sister?"

His brow creases. He scowls in the direction of his son, mulling over my words. "We'll tell your sister that I want to extend your contract. Just...a bit more time to figure things out."

My heart sinks. "I see."

He wants to keep sneaking around.

A sigh rips through Arlo's lips as he rakes his fingers through his hair. "No—wait. I didn't mean that."

I lean away from him, painting a smile on my lips. "No, it's okay."

It's not okay. Arlo wants to keep hiding me, pretending we aren't together. He wants our relationship to stay suspended in this strange in-between state, where we spend every night sharing a bed until the clock strikes six in the morning, and I'm on duty.

I was an idiot to think it was anything more. Apart from one night together years ago, I've known this man for three weeks. He's my boss. He's disgustingly wealthy. The differences between our situations are far, far too vast for any meaningful relationship to ever work between us.

That stupid fantasy of mine is playing out—again. I'm not going to find a man and skip off into the sunset with him. I'm going to have to start over again and pull myself up on my own.

As a cool breeze blows over my skin, the reality of my situation settles over me. Surprisingly, it's not a terrible realization. I've been here before. I've built my life from the ground up before; I can do it again. At least I have a bit of money now.

He turns to face me and takes my hands in his. "Bonnie, whatever you're thinking now, stop it."

A sad smile tugs at my lips. "It's okay, Arlo. I understand."

"You don't understand a thing." His words are harsh, his gaze sharp. "You—I don't want to hide you away, but…"

I pull my hands from his. "Really, there's no need to have this conversation right now. We have one more week together, and then we can figure things out."

There won't be any figuring out. When my contract is over, I'll leave. It's the only way.

"Come to the charity dinner with me," he blurts. "As my date."

I blink. "What?"

"I'm not sneaking around with you, Bonnie. I'm not trying to hide you. I want everyone to know you're with me."

My heart skips a beat. My mouth is dry. "What about Will?"

"Will adores you."

"You want me to be your date to an event that will host all

your family, friends, colleagues, and clients? Right before you take your company public? Isn't that a bit...risky?"

His smile is like the sun breaking through oppressive, dark clouds. "Probably. But losing you is an even bigger risk." He grabs my glove-covered hand and gives it a squeeze.

"Dad!" Will shrieks. "Bonnie! Look what I found!" He brandishes a wriggling worm, then cups it in his little hands to show it off. "It's a worm," he explains.

"Very nice," Arlo says. "But don't you think the worm would be more comfortable if you left it on the ground?"

Will considers, then nods. "Yes." He places the worm on a garden bed with more gentleness than I thought he was capable of, then smiles proudly as the worm starts writhing in the dirt. "He's my friend."

"He sure is," I reply.

Will slips his dirt- and worm-covered hands into mine and Arlo's, and the three of us head home.

THAT NIGHT, Arlo and I end up in his bed, our bodies tangled and sated. I run my fingers through his chest hair while he presses a kiss to my forehead.

"I have feelings for you, Bonnie," he admits.

I freeze, then slowly look up at him. "What?"

He tightens his hold on my waist, pulling me tight to his side. "You've made my life brighter in the past month than it has been for years."

Tears spring into my eyes. "Oh," I whisper. This dreamlike month hasn't all been in my head.

"I don't want you to move out. I don't want to hide you. I want to try to make things work between us." He brushes a tear that escapes down my cheek and gives me a soft smile. "I'm sorry for earlier today. You caught me off-guard. I never meant that I wanted to keep you hidden away. It's just been such an amazing time since you moved in, and I wasn't ready for anything to change."

"Well...nothing has to change, really. But I don't think I should be your employee if we're going to officially be together."

"No," he agrees. "Is this...going to cause any issues for you? With your sister?"

I bite my lip. One of my friends, Dani, was Linda's nanny a few years ago. She ended up with her client. It was all very dramatic, and I wouldn't want to bring any trouble to my sister's business by having that happen again.

"We could tell people the truth," I say. "We met at a business conference in London three years ago, and then ran into each other stateside."

He grins. "The rest is history."

"Exactly. Linda's name doesn't need to come up."

"My staff can be trusted." He trails a finger down my arm. "Maybe it's best if I cancel my contract with your sister's company entirely to head off rumors. I'll pay out the rest of the contract, of course, and I could give her a glowing recommendation."

I nod. "I'm sure Linda would understand." Once she got over the shock.

"I'd have to find another nanny from somewhere else."

"I don't mind filling in while you look for someone," I tell him.

Arlo's smile is soft and tender. He presses a kiss to my temple. "Thank you. And what about you?" Arlo asks softly. His lips brush my temple again, like he can't stop from feeling my skin against his mouth. "I know you're cooking up all kinds of ideas about what you want to do with your life. I have the money to help with any business ideas you might have, you know."

My lips curl, and I lean my chin on my hand where it rests on Arlo's chest. "Well. I have been thinking..."

MY SECOND SUNDAY OFF is spent with Nikita. She just started her new job at some fancy schmancy advertising firm and goes to great lengths to explain what a jerk her boss is, except her cheeks go pink when she does.

"You're attracted to him," I accuse.

She arches a brow at me. "Projecting, much?"

I laugh. "Stop trying to deflect. You have the hots for your boss."

Nikki throws up her hands. "Fine! Yes. He's attractive. But he's seriously not my type. He's so..."

"He's so..." I prompt when she fails to finish her sentence.

"Just not my type."

I lean back on her sofa and shrug. "I can't judge."

Her gaze sharpens. "No," she says, "you can't. Which brings me to my next question: What the heck have you been up to?"

When I tell her about the past three weeks, and about Arlo's invitation to his charity dinner, Nikki's brows climb higher and higher. She finally bites her lip when I stop talking and slumps down on the couch beside me, turning her head to look in my eyes.

"Are you sure about this, Bonnie?"

"No," I admit. "But...I don't know. It feels real. He says all the right things. He makes me feel so good."

"Sex has scrambled your brain. Again."

I grab a throw pillow and smack her with it. She laughs, catching it against her stomach and tossing it across the room.

"So what's the plan for next week? Are you still going to move in with me when your contract ends?"

I bite my lip. "I'm going to stay at his place."

Nikita lets out a long breath. "Wow. So it's serious."

Redness steals over my cheeks, heating my skin. "Yes."

"You have seriously been leaving out some details, missy."

Laughing, I cover my face. "I know." Biting my lip, I add, "He wants me to be his date to his charity gala. He wants our relationship to be public."

"Whoa."

"I think... I think I do too," I whisper. "So he's going to cancel the new nanny so that Linda has some plausible deniability about her agency being involved. I'll fill in while he looks for someone new, so our lives will mostly just stay as they are."

My friend straightens, worry pulling her features tight. "So you'll still be working for him?"

"No," I admit. "My contract is ending." Before Nikki can interject, I launch into the other part of the conversation Arlo and I had, the one that lasted deep into the night when I told him about all the secret dreams I've been cooking up since I left Holt & Holt.

I paint a big smile on my face and meet Nikita's gaze. "I've been thinking about what I want to do next, and I think I'm going to start my own financial advisory business. I'll focus on helping women become financially competent, as my own little personal rebellion around the boys' club of finance. I could inspire women to love finance, to secure their futures. Did you know that overall, women generally make better investments than men? But far fewer women invest in the market overall. I want to change that. I want to inspire women to secure their own futures. I just have to take one test and I can get certified, since I have the other qualifications and experience. After that, with a bit of seed money, I'll be able to launch an advisory firm, maybe some courses, a conference..."

My words come out in a rush—the blossoming business idea

that Arlo and I spent hours discussing—but by the look on Nikki's face, I know she won't be so easily distracted.

Nikki's eyes narrow. "That's great, Bonnie, but are you saying that in the meantime you'll be providing the same nannying services to billionaire mogul Arlo Noble, except now you're not going to be getting paid?"

I bristle. "We both want to keep living together."

"Right. But why cancel the other nanny's contract?"

This all made sense last night. I try to remember the conversation Arlo and I had, the reasoning we used. "Well...we don't want to sneak around."

"Uh-huh."

"He's not taking advantage of me."

Nikki says nothing.

Frustration and fear come out as anger. "Listen, I don't need your judgment right now, Nikita."

She throws her hands up. "I'm not judging. I'm just asking you to explain your plan, is all."

"The plan is to keep seeing each other and keep our lives as normal as possible. Keep things consistent for Will while we tell him that we're together now. And after I go to the Noble Foundation gala with him, it will all be in the open and he'll be able to hire another nanny while I start my business. It makes sense," I insist.

Nikki doesn't look convinced, but she paints a tight smile on her lips. "Yeah," she says. "Okay. And you know you can always come here if anything happens, right?"

"Nothing bad will happen."

"Right. Of course. I just want you to know that I'm here for you."

I nod, feeling angry and not really wanting to think about why.

Later, when I head back to Arlo's building, I look at the

opulence around me and start to worry that this whole thing is far too good to be true.

TWENTY

BONNIE

THE NIGGLING WORRY that I'm making a huge mistake gets pushed to the back of my mind when I'm with Arlo. I keep my bedroom downstairs but spend most nights in his suite. Our physical connection remains as scorching as ever, and I start to wonder if Nikki was right. My brain is slowly getting fried with every orgasm Arlo gives me.

Arlo is busy with work, and I'm busy taking care of Will, so another week passes in a blur of sex, routine, and happiness. Soon, it's been five weeks since I started with Arlo, and an entire month since passion exploded between us.

After dropping Will off at kindergarten, I busy myself studying for the financial advisor exam I've decided to take. My body is achy and my lids droop, but I force myself to study for an hour longer. Finally, when it becomes too much, I take a short nap —only to wake up when my phone rings.

It's Linda. The sight of her name makes my nerves tighten, because I know that Arlo must have spoken to her.

"Hey," I say after answering her call.

"Hey. Are you okay?"

I frown, wiping my eyes to rub the sleep from them. "Um. Yes?"

"I just heard from Mr. Noble that he's discontinuing his contract. Did something happen?"

I could lie. I could keep sneaking around with my boss and tell my sister that nothing strange has happened at all. But this is Linda—she took me in when I left Florida with a shattered ankle and no prospects. She hired me when I needed to put myself through college, and then again when my career collapsed like a house of cards.

If this thing between Arlo and me is real, I need to own up to it.

"Linda..." I take a deep breath. "Do you remember that guy in London about three years ago?"

There's a short pause. "The guy you spent the night with?"

I hum. "See, the thing is...it's Arlo."

There's another excruciatingly long pause, and Linda finally breaks it by saying, "I see."

"I'm sorry I didn't tell you earlier."

"And how has that...impacted your work? Is that the reason he's fired my agency?" Her voice is sharp, and it sends pain piercing through my chest.

I'm ashamed of myself. I've been so caught up in my life, in this whirlwind romance, that I haven't thought about the impact it would have on other people. On my sister, the most important person in my life.

"We've been involved," I answer quietly.

Another long, painful pause is broken by Linda's sigh. "I need time to process this, Bonnie. I'll talk to you later." She hangs up the phone before I can apologize, and I'm left in my beautiful bedroom, utterly alone.

. . .

ARLO FINDS me there an hour later, my arms curled around my knees as I stare into space. His thick brows tug together as he crosses the room toward the bed and takes a seat beside me. "What's wrong?"

"I told my sister about us."

Understanding clears the frown from his face. "Oh. She called you after speaking to me, then. She didn't take it well?"

I shake my head. "She said she needed time to process." I rest my chin on my knee and stare at the comforter. "I have this horrible feeling that I'm making a mistake, Arlo. Everything is beautiful when it's just the two of us, but how can this be real? My own sister won't speak to me now."

He tugs me into his chest, and I collapse against him. The stroke of his fingers through my hair makes me relax slightly, but I still can't shake the feeling that this is wrong. He's my boss. He's incredibly wealthy, and I'm incredibly not. The power differential between us is too big. What if he decides he doesn't want me anymore, and I'm left out in the cold with nothing?

Am I being a complete idiot? Should I break things off before he does?

"I worry that this isn't real too," Arlo finally says. "That it's all just an illusion, and it's going to shatter any minute."

I glance up at him. "You do?"

He smiles sadly. "It reminds me of how I met my ex-wife. I fell for her—hard. It felt kind of like this, exciting and overwhelming, but different too. I feel calmer around you, and whenever I get worried that we're moving too fast, I think about that feeling."

I mull over his words for a minute. "It shouldn't be comforting to hear that you have doubts, but somehow it is. It's validating."

He squeezes me closer, then loosens his grip. "One of the

reasons I was so blinded by Alice was that I pride myself on reading people. She was a grifter, plain and simple. She had a long-term boyfriend, and they chose me as a mark. She wrapped me around her little finger then fell pregnant right away, and I thought my life was clicking into place."

"Like I did with Galen."

Sad understanding floods his eyes. "Exactly like that. To learn that she'd been playing me all along threw me."

"I get that. I felt the same way."

"I felt like such an idiot." He blows out a breath. "And then there was the divorce."

"She didn't slink off into the darkness without a fight, I'm guessing."

Arlo huffs bitterly. "No, she didn't. She fought for custody of Will until I gave her the money she wanted, and then she disappeared."

I sit up, frowning. "So why did you think I knew her?"

"She's sent a few people sniffing around in the past couple of years. A housekeeper. A barista downstairs. I think she's trying to figure out if she can squeeze me for anything else, but our legal agreements are ironclad. She's not getting another penny from me, and she's not getting my son."

"I'm sorry."

He meets my gaze, finally, and his eyes are sad. "Me too."

"I'm not looking for a payout," I tell him honestly.

His expression softens, his lips gaining a wry twist. "Glad to hear it."

Unable to resist the temptation, I slide my palm over his cheek and pull him closer for a kiss. It's a soft brush of my lips against his, and Arlo's big body shudders beside me. His grip on me tightens, and I find myself sliding over so I'm straddling him, peppering his face and neck with kisses.

"I have to go back to work," he says, sliding his hands up underneath my skirt. "I only came back to warn you that I'd spoken to your sister."

I grind against him. "We'll be quick."

He smiles, capturing my lips in his. Our kiss deepens as his hands slide over my stockinged legs and onto my bottom, shaping my curves. I love the way he touches me. It's possessive while being utterly reverent. He makes my head spin.

Lust detonates in my core. After my conversation with Linda and all the doubts I've been mulling over for the past hour, I need this to be real between Arlo and me. I need to feel our connection —and the way we've always done that is with sex. Today, though, there's something raw shimmering in the air between us. Our mutual confessions about our doubts have unlocked some other layer of vulnerability, and all I want to do is bask in it.

Loving someone is a terrifying thing. I'm opening my heart to him, trusting that he'll treat it gently. Today, I realized that he's doing the same with me.

I need to show him that it's worth it—and show *myself* the same thing.

Reaching between us, I unfasten Arlo's belt. I free him from the confines of his pants while he tries to find the waistband of my sheer, high-waisted tights. He growls in frustration, the noise vibrating over my skin. I tug at his lower lip with my teeth while stroking his cock, a dangerous, raw sort of passion igniting between us.

When Arlo grips the crotch of my tights and rips them apart, I let out a shallow gasp.

"Stupid things," he growls, pulling me closer by the back of my neck to kiss me hard.

With his cock in hand, I tug the gusset of my panties aside and rub myself against him. He groans at the feel of me, and all my doubts disappear. It couldn't feel this good if it weren't real. We wouldn't have a connection as powerful as this one if our emotions weren't just as in sync as our bodies. I grind my hips against him until his shaft is slick, loving the feel of him sliding against all my most sensitive spots.

This can't be fake. There's no way. It can't be a mistake. Certainty washes over me, and I have to tell him exactly how I feel.

Grinding myself against him, I grip both sides of his face. "Arlo," I pant.

"Yeah?" His pupils are dilated as he meets my gaze, then drops it to my lips.

We've only danced around our feelings so far, but my heart is detonating for this man. It's an explosion beyond anything I've ever felt before, and it goes far, far beyond the physical. If this is real—if I'm going to deal with the fallout with all of our friends, family, colleagues, and associates—I want Arlo to know exactly what's in my heart.

I buck my hips and pant when the tip of his cock rubs against my clit with the perfect amount of friction. I could come right here, my body taut as a bowstring, my emotions shimmering like a cloudy haze around me.

But he has to know. I have to tell him.

I rock my hips and brush my lips against his, drawing another raspy groan from him. "I love you," I whisper. "I love you, Arlo."

A tug on my hair, and he's pulling me back to look in my eyes with a wild, euphoric expression on his face.

As I hold my hands on his jaw, I feel tears well in my eyes—and I say it again. "I love you."

Arlo trembles slightly, closing his eyes. His chest heaves with deep breaths, and then he pulls my face close enough that our lips brush. "I love you too, Bonnie. I love you so much it feels like I'm being torn apart with the force of it."

He brushes a tear from my eyes and kisses me softly—then hard. His other hand slides down to my ass and urges my hips back into motion. My body trembles and my breaths gasp, and I can hardly think of anything other than the fact that I love this man with every fiber of my being. I love his moods and his laughter. I love his sex. I love his supportiveness.

That can't be wrong, can it?

"Put my cock inside you," he rasps.

Not one to disobey those kinds of orders, I reach between us and fit him inside me. As I slide down on top of him, we both let out long, low moans. I'll never get tired of feeling Arlo inside me. Never get sick of the beautiful stretch of his intrusion.

I love him.

As I start to move, he gives me a few moments to get a rhythm going, and then Arlo takes over. He grips my waist with one strong hand and rolls his hips up into me. It feels so good I could cry. I grip his tie and the collar of his shirt, clinging on as our bodies move together to the end.

When I reach my peak, Arlo has a hand between us and is touching me where I need him most. His lips are at my ear as he whispers the most beautiful words I've ever heard. I cry out his name as he tells me how much he loves me, and my orgasm shatters through me like light reflecting off the shards of a broken mirror.

A moment later, Arlo finds his own ecstasy. He cries out as he clings to me, panting hard, and then holds me close until we both float back down to earth again.

When he leaves for work a short while later, I lie back on the mussed sheets and stare at the ceiling for a while.

I love him and he loves me, and everything is going to be okay.

TWENTY-ONE
ARLO

WILL RUNS toward his friends as we enter the restaurant's private room, reserved by one of his kindergarten classmates for a birthday party. He crashes into a pack of five-year-olds and is swallowed in a flurry of happy screams.

Bonnie glances at me, wrapped gift in hand. We head to the table of gifts and place it down next to the mound of boxes and bags.

"Are you sure you don't need to be at work right now?" she asks, brows drawn. "These kinds of parties aren't exactly fun for adults, unless you're a psycho who enjoys twenty five-year-olds in the throes of a sugar high."

She knows I'm taking my company public in a matter of days, and if this had happened two months ago, I would've been at work. Bonnie's presence has changed more than she knows; I've realized that no matter how much I try to dote on my son, I still spend too much time away from him.

Being with Bonnie has transformed my home life. It's not just me and Will against the world. I'm not building an empire to pass down to him. I watch him play with cars or action figures next to Bonnie, and I see a little boy drinking up her attention like he's been starved of it. His face lights up every time I tell him I'll be coming on a walk with them, and on the odd day I'm working too late to see him before he falls asleep, Will has always written a note for me in his lopsided, lovable handwriting.

I told myself I was being a good father because I spent weekends and most evenings with Will, and he seemed like a happy kid. I wanted to set up his future and protect him from all the people who might hurt him. But Bonnie showed me it hasn't been enough. My son has blossomed in the past five weeks, and I know part of that is that I've spent more time with him.

Bonnie did that for me. For my son.

I slide a hand over her lower back and grin. "Call this practice for the charity event."

"So I'm here as your date, not your nanny? That's news to me." She arches a brow, and her sassiness makes me want to turn her over my knee.

I growl. "Careful, Bonnie. That mouth will get you in trouble."

"Arlo!" A brown-haired woman wearing thick, black glasses approaches. She's the mother of the birthday boy. I met her when I was touring the kindergarten before Will started there, when she made sure to inform me that she was divorced. She smiles brightly. "We weren't expecting you to attend our little celebration. What a pleasant surprise!"

When she doesn't greet Bonnie or even glance in her direction, I clear my throat. "Chelsea, this is Bonnie." I put my hand on Bonnie's lower back, and the woman's brows jump as she follows the movement.

"Oh." She blinks at Bonnie. "My apologies. When I saw you

dropping Will off at the school, I didn't realize..." A tiny bit of frost enters her expression and is immediately banished. Her smile returns. "Would you two like a drink?"

We're swept up into the party, and for the most part, Bonnie is right. I end up sitting on a tiny plastic chair, watching my son run around with his classmates. I eat an overcooked hamburger and chat with the other parents, some of whom wince every time a particularly high-pitched squeal rends the air.

But Will glances over at me periodically, and his face lights up. He spends some time in the craft corner and comes over with a drawing of me, Bonnie, and himself, presenting it to me with a bashful expression on his face.

Every squeal that has pierced my eardrums during this birthday party is worth it, just to see my son smile while I praise his drawing.

As he tears off toward his friends again, Bonnie nudges her shoulder against mine. "He's such a good kid."

I slide my hand over her thigh and squeeze gently. "He loves you. I want to tell him about us."

Her eyes turn glassy. "Yeah?"

I nod. "I want us to be a family."

Is it fast? Yeah, it's fast. Is it happening at a time when my attention should be split between a thousand supposedly more important tasks and events? Sure.

But Bonnie is here, and I'm not going to let her slip through my fingers a second time.

Still, when it's time to take Will home and he falls asleep in his booster seat at the back of the limo, my ringing ears are glad to be sitting in a silent vehicle.

· · ·

THE NEXT COUPLE of days are spent working. We take our solar company public with lots of fanfare, and I go from being an extremely wealthy man to being an obscenely wealthy man. I thought I'd be happier—but all I want to do is go home and wrap my arms around Bonnie.

Rome calls me that evening, after the markets close. "Congratulations are in order," he says. "I saw the final numbers. Well done."

I lean back in my office chair and stare out at the city lights through the window. "Thanks, Rome. How have you been?"

There's a slight pause. "I've been fine."

I frown. "You sure about that?"

"Just...this temp we hired. She's driving me crazy."

"Why don't you get rid of her?" I ask, remembering Rome saying the same thing to me over a month ago when I told him about Bonnie.

He grunts. "I know. I should." *But I won't*, remains unsaid.

"What did she do?"

"She just...drives me crazy, is all." He huffs. "But enough about that. Are you celebrating tonight?"

"Nah," I answer, standing. "Just heading home. Gonna take it easy."

"What? Really?" He scoffs. "That woman has you twisted up, my friend."

I grin. "Doesn't feel too bad from where I'm standing. Maybe you need to be twisted yourself."

Rome grunts. "Doubt it."

"I'll see you next weekend?" The Noble Foundation event is coming up quick.

"Oh, I see how it is," Rome answers. "You won't meet me for a drink tonight, but you'll see me when you're soliciting huge donations for your precious charity."

I chuckle as Rome grumbles good-naturedly, then tells me he'll see me at the event. We hang up, then I pack my things and head out of the office with a smile on my face, leaving my staff to celebrate without me.

There's somewhere I'd rather be.

TWENTY-TWO

BONNIE

THE MORNING after Arlo's company goes public, after a night of very pleasant celebration, I wait for Nikki in the first floor living room. Not a minute later than I expected, the elevator opens and Nikita appears. She whistles as she walks into Arlo's home, eyes immediately drawn to the way the light reflects through the glass staircase. Then she turns to me with a wry smile on her lips. "No wonder you didn't want to move out."

I click my tongue, then let out a laugh. With Arlo and Will visiting his sister, he told me to invite my girlfriends to meet with the team Laura organized to get me ready for the charity dinner. The event is tomorrow, which I'm told is a lightning-fast turn-around for styling but still possible.

After grabbing sparkling water and a few snacks from the kitchen, we recline on the plush sofas. Nikki motions to one of the huge art pieces on the wall—not one of Beth's, but still gorgeous—and raises her eyebrows. "Either Arlo has good taste, or he knows someone who does."

I grin. "That would be option number two."

Nikki smiles and kicks her feet up on the table. We fall into easy conversation, and tension I hadn't noticed eases between my shoulder blades. As Nikki regales me with stories about how annoying her new boss is, Laura pokes her head into the room and introduces herself.

Nikki, not one to shy away from an awkward conversation, leans back in her chair and asks, "So, what's your opinion on Bonnie banging your boss?"

"Nikki!"

She laughs.

Laura glances at me, then back at Nikita. She shrugs, spreading her arms. "I knew something was up on that first day. Bonnie basically panicked and disappeared into the bathroom when she met Mr. Noble."

"That was not a good day," I cut in.

Nikita tilts her head, watching the house manager carefully. In a very casual voice, she continues her inquisition: "Is this something Arlo does...often?"

Laura fluffs a pillow on the other end of the sofa and refolds a throw blanket. She lets out a huff and shakes her head. "No."

I gulp, feeling uncomfortable. When Arlo and I gave into temptation, I hadn't thought ahead to these relationships. How should Laura and I treat each other now?

But Laura is more professional than I gave her credit for. She straightens and looks me directly in the eyes. "I've never seen Mr. Noble as happy and relaxed as he is with you, except maybe those first few months with his ex-wife. I understand the two of you met a few years ago, so although this entire situation is...unconventional, I'm willing to move forward if you are."

Relief sweeps through me. "Of course," I answer with a nod.

"Good. The stylist should be here shortly. Give me a buzz if you need anything." She sweeps out of the room, her shoes squeaking softly on the hardwood floors.

Nikita watches her leave before swinging her gaze back to me. The ice in her crystal glass clinks softly as she pokes it with a metal straw. She takes a thoughtful sip. "She carries herself like she's seen it all."

"I guess if you work for a billionaire, you have to be ready for anything."

Nikita's brow arches so sassily that she doesn't even need to speak words for me to pick up the nearest pillow and launch it at her. She bats it away with a laugh—and then the elevator bell dings.

The sound of a rolling rack clacking over hardwood floors, along with the rhythmic footsteps of a woman in heels, alerts us to the stylist's presence. A tall, dark-haired woman appears, her gaze sweeping over the two of us from behind her thick, black-rimmed glasses. She rolls the rack into the living room with spare, efficient movements. "Good. You're here. We've got a lot to go through. If any of these gowns need alterations, we'll have to rush it to the seamstress overnight, so we need to get started. I'm Mina. Please stand here, in the light, so I can get a good look at your coloring."

Nikita perks up at the sight of the clothing. I wonder how much she misses working in the vintage clothing store. I'll have to ask her how long she plans to work at her new job. My guess is... not long. Nikita plus corporate America just doesn't compute in my brain.

I stand where instructed while Mina reveals gown after beautiful gown, shaking out the skirts as she presents them to me, studying both my body and the gowns with a critical eye. Unable to resist, Nikita eventually gets up and starts giving her opinion. The two of them quickly start talking in lingo I don't really understand, things about silhouettes and shades and undertones and fabrics that are far, far over my head.

I'm stuffed into a dozen gowns, until one is proclaimed the winner. It needs some alterations, but they assure me it's perfect. By the time the two of them come to that decision, I'm so sick of trying on clothing that I just agree, not really seeing the vision. I just cross my fingers and hope that the alterations will be done in time for dinner tomorrow.

Mina rushes off again, and Nikki reclines on a sofa, sipping her sparkling water with a satisfied smile on her lips. "That was fun," she proclaims.

I arch my brows at her. "Maybe you should ask her for a job, seeing as you haven't stopped complaining about your new boss since you started working there."

Nikki's cheeks grow slightly red. She waves off my comment, then goes on the attack, changing the subject directly. "So, I gather things with Arlo are going well?"

I sit down across from her and kick my feet up onto the coffee table. I'm sweaty and oddly tired from trying on all those clothes, which is honestly kind of ridiculous. It's not like it was *that* physically taxing, but everything's been tiring me out lately. I guess I'm not used to running around after a five-year-old during the day, then staying up half the night with an insatiable lover.

Nodding at my friend's question, I let a smile bloom across my lips. "I really like him."

She studies me for a moment, then gives me a smile of her own. "Well, I'm happy for you."

"You are? You're not all mad and protective like you were last time we hung out?"

"I've never seen you look this good, Bonnie. You're glowing. I can see the happiness just bursting out of you, and that's not something I can stay mad about. You know that I'll always be there for you. And you know as well as I do that I've made at least as many mistakes as you have, so I can't judge."

A knot loosens in my chest. I'd been so worried that my relationship with Nikki would fray, and hearing her say those things means the world. After my sister's reaction, and the emotional aftermath with Arlo, it's nice to have a bit of stability in my friendship with Nikki. We spend another couple of hours together, until Nikki's phone rings and she has to leave.

Tomorrow, I'll be facing all of Arlo's family, friends, and associates—and I'll be doing it as his girlfriend, not his nanny.

If Laura can accept me, and Nikita can be supportive, maybe there's hope that my relationship with Arlo will go over well with everyone else. With that thought rattling around in my mind, I say goodbye to Nikki and head back to my bedroom. The latch snicks shut behind me with a soft click, and I pull out my phone.

My sister answers on the third ring.

I let out a long breath. "I was worried you wouldn't pick up."

She huffs. "I considered it."

Sinking down on the edge of the bed, I stare at the rich carpet beneath my feet and bite my lip. "I'm sorry I wasn't honest with you from the start, Linda."

"Between you and Dani, I'm worried my agency will start to get a reputation. I'm not sure if I'm providing childcare or matchmaking."

"I know," I say. "I'm sorry."

There's a long pause, and I hear a door close on the other end of the line. In a quieter voice, Linda asks, "Are you sure about this, Bonnie?"

"Yes," I answer. "But also no."

"I'm worried. It's not a healthy start to a relationship. And it's all happening so fast."

Half of me agrees with my sister's assessment. She's right, of course. No matter how passionate our relationship is right now, is it built on a good foundation? If our attraction wanes, will he lose interest? Will I? Is any of this real?

"Maybe you should pump the brakes," Linda suggests. "Move out of his place for a little while. Date him. See what happens."

My fingers rub over and back across my forehead as I consider her words. "Logically, I know you're giving me good advice."

"But you're not going to take it."

"It's just so *good*, Linda. A relationship has never felt this right with a man, ever. It was the same in London. We have a connection."

"It takes more than attraction to build a lasting relationship." Linda speaks from experience. She and her ex-husband were madly in love—until they weren't. "You both need to be on the same page, have the same values. Kids, marriage, career. Have you talked about all that with him? What about money? He has oodles of it, but how will you access it? Will you be dependent on him? What's the long-term plan here?"

A sick feeling churns in my gut. "I mean..." I drift off. We haven't talked about all that. All we've done is sleep together, talk about how much we like each other, and make dreamy plans about my future business. "He's had a vasectomy, so kids are out. As for the other stuff..." I let my voice peter out.

When Linda answers, her voice is excruciatingly gentle. "And you're okay with never having kids of your own?"

A lance pierces my chest, and I remember that picnic in the park we had a few weeks ago. I dreamed of having a big family. "I don't know."

"This is what I mean, Bonnie. You need space to clear your head. I know he's good-looking and wealthy and the whole package, but this is your *life*. Choosing a partner is the most important thing you'll ever do. More important than college. More important than any job. The person you share your life with will impact every single aspect of your existence in a deep, undeniable way. And I mean that in both directions—good and bad."

"You think I'm making a mistake."

Linda sighs. She pauses for so long, I'm not sure she'll answer at all, until she quietly says, "I think you're moving too fast."

My own fears are being echoed back to me from the one person who's always been in my corner. Can I really ignore it?

"I love you, Bonnie. If you need anything, I'll be there for you."

Tears prick my lids. My throat is suddenly thick, and I know I don't deserve my sister. She's letting me know, in no uncertain terms, that she'll be there to pick up the pieces when they inevitably shatter. Again. "I love you too."

"I have to get back to work, but I'll call you in a couple of days, okay?"

"Okay." The words come out a bit hoarse, so I clear my throat and put on a cheery smile that I hope bleeds through to my voice. "Sounds good."

When the line goes dead, a feeling of dread seeps through my gut like venom. If Linda is right, all my fantasies are just that—silly, girlish fantasies that will soon come up against hard, cold reality.

TWENTY-THREE
ARLO

THE HUBBUB DOWNSTAIRS DIES DOWN, which tells me that Bonnie is almost ready to go. I check my watch—perfect. We'll get to the Noble Foundation Gala just in time. I descend the stairs, making it halfway down before I see Bonnie—and have to stop.

She turns to face me, blond hair falling down her back in soft, golden waves. Her makeup is elegant and understated while still bringing out the beauty of her features. Her gown is...a gown. I can't really focus on it right now. All I know is it's a shade of blue, and the bodice nips Bonnie's waist perfectly before flaring out in a dramatic, draped skirt.

"It has pockets," Bonnie informs me, sticking her hands in said pockets. She smiles at me uncertainly when I remain speechless, still standing halfway up the stairs. "What do you think?"

I think she looks like a goddess. I think I'm the luckiest man to grace this earth, because not only did I get a night with this woman three years ago, but she also crashed back into my life when I least expected her. I think I want to make her my wife and never let her leave my side.

"You look beautiful," I manage to say, forcing my legs to keep moving down the steps.

A flush of pink deepens on Bonnie's cheeks. She looks me up and down, inspecting my tuxedo. "Not bad yourself."

I grin, sliding a hand around her waist.

She stays me with a hand on my chest. "No kissing. You'll mess up my makeup."

"I want nothing more than to mess up your makeup right now."

A shiver trembles through her body, which doesn't help keep me under control. Charity dinner? What charity dinner? Am I supposed to be hosting something?

Blue eyes blink up at me for a moment, then Bonnie drops her gaze to my bowtie and straightens it with soft, delicate touches. "Are you sure about this, Arlo?"

"About what?"

"About...me? Coming to this event on your arm?"

Unable to resist the temptation, I kiss the tip of her nose. "Never been surer of anything in my life."

It's the truth. This woman is everything I've ever wanted. It doesn't matter to me how she came into my life. I know in my heart that she's the one for me. Why else would our night three years ago have left such an impression on both of us? How else can I explain this urge to keep her by my side?

I told her the truth: I'm falling for her. Hard.

Unless I'm making the same mistakes I made with Alice...

Banishing the thought, I press a kiss to her forehead. My eyes drift down to her lips, and in a superhuman display of control, I tear my arm away from her waist and hold it out toward her. She places her hand on my elbow, and we head toward the elevator.

"Alex called a few minutes ago," Bonnie says. "Will ate dinner and is currently asleep in their spare room. He was very excited about all things baby related."

I grin. "Good. Now relax, Bonnie. I can see the tension in your shoulders. Everything will be fine tonight."

Both of my backup babysitters fell through at the last minute, and all my friends and family will be at the gala with me. I was lucky that Alex was available to watch Will for the night, even though she shouldn't be working. I'm lucky to have such loyal staff. I make a mental note to give Alex a generous holiday bonus this year, right before my thoughts are derailed by the light playing over Bonnie's skin.

I walk her to the elevator, then pause in front of it. "Before I forget..."

Her head tilts as I pull a box out of my breast pocket. Placing it on a console table nearby, I flip it open and reveal the glittering necklace I chose earlier today.

Bonnie sucks in a breath. "What's this?"

"This is a necklace. Mina told me you were wearing blue, so I got this one."

Bonnie is wearing a strange expression when I pick the necklace off its bed of velvet and hold it up. "You picked that one because it's blue," she repeats.

"Well, blue and sparkly."

Blinking, Bonnie stares at the piece of jewelry dangling between my hands. "Oh."

"Do you like it?"

"It's gorgeous, Arlo. It's... I've never seen anything like it."

"It's yours. Let me put it on you," I say, then let my gaze drift over Bonnie's slender neck as she lifts the gleaming sheet of her hair out of the way.

My hands tremble slightly as I clasp the necklace at her nape. Sliding my hands to her shoulders, I place a kiss below her ear, then urge her to turn around. Hundreds of diamonds twinkle in the light of my foyer, the deep blue of the sapphires gleaming between them.

Bonnie's fingers drift over the stones as she lifts her gaze to mine. "Thank you," she whispers.

"There's one condition to this gift," I tell her.

Her brow arches. "What's that?"

"Tonight, when we get home, you take everything off and leave the necklace on. Then I have my way with you."

Heat flares in Bonnie's eyes, and a coy smile tugs at her lips. "Deal."

TWENTY-FOUR
BONNIE

THE MIRRORED elevator walls show me a glamorous woman with a necklace that likely costs more than my old yearly salary at Holt & Holt. Maybe more. I have no concept of jewelry prices, but I do know there are a *lot* of diamonds and about a dozen almond-sized sapphires draped around my neck.

It's the most beautiful thing I've ever seen.

Hope is like a flower slowly unfurling in my heart. As the elevator plummets down, I begin to dream about everything that could be. The life that I could have with Arlo.

It's not the necklace that makes me feel this way, exactly; it's the look in Arlo's eyes when he gave it to me. The hint of vulnerability, followed by the satisfaction of seeing it clasped around my neck. Like he was staking his claim on me with these precious rocks, a signal to everyone we'll meet at tonight's event.

It feels good to be his, and even better that he's mine.

We're whisked off to the venue, which is a gorgeous Art Deco building. The foyer is dramatic and bursting with fresh flowers and swags of fabric. Through a dramatic, double-height doorway, I spy the main dining room. White tablecloths are draped over a hundred-odd round tables, elegant centerpieces decorating each one. Above, eight chandeliers light the space with warm, twinkling light.

There's a stage at the far end, with a big screen and a clear glass podium. In the back corner of the room, a harpist strums her instrument.

To the right, the room opens onto a gallery. This has Beth written all over it. Art pieces of all kinds are displayed, with well-heeled and well-dressed donors milling around, already placing bids on the silent auction. With a hand on my lower back, Arlo leads me toward the room.

People in designer gowns and tuxedos mill around, immediately accosting Arlo. With every new face, he introduces me by name and makes sure to include me in the conversations. I meet an heiress who's interested in starting an initiative about food deserts in the city. I meet an oil baron who is a regular donor to Arlo's foundation. There's a young tech entrepreneur who seems uninterested in the proceedings but is relatively polite.

My cheeks hurt from holding the edges of my smile up, but Arlo navigates through the room with ease. We slowly make our way toward the dining room, where more guests await. Some of them are already seated, but most people are talking and laughing in small clumps of glittering luxury.

Then I spot a few familiar faces on the opposite end of the room. I squeeze Arlo's arm. "I'm going to go say hi to some friends. I'll be right back."

Surprise darts across his face, until he looks across the room. "Right. You know Leif Sorensen."

"I do. Meet you at the table." I disentangle my arm from his, but before I can leave, Arlo tugs me closer and lays a kiss right on my lips, in the middle of his event, in front of everyone. I just stand there, heart hammering.

He grins at my startled expression. "Just so everyone's clear about what you mean to me."

Pulse rioting, I can't quite keep the smile off my face as I make my way across the room. Layla is the first to see me. She's Leif's wife, and since the two of them got married, we've only been able to catch up occasionally. She was busy with kids, and I was busy with my career, and then I got fired and I was too ashamed to reach out to old friends.

Penny is beside her. I met her the night I met Nikita. She's wearing a deep emerald dress that complements her red hair like it was made for her. And with Marcus Walsh as her husband—and fashion designer Raphael Garcia as a close friend—it probably *is* custom-made.

Finally, Dani spots me. Her face bursts into a smile. She spreads her arms and rushes forward, wrapping me in a tight hug and squeezing so long and hard it becomes difficult to breathe. She pulls away when I wheeze, tears wetting her eyes.

"You've been avoiding me," she accuses. "What are you doing here? You look gorgeous. That *necklace*! Bonnie!" Her eyes are bright. "I'm so happy to see you! Did you get a new job? Are you here with your company?"

"No," I say. "I'm here with Arlo, actually."

Her head tilts. "Arlo Noble? As in, the Noble Foundation's Arlo Noble?"

A blush heats my cheeks. "The one and only."

"Girl." Her gaze flicks to Layla, then Penny. "Did you two know about this?"

"Bonnie hasn't taken my calls in three months," Penny pouts. "I've been worried. Nikki told me you were going through a hard time, but still."

Shame rises up inside me in a scorching wave, and I let my shoulders drop. "You're right. I've been a bad friend. It's just...I didn't want to burden you all."

The three of them have kids and husbands and beautiful, glamorous lives. Somewhere along the way in the past few years, I got left behind.

Or at least, I thought I did. Maybe I shut myself out, when the three of them would have opened their homes and lives to me if I'd only asked for help.

Have I been burying myself in self-pity all this time? Was all my misery self-inflicted? I've been so focused on wallowing in the fact that I had to start my life back at zero...did I miss the fact that I wouldn't have needed to do that at all?

"What has been *happening?*" Dani asks. "Where's the woman who took me speed dating and dumped a pitcher of water on a creep's head?"

I laugh, if only to stop myself from crying. "My life kind of fell apart," I admit. "I'm only clawing myself out of it now."

That's when a voice sounds behind me, the familiarity of it crawling up my spine like spindly fingers. "You seem to have landed on your feet, Bonnie." I turn to see Galen Deely smirking behind me. His gaze flicks from me to my old friends, and back to me. "Saw you walk in with Noble. Didn't take you long to sink your claws into someone else, did it?"

If I were a better, cleverer person, I'd have a witty comeback. I'd be able to tear Galen to shreds with nothing more than a haughty look and a few well-chosen words, using all the righteous indignation borne of what he did to me. But I see him there, in a tuxedo, wearing a cruel smile that I remember from the night everything fell apart—and I freeze.

"Nothing to say?" he asks, still smiling, though his eyes are very, very sharp. "He asked about you, you know."

"What are you talking about?" I croak.

"Who the hell are you?" Layla cuts in. "Go away."

Galen ignores her. "Arlo. We had lunch a few weeks back, and he told me he was considering hiring you." His gaze flicks down my body and back up again. "Is that what this is?"

"Okay. That's enough." Penny stomps toward him. She's short, and she's not usually angry, but since she got with Marcus and had a child, her confidence and assertiveness have skyrocketed. She puts a hand on Galen's chest and urges him to take a step back. "Leave, or we'll call security."

Galen snorts, then turns on his heel and walks away.

That's when I realize I'm trembling. Dani grabs me around the waist and hauls me down a nearby hallway, stuffing me into a washroom while we all crowd in. Layla closes the toilet lid, and Penny puts her hands on my shoulders and makes me sit down.

The effort it takes me to keep from blubbering and ruining my makeup is immense. But once I open my mouth, the whole story comes out. I tell them about Galen, about losing my job, about having to sell my apartment, about being completely, utterly broke. I tell them quickly, like I'm reading out bullet points outlining how my life fell apart one by one. "Then Linda found me, gave me a temporary job. And I walked in and saw that he was the guy from London."

"*Mr. Sexalicious?*" Layla screams. "Arlo Noble is Mr. Sexalicious?"

The squeals and shrieks of three women echo in the tiny bathroom, and all I can do is melt into laughter while praying that my eardrums recover. "He is. We sort of...picked up where we left off."

"Oh my goodness." Dani slaps a hand on her forehead. "I can't judge because we all know how things happened between me and Emil, but gosh. Just hope you don't get pregnant and blow the whole thing up, because let me tell you, that is *not* a fun time."

I snort. "Well, Arlo's been snipped, so there's no risk of that."

"Vasectomies aren't foolproof," Penny says, shrugging. "Never say never."

"I'm saying never," I tell them, holding up a hand. "My nerves can't handle much more."

"I'm going to talk to security about getting that guy kicked out," Dani says. "Come on. Let's head back before people think we're doing something other than cornering our reclusive friend in the bathroom for long-overdue gossip."

She tugs open the door, and fresh air flows in. I inhale deeply and let my friends tug me back to the main room. Pausing before we enter, I look at the three of them in turn.

"Thank you," I say solemnly. "I know I've been a terrible friend. I know I've been dodging your calls and avoiding you. I was ashamed of what happened in my life, but I should have known you wouldn't judge me."

"We have done worse," Layla says, a sardonic twist to her lips. "Or have you forgotten?"

I snort, blinking tears away. It wouldn't do to ruin my makeup now. "No, you're right."

"The important thing is you're here now, and we know what's been going on," Dani says. "Now let's go eat some delicious food and listen to some boring speeches. It's so rare I have an evening away from the kids, and I want to make the most of it."

"There you are," a deep voice calls out. Emil Van der Berg smiles at his wife, sparing a quick glance for the rest of us. The way his gaze returns to Dani, though, makes me think he might have more baby-making on the brain. Not that they need more— between Emil's two kids with his late wife and the three they've had together since, they already have a full brood.

Dani leans on her husband, smiling, and Leif and Marcus appear next. They lead their ladies to a table, and I scan the space for Arlo. When I don't see him, I make my way across the big room to the table just to the left of the podium, and I find my name written in cursive on an elegant, folded card.

Sitting down, I accept a drink from a passing waiter, grateful when Beth plops down in the seat beside me. She wraps an arm around my shoulders and gives me a quick, one-armed hug.

"I knew there was something between you and my brother," she says with a wink. "Glad you two figured it all out."

"So you're okay with it?"

Beth huffs. "Arlo needs someone to show him how to enjoy life. And I knew as soon as I saw his reaction to you dancing with another man that you'd be able to do it."

I laugh. "He has a bit of a possessive streak."

Not wanting to delve too deeply into my relationship with Arlo at this event, I open a brochure placed on the table and hum at some of the pieces Beth sourced for the silent auction. She leans in and tells me details about the artists and their pieces, and we fall into easy conversation. She has great taste and a nose for trends. I have no doubt the silent auction will be a success.

The budding hope in my chest unfurls a little bit more. Galen is nowhere to be seen, and my friends have reminded me that they're here for me.

Maybe—just maybe—things will turn out okay.

TWENTY-FIVE
ARLO

I SHOULD BE SITTING beside Bonnie. Or maybe I should be preparing for my speech and making sure all the last-minute problems that inevitably crop up at an event are sorted out.

Instead, I'm stuck in the foyer of the building talking to a hedge fund manager, of all people. Does this guy not take a day off? Galen cornered me a moment ago, when I had to deal with a mix-up at the entrance to let a guest inside, and he seems like he has something on his mind.

He's been dithering for the past thirty seconds, telling me how impressed he is with the venue and the event.

"Thank you," I tell him with a tight smile. "I should be getting back in there."

"Saw you were here with Bonnie Delmar," he blurts.

I freeze, frowning. "Yes. I am."

"Didn't look like she was an employee after all."

Danger is a distant ringing in my ears. I don't like the look in the other man's eyes, the gleaming in his irises like a light shining on sharpened steel. "No," I answer after a beat. "She isn't."

He straightens. "I think I should be a little bit more upfront about what we talked about at lunch. Tell you the whole story." His eyes are shrewd, studying my face. There's an odd twist to his lips, like a snarl wants to burst through but is being held back.

"I really need to be getting back," I tell him, turning away. "I'll be making a speech soon."

"This is what she does, you know." The words are lobbed at me, a rocket whistling through the air.

I freeze.

Galen stands at my back and speaks the words I don't want to hear. "Bonnie. This is what she does. She did it to me."

I turn slowly, meeting his gaze. I say nothing.

"She uses sex to get ahead." He spreads his arms. "We were just coworkers, until I got promoted. Then all of a sudden, she wanted more."

"That's not what she told me."

"It wouldn't be, no," Galen says with a bitter huff. "I'm just trying to tell you, man to man, to watch your back around her."

"That's very decent of you," I say in a dark tone. "Man to man."

He knows I don't believe him. Galen arches a brow and shrugs his broad shoulders. "I know you're still on the fence about hiring us to manage your assets, so let this be the first sign of trust. All I want is for you to have all the information."

"She told me you came on to her. Seduced her."

"She would say that, wouldn't she?"

There's a ringing in my ears. He's lying—he has to be.

But why?

Wouldn't it be easier to sweep the past under the rug and keep trying to woo me into handing my assets over to his fund? He's making his own life harder by admitting these things.

Unless they're true.

"So what really happened?" I hear myself ask.

"It was a company holiday party two years ago," Galen tells me, taking a step closer to me. "We were at the director's house, and everything was normal. My promotion was announced, and not ten minutes later, Bonnie dragged me into one of the bathrooms. She was—well. You've probably experienced it too."

An image pops into my head, of Bonnie pushing me up against the wall outside the elevator in my home. Dropping to her knees. A living, breathing fantasy.

Galen must see the tension in my jaw, because he gives me a pinched-lip smile. "Sorry, Arlo. But this is what she does. She sleeps her way to the top. I'm not sure how the two of you met, but I'm sure that when she found out who you were, she was probably angling to get with you."

Did she know who I was three years ago? Has she been lying to me this whole time?

If I were thinking logically, I would take a step back from this situation. I would ask Bonnie for her side of the story. I would find out the truth.

But all I can think about is Alice, wrapping me around her little finger. Alice, promising me love and devotion. Promising me the world.

Alice, lying to me the whole time.

If Bonnie is doing the same thing, the wrath I mete out will be unending. Have I fallen for the same tricks *again*?

Blood pounding in my ears, I nod to Galen and mumble words that may or may not make sense, then I head for the dining room. I'm not sure what my face does while I try to tamp down the boiling mass of dangerous emotions churning in my chest, but it can't be good.

Halfway across the room, I see Bonnie smiling at my sister,

and I wonder if this is another ruse. Did she ever care about me? Was *anything* she said true?

Is Galen lying? Why would he?

Bonnie looks up when I approach. A smile spreads over her lips—then freezes. "Is everything okay?"

I nod. "Time for a speech."

"You'll do great," she says, then stands to straighten my bowtie. Her touch is excruciating. I study her face, my teeth clenched, as if I can see the truth written on the lines of her face.

She studies me right back. "Are you sure everything is okay?" Her hand smooths over my lapel, intimate, soft.

I take a step back. "I'd better get up there."

"Arlo," Beth cuts in, standing beside Bonnie. Her brows are drawn low over her eyes. "What's wrong?"

"Nothing," I lie. "Excuse me." I walk to the small stage and wait for the lights to adjust. When the lights are on my face, I can no longer see Bonnie and my sister's faces at the table in front of me. It's a relief. I paint a smile across my face and read the teleprompter to give my speech. It's a blur. When I step down from the stage a while later, applause ringing in my ears, I don't sit down at my table for dinner.

ARLO IS ACTING STRANGE. He doesn't sit down for the delicious meal that's served, and I don't see him at all for the second half of the evening. Even Beth notices, head swiveling as she tries to spot him.

"Usually he's very visible at these things," she tells me.

He reappears on stage to direct people back to the silent auction room, and I try to catch his eye when he descends the stairs—with no luck. Trying to push the squirmy, uncomfortable feeling out of my gut, I find my friends and do my best to put on a happy face. But something is wrong.

That fact is confirmed when Arlo reappears at the end of the night and takes my arm without a word. The muscles in his neck are stark, and he won't look me in the eyes. We enter his limo and sit in our usual seats, but the air in the vehicle is oppressive.

"Did something happen tonight?" I ask a moment later, when the limo gets stuck in a bad snarl of traffic and I can't take the tension anymore.

"What exactly happened between you and Galen?" His voice

is low, monotonous, and unfamiliar. City lights slice across the planes of his face, shadowing his eyes.

I rear back. "I told you what happened."

"You didn't tell me about your company holiday party."

The sick feeling in my gut intensifies. Leather squeaks beneath me as I shift uncomfortably, mind whirling. I lift my gaze to try to meet his, shaking my head. "What's this about? What did Galen say?"

"He said you use people. That you were probably using me."

"And you *believed* him?" The words explode out of me. "After all the time we've spent together? After everything I've told you?"

"What happened at the holiday party?"

My breaths are shallow, but I try to keep my emotions in check. This is just a fight. It's not the end of anything. Arlo has been hurt, and he's afraid that I'll take advantage of him. Maybe he's forgotten just how much power he has in this relationship.

"Bonnie. You need to tell me."

Scratch that. His tone is hard, and he knows exactly how much power he has.

"Galen got the promotion I wanted," I tell him, voice flat. "We'd been sleeping together for four months. I was infatuated. I had a couple of drinks at the holiday party, and half of me was hurt that he got the promotion, but the other half was happy for him."

I close my eyes, slowly opening the lid on those memories. After three deep breaths, I'm able to speak again.

"We hadn't been able to keep our hands off each other up to that point," I say, and watch Arlo's hands tighten on the end of his seat. Suddenly, I feel tired, and I just want to tell him the rest so it'll be done. "I thought we were a couple, so after the announcement was made, I followed him down one of the hallways to congratulate him. He tugged me into the bathroom, and we had sex."

I close my eyes, squeezing them shut. I feel dirty all over again, exactly how I did that night when I went home.

"Anyway, when it was over, he zipped himself up and gave me this weird look. I asked him what it was about, and he said, 'It's not going to work, Bonnie.' I was confused, obviously, because what the heck was he talking about? We hadn't had the talk about exclusivity, but for all intents and purposes, he was my boyfriend. I sure wasn't sleeping with anyone else. I shared everything with him. All my work. My bed. My dreams."

A breath shudders out of me, and I lift my gaze to meet Arlo's dark one. "Then Galen said, 'Sleeping with me won't get you anywhere, even though I'm your boss now. We won't be doing this again.' And he walked out of the bathroom. Someone must have seen me walk out afterward, because that's when the rumors started. Or maybe Galen started them himself. I don't know."

The stillness of Arlo's body is unnatural, but I suddenly feel so tired that I don't care. I endured so much derision, so many whispers, in the weeks that followed that party. I felt dirty, even though I'd consented to sex. Even though I wanted it at the time. The way Galen flipped a switch on me left me reeling.

Now Arlo's switch has flipped too, and my body is beginning to ice over. I can't go through this again.

But a breath shudders out of him, and he unclips himself, stepping over the center console to join me on this side of the limo. He puts an arm around my shoulders and tugs me into his chest. "I'm sorry," he breathes in my hair. "I'm sorry, Bonnie. I've been a dick to you tonight."

His apology is a balm, but it doesn't quite soothe the ache. I lean my head against his shoulder and wonder once again if I'm making a huge mistake. His warmth finally permeates through me, and I let out a long breath. "I'm guessing that's not the story Galen told you?"

"No," he says. "It's not."

"But you believe me?" The question comes out smaller, thinner than I'd meant it to.

"Yes." His arms tighten around me.

A weight drops off my shoulders, and suddenly I'm crying. Arlo lets out a pained sound, then cups my cheeks and kisses my tears away. "Stop crying," he pleads. "I'm sorry, Bonnie. I'm sorry. I'm sorry."

"It's not you," I say, smearing my makeup with the backs of my hands. "I just haven't thought about that night in a long time. I blocked it out, and now I'm remembering the way I felt...the rumors..."

A curse tears through Arlo's lips, and he unclips my belt and hauls me onto his lap. He holds me tight and rains kisses down on my face, my jaw, my lips.

"This is really unsafe," I say, my body becoming languid. "We should be wearing seatbelts."

"We're home already," Arlo says, and then the car stops. A few minutes later, we're zooming up the elevator and Arlo hasn't stopped touching me. He strokes my arms with his warm, broad palms. He kisses my jaw, my neck. He wraps me in his arms and squeezes.

It feels so, so good to be loved like this. Too good, maybe.

Arlo carries me to his bedroom in the quiet, empty house and lays me down on top of his down comforter. We make love, and I let the pleasure of his touch carry me away. I cling to him with all my strength, trying to wash away the memories of another man, another time.

But later, when Arlo snores softly beside me, I lie awake and stare at the twinkling city lights through the window, and I wonder if I'm making a terrible mistake.

Galen got under Arlo's skin with a single conversation. What if Arlo hadn't believed me? What if I'd been kicked out and shunned, just like before? Can I really trust Arlo? Can I live with myself if I hand over my autonomy to a man so much wealthier and more powerful than me?

A restless sleep follows, and I wake up feeling nothing but dread.

ON MONDAY, Penny invites me to a late lunch at her place and makes it clear that it's not an optional invitation. "You've dodged my calls for long enough, Bonnie," she says, and she sounds uncharacteristically solemn.

Will is at kindergarten today, and Arlo tells me he can handle his own son for a few hours afterward. He's being so sweet to me since Saturday, remorseful and affectionate.

It makes me feel even worse for having doubts about him.

When I leave his apartment, I'm ashamed to feel a weight lifting from my shoulders. It's a relief to be away from Arlo, from all the expectations and uncertainty. I make my way to SoHo, to Penny and Marcus's refurbished factory that has—somehow—turned into a beautiful family home. Timothy, her son, is now a rambunctious four-year-old. He's hilarious, enjoying playtime with Layla's and Dani's many kids as we sit at the kitchen island and sip hot tea and coffee. Nikki arrives in a flurry of polka dots, dropping her purse on the polished concrete floor with a dramatic huff.

"I never want to work for anyone ever again," she proclaims.

"Where can I find one of these billionaires you all seem to be marrying?"

I laugh, but secretly, I'm relieved she's here. We're the only single and childless women here, and I feel those differences in my bones.

Penny's dog Bear comes to investigate Nikki's arrival, sniffing her purse and her fingers. She scrubs him behind the ears as a cost of admission. Satisfied, the dog pads back to the children to let her join us. He falls in a heap on the floor, presenting his stomach to Timothy, who starts driving a toy car over his fur.

It's so cute it makes my eyes prickle.

Tearing my gaze away from the dog and the kids, I fill my friends in on a more detailed version of what's been going on in my life. They're all horrified at what I went through at my old job, chiding me softly about not asking for help when I had to sell the apartment and didn't have anywhere permanent to live. I never had them over at my crappy apartment, because they're billionaires' wives and most of my roommates were cockroaches.

"I was embarrassed," I admit.

Penny puts her small, freckled hand over mine. "We're here for you, Bonnie. Don't ever hide away from us again."

A long breath slips through my lips, and to my horror, tears start flowing again. I don't know what's wrong with me; I'm so weepy. Even crying makes me want to cry some more. While I try to wipe my tears, I happen to glance over at the kids and see Layla's daughter Madeline give Timothy a hug and a kiss, and my sobbing intensifies.

"They're just so cute," I wail, like that makes any sense at all.

My friends crowd around me, and through my tears, I tell them about Saturday night. Outrage gives way to reluctant acceptance of Arlo's apologies, but I still feel unsteady inside, like a little dinghy thrown around on stormy waters.

When I finally get a hold on myself again, I let out a long breath. "I feel like a crazy person," I say, taking a deep breath. My crying fit has passed, and now I don't recognize the person I was a couple of seconds ago.

Honestly, I think sex with Arlo *has* killed some brain cells. Why else do I feel so out of control? Even yesterday, when I burst into tears on his chest and then stayed awake all night stewing in my own anxiety...that's not like me.

I've been through bad situations enough times to know that I can pull myself out of them. Generally, I'm not a crier. I didn't even cry when I lost my apartment. I just signed the papers to sell it, discharged the mortgage, and looked for cheap rent somewhere halfway convenient. I felt like death, of course, but I didn't cry.

Now I can't seem to *stop* crying.

I frown at my hands. "Do orgasms make you suddenly more emotional?" I ask. "I haven't had sex with anyone since Galen, and now I'm having sex all the time. So...is that what's going on? Is that why I feel like I'm going insane?"

Dani narrows her eyes at me, tilting her head. She glances at Layla, who arches a brow. Penny seems to be mulling over something, tapping a finger on her bottom lip.

Nikki stares at them all, then at me, and frowns. "What's going on? Why does everybody look like they're trying to figure out the best way to break some bad news?"

Dani smooths her hands over the cool marble of the island and takes a deep breath. "Well, see, here's the thing." Then she stops talking.

Layla picks up the thread. "It's not the *orgasms*, precisely, that make you feel like a crazy person..."

Penny bites her lip, arching her brows as she nods.

I look at them all in turn, then at Nikita. She shrugs.

Dani clears her throat. "You said Arlo got a vasectomy, right? Did you use any other protection?"

Understanding is like a meteor blazing across a dark sky. "I'm not pregnant," I blurt.

Layla's smile is tight. "No? Are you sure?"

"I cried at a commercial for automated blinds when I was pregnant with Tim," Penny tells the group. "They were just so *convenient*. I couldn't handle it."

My breaths are shallow, sawing in and out of my lungs like sharp little blades. "No," I say. "Nope."

"You could take a test?" Layla suggests.

"Arlo got the snip!" I yell, louder than intended.

Nikki's staring at her phone. "Okay, so, vasectomy failure rates are rare. Less than one percent, apparently, and usually in the first year. When did Arlo get his?"

"After Will was born," I say, "so five years ago."

Nikki scrolls. "Wow. The vas deferens can reconnect even ten years after the procedure."

Now my breaths are in the hyperventilation range. I shake my head. "No. I don't accept that."

"I have a test," Penny says brightly. "Marcus and I have been trying for another kid, so I have a bunch of them. Let's just do it, and you'll know for sure."

"I'm not pregnant," I protest.

Penny smiles, nodding. "But don't you want to know for sure?"

I stare at her, then down at my stomach, then back at Penny. "No."

Her shoulders drop, and she gives me a sad little smile. Her arms come around me, and even though she's shorter than I am, it feels like I'm a child in her arms. More arms appear around us, and suddenly I'm in a big group hug.

Bear, the dog, comes bounding closer, stuffing his snout

between legs so he can get in on the action. When everyone pulls away, I meet my friends' gazes one by one. My shoulders drop. "Fine," I say. "I'll do it."

Penny disappears down the hall, then comes back and produces the long, slender pregnancy test. I take it between my fingers like it's going to tear open and attack my face like a murderous alien.

"Okay, you'll have to wait three minutes," Nikita informs me, reading the instruction leaflet. She's just full of helpful information. "Pee on the end of it, put the cap back on, and then wait until the windows look like this." She points to the paper, where I see a diagram showing what the test will look like. "You're supposed to do it first thing in the morning for best results but let's just do it now and get it over with."

"I like the way you think," I say with a grim smile.

We tromp down the hallway together while Penny stays in the main room to watch the kids, and the rest of my friends wait outside the bathroom. I pee on the test, put the cap back on, start the timer, then wash my hands. When I open the door, four heads poke into the opening. We watch the timer on my phone count down, millisecond by millisecond.

Silence settles over us all as one minute turns to two, then three. The alarm rings, and I turn it off with a tap of my index finger. The pregnancy test is on the end of the vanity, and I pause, afraid to look at it.

"You want me to check it?" Nikita offers.

I square my shoulders. "No. I can do it." I take a big step forward, then peer into the little window. Then I start hyperventilating for real.

TWENTY-EIGHT
ARLO

ROME THROWS my son over his shoulder and tears around the room. Will thinks it's the most hilarious thing that's ever happened and giggles uproariously while he waggles all his limbs. When the two of them land on the sofa in a heap, Will slides to the floor and hops from one foot to the other. "Again!"

Rome groans. "I'm too old, Will. My body is broken."

Will grabs his arm and tugs. "Again! Again!"

"Give Uncle Rome a break, kiddo," I say. "You want a snack?"

Without answering, my son tears down to the kitchen, where I hear my chef greet him. I poke my head in, and Steve waves me away, telling me he'll put something together for my son.

I return to the living room and flop down across from Rome, arching my brows. His stubble is longer than usual, and there are bags under his eyes. "What's going on with you?"

"I was going to ask you the same thing," he deflects. "You seem distracted today."

Shrugging, I grab a bottle of water from the bar in the corner of the room and toss it over to him before taking one for myself. "The event took it out of me this year," I lie.

Rome cracks the lid on his bottle and takes a swig, then studies me intently. "How are things going with your girl?"

A sigh slips through my lips before I can stop it. "I think I messed up on Saturday night." I tell Rome about my confrontation with Galen, then reveal as much as I can about Bonnie without telling him anything too personal. "I snapped right to believing the worst instead of just asking her what was going on."

"But she's okay, right? She accepted your apology?"

Discomfort churns in my gut. "Yeah. But...I don't know. She seemed distant ever since."

Rome lets out a breath. "Don't worry about it. These things happen in relationships. You just gotta work through it."

I arch a brow. "You're a relationship expert now, are you?"

In all the time I've known him, Rome hasn't had a girlfriend last more than a couple of months. He waves away my comment. "You know what I mean."

"You think she'll come around?"

"She probably just needs to feel safe here. Secure."

I think about all the times Bonnie has had to start over, all the blows she's suffered over the past ten or fifteen years of her life, and I know Rome is right. What Bonnie needs is to know that she always has a place in my home.

Can I give her that? Can I get over my own fears and trust her, when my first instinct is always to push her away?

I feel like an ass for believing Galen, but part of me still stews in trepidation over the speed with which my relationship with Bonnie has developed. Can something lasting really start so quickly? Is it just lust? Am I being an idiot to invite this woman into the most intimate places in my life, my son's life?

As if he can sense my thoughts, my son lets out a loud laugh from the kitchen. I turn my head toward the hallway, heart squeezing. He loves Bonnie. What if she hurts him?

"Look," Rome says. "Your PI cleared her, right? And it's not like you're marrying the woman. Just enjoy your time with her, yeah? Your company just went public. Your charity is swimming in money. You're on top of the world, and a beautiful woman dropped into your lap. Don't ruin it for yourself."

"You think that's what I'm doing?"

Rome shrugs. "What's the worst that could happen?"

"I fall for another woman who's just playing me?"

He purses his lips. "You really think she's doing that?"

"Alice used to twist me up like this too," I tell him.

My friend frowns. I haven't told him everything that went on in my whirlwind relationship with my ex-wife, but he was there. He saw me destroyed by the end of it. He helped me pick up the pieces in the aftermath.

"Whenever I started asking her questions about her life, her motives, Alice would start crying. She knew I couldn't stand to see her tears, so anytime I brought something up she didn't like, the waterworks would start."

"You're worried that's what happened Saturday night?"

"I don't know," I admit. "I just don't know. Bonnie seemed sincere. She was hurt, and I felt like an ass...but what if I'm just falling for the same old tricks? My relationship with Alice was *so* similar. I fell for her so fast, and then she pulled the rug out from under me. I *want* to trust Bonnie, but..."

"There are too many similarities."

I sigh, nodding. "Yeah." The word burns on the way up my throat, but I can't take it back once I've said it.

Because it's the truth. There *are* similarities between my conniving ex-wife and the woman I'm falling for now. The unsteady, world-tilting feeling I get with Bonnie is a more intense version of the affection I had for Alice. The desire to give her everything. The crushing guilt I felt when I saw her tears.

It's all so familiar, it makes me sick.

"Just because someone cries doesn't mean they're manipulating you," Rome says quietly. "You did accuse her of some pretty dark shit."

I drop my head in my hands. "My ex actually *did* that dark shit, Rome, and I never saw it coming. It's not so unbelievable to me that it would happen again."

"Maybe you should slow down with Bonnie, then. Take some space. Clear your head."

"Things are moving too fast," I agree.

"Yeah. Move her into another apartment and start dating her. Slow things down to a pace that feels comfortable. You guys have barely known each other for a month." He holds his hands up when I open my mouth. "A one-night stand three years ago doesn't count, Arlo."

I huff. "You're probably right."

His phone rings, and he groans, glancing at the screen. "I have to go. Let's catch up for a drink later this week."

"All right."

The elevator dings a moment later, and Bonnie steps into the lobby. Rome gives her a polite nod, then disappears behind the closing doors.

Bonnie's face is white.

I put my hands on her upper arms, searching her eyes. "What's wrong?"

Even as the question comes out of my mouth, I remember another hundred moments just like this with Alice. There was the time her "brother" got in a car accident. That was the first time she asked me for money. I was all too happy to pay whatever hospital bills came up, and I trusted her enough to send her the money directly. After the divorce, I found out there was no brother. There was no accident.

Or there was the time she lost her job and had no health insurance, and I offered to put her on mine. I moved her into my house not long after. Or the time an aunt had a fall and broke her hip, and she needed to rush out of the city to be with her. I paid for flights and spending money, only to discover years later that she'd actually been on a tropical vacation with her boyfriend. I gave her everything she wanted, and I didn't question any of it.

There were a hundred emergencies, and Alice used them as ammunition to stuff me into the role of provider. None of them were true. None of it was real.

Until Will. He was real, and the news that she was pregnant was what tipped me over the edge. She said she wanted to get married before he was born; it was important to her. She had already closed the jaws of her vise around my heart, and with her pregnancy, she squeezed. Alice took things further than I ever thought possible, all because she wanted to suck me dry. I found out later that she'd stopped taking her birth control, hoping to get pregnant with my child. Every second of our relationship was designed to manipulate me, to knock me onto unfamiliar, unsteady footing.

That's why I got a vasectomy. I didn't want to ever be in that position again. I love my kid, but I hated the way he was conceived.

But Bonnie is different. She has to be. She wouldn't do that to me. Her tears were just tears; they weren't manipulation. She wouldn't manufacture some emergency just to wriggle her way into my heart. She was telling the truth last night. She's not here to take advantage of me. She's genuine.

Galen was the one who was lying.

Right?

TWENTY-NINE
BONNIE

NAUSEA RISES within me like a rogue wave. I push past Arlo and rush to my favorite powder room, making it to the toilet bowl not a minute too soon. Vomiting hurts, it's so violent. Leaning back on my heels as my stomach rolls, I flush the toilet and let out a breath.

Arlo appears at my shoulder with a bottle of water. I swish it around my mouth and spit it out, then do it again. I lean against the vanity and stare at the glass bowl of the sink, sensing Arlo's presence in the doorway. Lifting my head, I meet his gaze in the mirror.

His brows are drawn, but there's something strange in his eyes. "Are you okay?"

I'm not sure what to say because no, I'm not okay. I'm very far from okay. Another swig from my water bottle buys me a few more seconds of time to gather my thoughts.

I lingered at Penny's house for as long as I could, soaking up the support my girlfriends provided. I can't believe I pushed them away. I could tell Dani, especially, was hurt by the distance I'd inserted between us. She promised me she'd have a spare bedroom with my name on it set up as soon as she got home and wouldn't listen to any of my protests.

Penny piped up and said the same. Nikki offered her couch, making a quip about it not being as nice as the other offers but still a remarkably comfortable couch.

I was overcome with affection and love for my friends, and for a moment, I felt like I could handle the news of my pregnancy.

But now I'm here, and the father of my unborn child is standing in the doorway, staring at me like he's hiding some dark secrets behind those shuttered eyes.

"Bonnie?"

I let out a sigh and turn around, leaning against the vanity to face him. The toilet gurgles beside me. Lifting my chin, I meet Arlo's gaze. "I got some...unexpected news today."

His brows draw together. Is that suspicion in his gaze, or concern?

With a shake of his head, he takes a step back and waves his hand for me to exit the bathroom. I follow him into the hallway and lean into the hand he places on my lower back, soaking up every bit of warmth and comfort I can get from it.

The girls told me I should take a few days to sort my emotions out before I told him. They said that I should go to the doctor to confirm the test, because it's possible it was a false positive.

But now that I'm here, in Arlo's home, I know I'll never be able to keep the truth from him.

We sit on the sofa, side by side, and I twist the cap off my water bottle to take another sip. Slowly, I screw the cap back on and read the label on the bottle. Arlo's thumb strokes the side of my neck where it meets my shoulder, the weight of his arm a comfort across my shoulders.

Closing my eyes, I focus on that tender touch, and I find the courage to speak. "I'm pregnant, Arlo."

His thumb stops. When Arlo says nothing, I open my eyes and look at him. In that moment before I see the look in his gaze, I indulge the nascent hope budding in my heart. Will he be happy about another child? It's fast, and unexpected, but it's not the *worst* news in the world, is it? We both love kids. The past five weeks have been magical. It'll be a challenge, and there will be a lot of emotions, but maybe, if our affection for each other is true... maybe it'll all work out?

I lift my gaze to his and meet his eyes—and my hopes die a gory death.

Arlo's jaw is diamond hard. His eyes are dark—darker than I've ever seen them—and there's no hint of affection written in them. He pulls his arm away from my back, the ghost of his touch heavy against my skin. Arlo pushes himself off the sofa and stalks to the big windows overlooking Central Park, leaning his palms directly on the glass. His shoulders heave.

My heart beats so hard it hurts. I wait, terrified, for the hammer to fall.

Arlo takes his hands off the windows, leaving two palm prints on the glass. He spins around, and his face is terrible, twisted into an ugly grimace. Then he seems to gather himself, and a mask falls over his features. It's almost worse than the other expression, because it's so cold, it crackles around the edges.

"I'll have my lawyers draw up the papers," he says.

I freeze. "What?"

"I'll want full custody. You can tell my legal team your terms."

"My...terms?" Mind whirling, I stare at the man silhouetted by the windows behind him. "What are you talking about?"

"I'll want a DNA test, of course, but the lawyers will sort out the details. It goes without saying that you can't live here while we discuss the particulars."

The heart that had been beating a riot in my chest suddenly stops. I put a hand against my sternum and suck in a breath while it restarts unsteadily, thumping sluggishly in its cage. "What are you talking about, Arlo?" I repeat.

"I assume this was your aim all along. Congratulations. If you'll excuse me, I have to speak to my doctor and my lawyers. It seems there are some loose ends I need to tie up. Fernando can drive you wherever you need to go, and my legal team will be in touch."

Then Arlo just...walks away. I watch him enter the kitchen, and I hear Will's voice float out from behind the door. A moment later, the elevator dings and Laura emerges. Her face is drawn. She gestures to the stairs. "I'm to accompany you to your room while you pack."

On shaking legs, I stand. "Wait." I put a hand to my forehead and grip the arm of the sofa for balance. "Wait," I repeat, breathless. "What's going on?"

"You need to pack your things, Bonnie. Fernando is preparing the car." Her features are drawn. She meets my gaze, and a hint of sympathy enters her expression. "Do you have somewhere to go?"

A deep, yawning void opens up in the pit of my stomach. I grip the end of the couch for support until my legs stop shaking and wait for the world to stop rocking. When everything seems steady, I suck in a deep breath. Laura says something I barely hear. I stumble after her, gripping the banister with white-knuckled fingers while I descend to the first floor of the penthouse.

My room is as beautiful as it was the first day I saw it, but it makes me sick to be in here. It makes me sick to see the bed where we first made love. To think about the nights I spent in Arlo's arms when he would just kick me out like this. When he wouldn't even *speak* to me after I told him about the baby.

I don't even know if I'm pregnant for sure! It could be a false positive!

I should have listened to my friends.

With shaking hands, I haul my suitcase out of the walk-through closet and let it fall open on the floor. My vision tunnels, and all I can do is move robotically through the room as I grab my things and start packing. Consciousness leaves my body, and I find myself packing slowly, methodically, folding my clothes with care. Colors are brighter than they were before. The feel of fabric beneath my fingertips is enhanced, each thread feeling rougher than it should.

Laura watches, saying nothing.

I throw everything in my bag, including the beautiful gown and the necklace Arlo gave me. I don't have the brain capacity to think about anything other than putting items in my bags. An eternity later, I'm zipping up my suitcases and rolling them down the parquet floors toward the elevators.

Fernando meets me in the elevator lobby, like Arlo's team doesn't want to let me out of their sight even for the length of the elevator ride.

Half an hour later, I'm walking into Dani's building. When my name is passed up through the receptionist to another penthouse residence, I'm whisked up the elevator and vomited up in another beautiful lobby I'll never be able to afford to live in.

Dani's waiting there for me, and she wraps her arms around my shoulders and holds me tight for long, long minutes. Then she pulls away and reads the devastation in my eyes, tears gathering on her lower lids. "He didn't take it well?"

"No," I croak, and it's the first word I've spoken since I followed Laura down the stairs.

Her home smells like chocolate chip cookies. Her stepdaughter, Talia, is nearly a teenager now. She'll be turning fourteen in only a few months. She stares at me from the kitchen, a spatula in hand, half a tray of chocolate chip cookies transferred to a cooling rack before her. Her brother, Francis, is nine. His big eyes study me from behind a new pair of glasses. A nanny pokes her head up from behind a sofa, where Dani's three other kids are playing with blocks and bright, plastic toys.

"Bonnie's going to be staying with us for a while," Dani explains.

Kathryn, their house manager, bustles in and grabs my bags. "Follow me, honey," she says quietly, her face wrinkled and kind.

I'm led to another unfamiliar room, with another bed that isn't my own. But that's not so different, is it? I haven't had my own bed in over a year. Not since Galen turned on me and everything fell apart. I should have known that when I sold my apartment and gave the keys to the buyers, that was the last time I'd feel at home anywhere.

Kathryn settles me in the room, then Dani appears and closes the door softly behind her. She gathers me against her chest like I'm one of her five kids and rocks me until I dissolve into tears in her arms.

THAT EVENING, when all the kids are in bed and the staff has vacated, the rest of our girlfriends arrive one by one, bearing ice cream and chocolate and bags and bags of outrage. I tell them everything I remember from this afternoon, trying to recall Arlo's sentences word for word. Horror floods their faces.

"I'm calling Leif," Layla says, pulling out her phone. "We're pulling our donation to his stupid charity. Really, a children's hospital, when he treats the mother of his child like *that*? No way."

"Me too." Penny gets her own cell phone out—the latest, fanciest model with all the bells and whistles, courtesy of Marcus—and starts poking at it until it works. Her brow furrows until she gets it to call her husband. "Marcus," she says. "Yes, everything's fine, except that Arlo Noble is a piece of crap and I refuse to give him any money. Yes, I'm serious. Uh-huh. Love you too. Bye-bye."

Dani is putting her phone face-down on the table when Penny hangs up. My oldest friend nods decisively. "I just texted Emil. He's already pulled our donation, and he's telling all of his contacts to do the same."

Tears flow down my face. "You shouldn't do that. What about the children's hospital?"

"We're donating directly," Layla says.

"Same here," Penny adds.

"Yep." Dani crosses her arms.

Nikita arches her brows as she looks at the three women, pursing her lips as she nods. "Not bad, ladies. Hit him where it hurts."

"He's trying to use his money to push *our* friend around? Ain't gonna happen." Dani harrumphs. "He won't see a dollar from us or any of our friends."

"Serves him right." Penny's lips are pursed, her blue eyes flashing.

"You'll use our lawyer, of course," Dani proclaims. "I've already told Emil to set it up. You won't have to worry about a thing."

"He's not going to take that kid away from you," Layla says fiercely, putting her hand over mine.

Nikki tilts her head at me. "That's assuming you *are* pregnant...and that you want to keep the baby."

Burying my head in my hands, I do my best to hold back the

tears prickling my lids. "I don't know," I admit. "Everything is happening too fast."

"Have some ice cream," Penny suggests, pushing the tub toward me. "That usually fixes things, at least for a little while."

I have a bite of mint chocolate chip, letting the sweet, cooling flavors melt on my tongue. I smile at Penny. "It does taste pretty good."

She pats my hand with a sad curl tugging at her lips.

"Thank you," I tell them all.

"We're just happy you called, Bonnie. You've been carrying all this on your own for too long." Dani wraps her arms around me and gives me a quick hug. "We're here for you."

There's a knock on the door, and Dani shoots me a quick glance, then bustles over to open it. My big sister stands in the doorway, her eyes cutting straight to mine.

I burst into tears.

Linda hurries to my side and wraps her arms around me. "Hey," she coos. "Come on, now, Bonnie. Everything's going to be okay."

"I'm sorry," I wail, unable to stop myself. "I'm so sorry, Linda."

My sister is a five-foot-four powerhouse. She's been the only constant in my life since I was eighteen years old, and I've been nothing but a pitiful wreck. Her light-brown hair is tied back in a low bun, and she watches me from behind her glasses with serious, gray eyes. She puts her hands on my shoulders, and a wave of shame nearly knocks me down.

"I'm sorry," I repeat.

Linda pulls a small travel-sized packet of tissues from her purse and hands one over. "Stop it now, Bonnie. You have nothing to be sorry for."

"I do, though. I took the opportunity you gave me and threw it back in your face."

"You were taken advantage of by a client, who has now been blacklisted from my agency. I've put in the call to my colleagues as well, to let them know what kind of man Arlo Noble truly is."

"He's not that bad," I sniffle. "His kid is great."

"Don't defend him," Dani cuts in with a vehemence that makes me meet her angry gaze. "That asshole seduced you, impregnated you, then kicked you out. He deserves everything he gets."

Linda grunts in agreement. She takes the soaked tissue from my fingers and replaces it with a clean one. "Damn straight," she says, which is how I know she's serious. Linda never swears.

Swimming in the love and support of the women around me, I feel my spine straighten. Slowly, vertebrae by vertebrae, it curls up until I feel almost human again. The weight of everything that's happened today is shared across our six sets of shoulders, and I'm able to take the first full breath I've taken since the girls first mentioned the word "pregnant" to me all those lifetimes ago. Was it really only this afternoon?

Glancing out at the night sky and the glittering lights of the city, I blow out a breath. "I have no idea what I'm going to do."

"Well," Linda says, "it's a good thing you don't need to figure it out right now. All you need is a good sleep, some food, and time to sort through all these emotions."

I meet my sister's steady gaze and shake my head. "You're too good to me, Linda. All I ever do is disappoint you."

Her eyes are sad when they meet mine. "It breaks my heart that you think that, Bonnie, because I am in awe of you every day. You've been knocked down so many times and you've *always* gotten up again. I was nearly destroyed by my divorce, but I still had my business and my kids to keep me centered. You've faced worse trials than I ever did, and you always come out of it with your head held high, stronger than you were before. You are the furthest thing from a disappointment to me, Bonnie. You're an inspiration."

My eyes are leaking again. Another clean tissue appears in my hands, stuffed there by one of the friends I've neglected so badly. "I feel like a terrible person. I haven't been there for you all when you needed me."

"You opened your home to me when I was homeless," Dani points out.

"You helped me get over my fear of going out," Penny adds. "Your Halloween party was the first invitation I accepted in nearly a decade."

"I wouldn't have taken that night class on management without your encouragement," Nikita tells me. "But I saw you working on Wall Street, talking about your MBA like it was no big deal, and so I went for it."

"You took care of my kids when I went through my divorce, and you stepped up when I started my business," Linda says softly. "I know you think it was me doing you a favor to hire you when you were in college, but Bonnie, the business wouldn't have made it through those few years without the hours you put in."

Layla smiles at me. "I just think you're really smart and cool," she provides.

I snort-laugh, shaking my head. Meeting each of their gazes in turn, it hits me that they're telling the truth. Is it possible that they see me in such a different light than I see myself? All the times I've felt like a burden to them all...was it just a lie I told myself?

"Here's what's going to happen," Nikita says, clapping her hands. "We're going to eat all this ice cream. Then you're going to go to bed, and you're going to sleep in tomorrow. Tomorrow is Tuesday, which means salsa dancing at Charlie's Bar. Wednesday is Iguana, and there's a new spot Teddy told me about for Thursday. We're going to dance until our feet fall off every night, and then you're going to sleep and eat to your heart's content. In a week or so, when your emotions have stabilized, we're going to revisit all this." She waves in the general direction of my abdomen. "And hopefully by then, you'll remember that you've been as good a friend to us as we've been to you."

My shoulders drop as the corners of my lips curl. "My ankle won't enjoy that much dancing."

"Your ankle can get its shit together and stop being a little wuss," Nikita mock-snarls.

I laugh, then nod to the mint-chip pint in front of Penny. "Pass that over here. We'd better get started on the first item on that list right away."

THIRTY

ARLO

"WHERE'S BONNIE?" Will stuffs a spoonful of cereal in his mouth and munches loudly. He swallows and glances at me when I don't answer his question. "Daddy?"

I clear my throat, mixing more honey into my coffee. "She's gone home, kiddo."

Will falls back against the back of his seat, shocked. "Without saying goodbye? Why?"

"She had some things to do," I respond, shifting uncomfortably. "I'll take you to kindergarten this morning."

"Okay." Will frowns into his cereal, dragging the spoon from one side of the bowl to the other. "Is she coming back?"

I sigh. How do I explain this so a five-year-old will understand? It doesn't help that I woke up this morning feeling the first twinge of guilt. Did I act too brashly? Bonnie's face betrayed intense shock...did I misread the situation?

No, I decide. I have to protect my son and myself. I won't go through what Alice put me through again.

"She's not coming back, Will," I say. "You'll get a new nanny."

Somehow. Although I've already heard that the Delmar Agency won't work with me anymore. I have Laura calling other agencies to try to find a replacement, so I should have someone lined up for tomorrow.

"I don't want a new nanny." Will throws his spoon on the floor and glares at me with all the vitriol in his five-year-old heart. "I want Bonnie!"

"Will," I say, trying to sweep up the remnants of my patience. "Bonnie was a temporary nanny. Remember?"

"But..." His lip wobbles.

Sighing, I slide a chair beside William's and wrap my arms around him. Hauling my son into my lap, I hold him as he bursts into tears. It hurts to feel his little body wracked with sobs. I feel like a terrible father. I'm the one who put him in this position. I'm the one who brought Bonnie into our lives, who let her wriggle her way into my son's heart.

A shell forms around my own heart, reinforcement around the defenses that Bonnie had managed to crack. My son is sobbing because of me. Because I failed to protect him—again.

Soothing William, I hold him until he pushes off me, and then I help him get ready for school. He's crushed. I can see it in the curve of his shoulders and the way he drags his feet. He doesn't smile once as we drive to his kindergarten—not even when he sees his favorite teacher and all his friends. I place a kiss on the top of his head and walk him inside.

Chelsea, the mother from the birthday party Bonnie and I attended, sees me enter. When Will hangs his backpack up on his hook and walks over to his friends, she sidles up beside me, glancing over my shoulder. "Where's your...friend? What was her name again? Bethany?"

"Bonnie," I correct, her name burning on my tongue. "She's not...around anymore."

"What a shame." Chelsea's hand drops onto my forearm, squeezing gently. "Would you like to grab a coffee and talk about it?" Her eyes are earnest, but there's a shrewd edge to them.

Another woman trying to sink her claws in me—except, while Chelsea stares at me, I realize that Bonnie never once looked at me like that. Was Bonnie just a better actor?

Or was I wrong about her after all?

I shake the woman off. "No." Then, when I remember I'm not an ogre, I add, "Thank you."

She shrugs and lets me walk away without another word. I slide back into the car and tell Fernando to take me to the office.

Once I get there, my day gets worse. Combing my fingers through my hair, I growl at the Noble Foundation manager sitting across my desk from me. Wanda is a tall, broad woman in her early fifties who runs the foundation with an iron fist. Her dark hair is twisted into a dozen neat braids that wrap in a big bun at the crown of her head. Her brown eyes stare at me from behind blue-framed glasses, one eyebrow arched.

"Seventeen *million?*" I repeat, staring at the figure on the page.

"We're still getting phone calls about more donations being pulled, so the number might get bigger by the end of the day. I'm projecting somewhere just shy of eighteen."

I scrub my face. "And none of them gave any reasons?"

"Mr. Van der Berg claimed that new information came to light about the ethics of..." Wanda clears her throat. "There were concerns about you, personally."

"Me?" I drop my hands, giving Wanda my best scowl.

Normally, people shy away from me when I look at them like that. Wanda just meets my gaze with one of her own. "You," she confirms. "And Marcus Walsh's team seemed to intimate the same thing, as did Mr. Sorensen's."

I freeze. "Sorensen. Leif Sorensen?"

Wanda nods. "The one and only."

An image flashes in my mind: Bonnie, silhouetted by the windows in my small, second-story home office, telling me about her friend Leif Sorensen designing the building I live in. Then I remember the people she crowded around at the Noble Foundation Gala, and a sick feeling churns in my stomach.

They were the wives of some of our biggest donors. Emil Van der Berg. Marcus Walsh. Leif Sorensen. Those three men are titans of their industries, and it's not impossible that they'd have influence over other donors too. In the stratosphere of Manhattan society, the air is thin and relationships are important. Those three men would be able to pull eighteen million dollars' worth of donations with a few phone calls.

"They're pulling their donations because of what I did." I don't mean to say it out loud, but it slips through my lips and draws a sharp gaze from Wanda.

Her eyes narrow. "What did you do?"

My mind whirls. For the first time in nearly twenty-four hours, I consider the possibility that I was wrong about Bonnie. She told me she was pregnant, and all I could think about was Alice. I was transported to six years ago, when Alice came to me, teary-eyed and afraid, telling me her birth control had failed. In those few moments when Bonnie sat beside me on the sofa, I re-lived the months—the years—of torture that my ex-wife put me through.

And I snapped. I blamed Bonnie for what Alice did. My worst fears were confirmed.

But...

Groaning, I rub my forehead to try to ease the ache building beneath my skull.

Bonnie has friends—powerful friends—who are shutting me out because of the way I acted. She's not some grifter who happened to get under my skin. She doesn't need me or my money.

She's on a first-name basis with Leif fucking Sorensen, for God's sake. Three of her closest friends are as wealthy as a small country.

I meet Wanda's gaze, and speak the words that shine like a blaze in my mind: "I think I've made a horrible mistake."

An hour later, I get a phone call from one of the most influential family lawyers in the city. She's representing Bonnie Delmar, she tells me, and all communication about our affairs goes through her.

After I hang up the phone, I spin my chair around, lean back, and look out over the city. People scurry like ants. Cars honk. Pigeons coo.

Sitting on my perch on top of the world, I realize that it's a long way down to the bottom.

THIRTY-ONE
BONNIE

MY FRIENDS DON'T LET me forget that they're there for me in the week that follows. True to her word, Nikki takes me out dancing to all our favorite spots. I see Teddy and Mark and all the other dance partners I've met over the years. My ankle aches like the devil by the time the next weekend rolls around, but my body is sore and tired in a delicious kind of way.

Dani organizes my appointments with her doctor and doesn't hear any of my protests about cost. Not to mention the lawyer. I don't even want to know the kind of fees she's charging to represent me.

On Sunday night, when I've begged off salsa dancing with the intention of staying at Dani's for dinner, I corner her after the kids are in bed. "You have to tell me how much this is all costing."

My friend smiles at me, and the edges of it are tinged with sadness. "It's a drop in the bucket, Bonnie. Just let me do this for you." She kicks her feet up on the coffee table and leans her head on the back of her couch—which is where Emil's old white couch used to be before Dani changed it to a more sensible—and child-proof—dark-brown leather. "What did the lawyer say when you met on Friday?"

I take a sip of fizzy water and set it down on a coaster on the side table to my left. "She told me we'd get a DNA test done first of all, and then go from there. She thinks Arlo will fight for at least fifty-fifty custody."

"Why the grimace?"

I put a hand to my abdomen and stare out the windows. One of those twinkling lights spread out across the city belongs to Arlo. Is he staring out, thinking of me? "It's just happened really fast. Such an intense high, and then it all collapsed."

"Has Arlo reached out at all?"

I shake my head. "No." I tilt my head. "Well, I don't know. I blocked his number."

Dani hums.

Blinking, I meet her gaze. "You have to let me repay you somehow, Dani."

Reaching over, my friend pats the back of my hand. "Bonnie, friendship isn't transactional. I'm doing this because I care about you, and because you'd do the same for me." She gives me a wry glance. "Oh, wait. You've *already* done the same for me. Or have you forgotten what happened when I was pregnant with Ambrose?"

"That was different."

"It wasn't."

"Agree to disagree," I say, then push myself up to my feet. My body aches, and I don't know if it's dancing, pregnancy, or the broken heart I've been trying to ignore. I dart to my bedroom, then come back out, tossing a velvet box on Dani's lap. "There."

She frowns, then flips the box open. Her eyes widen. "The necklace you were wearing at the charity gala."

"It's worth eight hundred thousand dollars, give or take," I tell her, feeling slightly ill when I say the number out loud. "I had it valued this week. The sapphires are of Kashmiri origin and of a particularly rare hue of blue, and the diamonds are worth a couple of hundred thousand on their own, apparently. Between medical expenses, legal fees, room, and board, I figure that should just about cover it."

Dani snaps the box shut and thrusts it back at me. "I'm not taking this."

"I'll never wear it again," I tell her, going for a casual shrug. "You might as well keep it. Break it apart and sell the gems. I don't care."

The truth is, giving the necklace away makes me want to cry. But keeping it feels even worse. In my whirlwind week, when my friends have rallied around me like never before, I haven't had much time to think about what's going on in my life. I've been pumped up with their outrage on my behalf, their kind words, and their support.

But when I settle into my bed at night, or when I wake up before dawn in the morning, everything hurts. In my infinite weakness, I miss Arlo. I miss those languid wakeups, in the hour before I had to sneak back to my own room.

And how messed up is that? We were always sneaking around. I was always a dirty secret to him, and the minute we brought our relationship out into the light, it fell apart.

We never stood a chance.

But my heart still hurts whenever I stop moving long enough to notice.

Dani puts the velvet box on the arm of the sofa beside her, looking at it like it'll grow teeth and bite. She turns to study my expression, which I try to keep blank. She's already so worried about me; it wouldn't do to show her just how badly I'm hurt.

"I'm sorry, Bonnie," Dani says quietly.

I huff. "For what?"

"You haven't had it easy."

"That's life," I answer, more bitterness than I intended seeping into my tone.

The front door opens, and Emil strides in, pulling his tie loose. He cuts straight to Dani, planting a kiss on her forehead. "Hello, love."

"Hi." Dani smiles and tilts her head to accept a kiss on the lips.

And that's my cue to leave. It's not that they're being inappropriate, it's just that being near two people that love and respect each other that much hurts like hell. I'm sure the pain will dull with time, but right now, I'm finding it hard to breathe.

"I'm going to go to bed," I tell the room at large, mumbling goodnight to the two of them as I disappear down the hall. When I'm safely in my room, I do what I've done every night since I left Arlo's home and silently cry myself to sleep.

THIRTY-TWO
ARLO

MY PRIVATE INVESTIGATOR told me Bonnie was staying at Van der Berg's place, so I've been waiting in the lobby all morning. I tried calling Bonnie, but she's blocked my number, my office number, and Laura's number, so I have no choice but to wait for her. I'll wait all day if I have to.

She has to leave the apartment sometime, doesn't she?

Another hour crawls by, and sweat soaks all the way through the back of my shirt, evidence of my growing anxiety and restlessness. What am I doing here? Why the hell did I come?

Then the elevators open, and she's there. A goddess given human form. Her sleek ballerina bun on the crown of her head, a black pea coat wrapped around her body. Her sheer black tights make her legs look slender and long, and her little black booties click on the marble floors. She's limping slightly, but she's trying to hide it, which makes me want to break something. Her ankle is bothering her, and I can't do anything about it.

She walks with a confident stride—until she sees me, and stops.

"Bonnie." Suddenly I'm in front of her, and I have no recollection of actually moving. I stop myself from reaching for her at the last moment when she looks at me with wide, frightened eyes.

I put that fear in her gaze. I created this distance between us.

All because I'm an idiot who was so wrapped up in my own past to notice what was right in front of me.

"Bonnie," I croak once more, because her name is the only thing that makes sense to me.

"What are you doing here?"

"You haven't been taking my calls."

"Hmm," she answers sarcastically, tilting her head so the light catches every beautiful plane of her face. "I wonder why that is."

"I'm sorry," I blurt. "I'm—can I take you out for...for coffee? Lunch?"

Emotion flashes across her face. I read hurt in the tilt of her lips and sadness in her eyes. All my fault. She shakes her head. "No, Arlo. You can't."

My gaze circles her face, then drifts down to her feet. "Your ankle is sore."

She takes a step back. "That's none of your concern."

"Have you been dancing on it?" My brows angle downward. Has she been dancing with other men this week?

"I'm not supposed to talk to you. My lawyer specifically said I shouldn't." Angling to get around me, Bonnie flinches when I reach out a hand.

Desperation claws at me. My breaths are shallow, and my vision goes dark at the edges. All I see is Bonnie. Her perfect bun. Her beautiful face. The hurt I put there.

"I'm *sorry*," I whisper, because that's as much as my vocal cords will work. "I'm so sorry, Bonnie. Please. Please, just talk to me."

She hesitates for a brief moment, and hope flares to life so fast I nearly fall to my knees.

Then Bonnie's shoulders drop, and she shakes her head. "It was never going to work between us, Arlo," she says quietly, resigned. That tone of voice is almost worse than the one that betrayed her pain. She gives me a sad smile and reaches for me, placing a delicate palm against my cheek. "We come from different worlds. We could never have a relationship as equals, and I refuse to live my life with the fear that everything will be taken away from me again."

"It won't," I blurt. "I promise, Bonnie. I'll make sure that you feel safe. I was wrong. I was so wrong, and I know it. Please..."

Her thumb coasts over my cheek, and her look is almost...pitying. "I believe that you believe what you're saying, Arlo. But I just can't take the risk." Then she drops her hand, skirts around me, and walks away.

I stare after her, watching her slight limp, feeling more powerless than I've ever felt in my entire life.

THIRTY-THREE
BONNIE

IT TAKES every ounce of self-control I possess to keep my back straight and my steps steady. But as soon as I'm on the street and around the corner, I duck into the nearest door—a Starbucks—and steal into the bathroom, locking myself in a stall while I gulp down deep, shuddering breaths.

The past week has lulled me into a haze of thinking I could handle this...this breakup? Can I even call it a breakup when we weren't even together for two months?

I lean against the stall door and close my eyes, trying to sort through the riot of emotions pounding against my bones.

It hurt to see him, looking so handsome and tortured. I hated that he could tell my ankle was bothering me with nothing more than a glance. I hated how much I wanted to go into his arms for help and comfort and love.

But how can I accept those things from him when he wields them like weapons? I *trusted* him. I fell for him—hard.

And now what?

Now I'm lost. Because what if he was just trying to weasel his way back into my life so he could take my child away? I curl my arms around my stomach as tears leak from my eyes.

I'm so *sick* of crying by myself like it's some shameful secret that I'm hurt and heartbroken. My emotions are wild animals, thrashing against the bindings I use to try to strap them down.

A week ago, I had dreams of living with Arlo, of making a life with his son, of being happy.

Now, even when he apologizes and offers me that life back on a silver platter, I can't accept it—because I've seen the precariousness of putting myself in his life—under his thumb.

I was so *stupid* to believe that things could be different with Arlo. So naive to think that it could work out for me.

Hands shaking, I pull out my cell phone and dial Dani's number. She answers on the first ring.

"I'm hiding in the Starbucks bathroom," I tell her, sniffling. "Arlo was in the lobby."

"I'm coming down," she says.

Minutes later, Dani is there, gathering me in her arms, leading me back up to her home. When we get there, I break down and cry in my friend's arms, letting her soothe me with steady strokes up and down my spine.

"It's all going to be okay," she tells me, and it sounds like a pretty, fanciful lie.

ANOTHER WEEK PASSES. The doctor tells me I'm approximately six weeks pregnant, and I curse myself for being so irresponsible. After our first night together, Arlo and I didn't speak about condoms or protection. We both assumed the vasectomy would be enough. What was I thinking?

That's the main theme I keep returning to. *What the hell has been going through my mind all this time?*

In my third week at Dani's house, in a bid to pull myself together even the slightest bit, I register for the financial advisor exam and throw myself into my studies. My friends are encouraging, and Penny even gives me the contact details of the graphic designer that did her logo for her dog clothes business. Linda makes time to sit down and create a business plan with me, even though she must be busy with her own business.

"Are you sure you don't need me to help with your agency?" I ask her one evening. "I know you're still short-staffed."

She shakes her head. "I've gotten a wave of applications," she tells me. "Just hired three new nannies on a probationary contract, a new bookkeeper, and an administrator."

My brows jump. "Wow."

She gives me a small smile. "It's been a good couple of weeks," she admits. "I don't know where all these candidates came from, but I'm not going to look a gift horse in the mouth. We got a dozen resumes last week alone, all of them highly qualified."

I blow out a breath and turn back to the screen in front of me, where my tentative business plan is laid out. "I guess you don't need me, then. I have no excuse."

Linda grins. "None at all."

I'm not sure if I want to work in finance forever, but the thought of starting my own business *does* excite me. I've never had something of my own like this. Not since my ankle ruined my running career.

A business where I help other women become financially literate sounds like something that could be mine—all mine. Something that would give me a platform that no one could take away from me. I'd never have to start over again.

Slowly, day by day, week by week, I find my center. Leaning on friends I've done nothing but neglect for a year, I drag myself out of the darkness and start moving. In a way, it doesn't even matter *what* I do, just that I'm doing something.

I dance with Nikki. I study for my upcoming exam. I bury myself in website creation and logo design and business development.

All the while, a life grows inside me. Being around Dani's, Layla's, and Penny's kids helps me get excited about motherhood instead of feeling only terror.

Yes, I'm starting over again...but I no longer feel alone. I have friends. I have a baby on the way. I have dreams.

Winter arrives while I busy myself building my new life. I watch the first snowfall from Dani's living room, my laptop on my knees, feeling a grim, determined sort of hope growing inside me.

As long as I don't think too much about my weeks with Arlo, I think I'll make it. I'll be okay.

At least, that's what I tell myself to keep the heartbreak buried somewhere deep and inaccessible. If I don't think about how much I miss him, those feelings will fade. They have to.

THIRTY-FOUR
ARLO

CHESTER HOLT GREETS me with a polite handshake and a gleam in his eyes. He straightens his tie and gives Galen a subtle nod as we all take our seats at a long table in one of the boardrooms in my office building. It's December, and the city has had another snowfall. It's not quite cold enough to stick on the roads, so the world outside my office windows is gray, black, and slushy.

There are a number of places I'd rather be than in a conference room with the people at Holt & Holt, but there's something I have to do. Before they can launch into their pitch, I hold up a hand. "I'd like to talk to Mr. Holt in private before we begin," I say to the room at large.

My own legal team pushes their chairs back immediately, but Galen remains seated. I turn to stare at him as the seconds bleed into each other, and he finally, reluctantly, stands. "Whatever you say to Mr. Holt, you can say to me," he says, a little petulantly.

"Leave us, Galen," Chester says with a wave of his hand.

Chester Holt is a white-haired man of considerable girth. He leans back in his chair and studies me with shrewd gray eyes, braiding his fingers over his round stomach. His mouth spreads into a genial smile. I've seen him switch from a Jolly St. Nick persona to a shark, so I know his easy grin isn't all it seems.

"What's this about, Arlo?" His question is cheery, but his eyes are sharp.

I lean an elbow on the arm of my chair and rest my chin in the cradle of my hand. Blinking at the spiral-bound proposal sitting on the desk in front of me, I shift my gaze to look at the director of the biggest hedge fund in Manhattan and say, "I'm not going to hire your firm."

The older man goes utterly still for a moment. Then he blinks slowly, like a big cat, and taps his index fingers against each other. "I see. It can't be due to our performance, which is flawless. So, why the sudden change of heart?"

Men like Holt wield a lot of power in the city. Yes, he's been wining and dining me, wooing me so he can get juicy fees for managing my money, but he could just as easily attempt to cripple one of my businesses. So when he lobs his question at me, the instinct is to answer obliquely.

But I don't want to be vague. I want him to know exactly why I've finally decided to end this charade.

"I received information that your employee"—I tilt my head ever so slightly toward the door, so it's clear that I'm talking about Galen—"appropriated the systems he now uses to make investment decisions from a former employee of yours and passed the work off as his own. I only work with people I trust, and I find that I can't trust him."

The sharp look in Chester's gaze intensifies. He lets out a slow hum. "And have you any proof of this accusation?"

The only proof I have are my own instincts, and the fact that my private investigator found another ex-employee of Holt & Holt, who was seduced by Galen years ago the same way Bonnie was.

Not that I needed the confirmation. The moment I heard about the donations being pulled by Bonnie's friends, I knew I'd messed up. I've just been scrambling to find a way to fix it ever since.

"No, I don't have evidence," I admit. "But I'm sure that if you look at your company files and emails, you'll find the paper trail you need. Galen Deely stole work from a former employee and passed it off as his own. He's not as clever as he seems."

Chester rocks the chair forward, setting his feet firmly on the ground. He leans forward, eyes on mine. "This is about Ms. Delmar, isn't it?"

Anger starts a slow journey through my gut, winding its way up my chest like a boa constrictor. I don't like hearing Bonnie's name on any of these people's lips. Not when it's spoken in that tone. "It's about me trusting the people who will be handling ten figures' worth of my portfolio."

"Galen told me she was at your event, and Arlo, I have to say, Bonnie isn't exactly a trustworthy source—"

"What you say next will have consequences," I say, my voice dark.

Chester narrows his gaze. "You're telling me that *Bonnie* was the mastermind behind the systems we've implemented across the fund?"

I want to throttle him for saying her name like that, for his doubt, for *my* doubt. But I just shrug at the other man. "I'm saying it wouldn't hurt to go back through your company servers and find out how Galen came up with *his* system for identifying under-valued equities. If my accusations are unfounded, you'll find that he created them on his own computer, won't you?"

"Bonnie is the one who was trying to climb—"

My hand bangs against the table before I even know I've lifted it. Chest heaving, I stand. Rallying all my self-control, I manage to grate, "We're done here. Whether or not you believe me, I won't hear you speak Ms. Delmar's name in my presence. Look through your company's email archive or don't. Either way, you won't be handling my finances."

Chester Holt gives me a dark look, then stands. He doesn't shake my hand when he leaves.

When everyone from the hedge fund has left, I collapse onto the couch in my office and bury my head in my hands.

I'm lonelier than I've ever been. I'm ashamed of myself.

My mind takes me back to the touch of Bonnie's hand on my cheek, the pitying look in her eyes. She made her choice, and I'm not part of her future.

I can't believe I thought she was trying to swindle me the way Alice did. I can't believe I threatened her with lawyers the moment I found out about the baby. I can't believe I acted like such a heartless bastard, when Bonnie is the only woman who's ever made me feel whole.

I deserve vitriol and hatred from her, but what she gave me instead was a gentle touch on the cheek and a soft goodbye.

She was always too good for me. I should have known it from the moment she walked into my house—or from the moment I sat down beside her at that bar in London all those years ago.

I was never good enough for her to give me her body, let alone her heart. It's only right that I've lost both.

WILL IS quiet and subdued that evening, and I don't know if it's because he still misses Bonnie or because he's picking up on my mood. When I put him to bed, I tuck him in, then walk out to the playroom. I notice Mr. Freeze tucked in the couch, only his plastic feet sticking out from between the cushions, like my son stuffed him there in disgust, or heartbreak, or both.

I take the action figure to my room and place it on the dresser, like it will stand vigil above me, reminding me of all the mistakes I've made.

My phone rings just as I'm adjusting the figurine's legs so he's balanced. Chester Holt's name is on the screen.

"You were right," the old man says, and his voice sounds more tired than I've ever heard it. "Galen took Bonnie's work and passed it off as his own."

I didn't need to hear the confirmation to know I'm a piece of shit, but I still have to sit down on the edge of the bed to process it.

Galen, me, Bonnie's college ex-boyfriend, her parents...we're all the same. We treated her like she was disposable.

I'm so ashamed of myself my throat burns like I've swallowed liquid fire. I listen to Chester Holt tell me everything they found in their company email archives, all the work that Bonnie shared with Galen in the months that led to Galen's promotion.

That night, it takes me a long time to fall asleep. Mr. Freeze watches me from his perch on the dresser, and he doesn't need to fire his weapon for me to feel ice crackling over every inch of my skin.

THIRTY-FIVE

BONNIE

AFTER FOUR WEEKS at Dani's place, I sit down in front of an elegant little cake and give my friends a full-wattage smile. It feels slightly brittle around the edges, but I've been living by the motto of "fake it till you make it" for so long, I'm almost certain my expression looks genuine.

"Congrats, Bonnie," Dani says, nudging my shoulder. "We knew you could do it."

"You kicked that test's butt!" Penny adds, fist pumping the air.

"Certified financial advisor, who?" Layla cuts in, grinning.

I laugh, grabbing a knife from the table. "Let's dig in. Thanks for the support, ladies. And the cake."

"Most importantly, the cake," Nikita agrees.

We eat a deliciously moist chocolate cake with ganache filling, then recline on Dani's living room furniture and gab for an hour. It's the middle of the afternoon, and the midwinter sun shines weakly over the city. The holidays are almost upon us, and I dread the next few weeks of cheeriness. That'll be a lot of faking it and not a lot of hope that I'll be making it.

But as my friends laugh around me, a now-familiar ache is slightly lessened in my heart. I might have lost the affection of the first man I thought I loved, but at least I reconnected with my friends.

"She's not even listening," Layla says, tossing a pillow at me.

I catch it against my stomach. "What? What'd I miss?"

"We're masterminding your new business's launch," Dani explains. "We've been talking it up to everyone we know."

"I don't even have a business yet," I protest. "How can I possibly launch it?"

"Oh, *pah*," Nikki spits. "You've been cooking the idea up for weeks now, and Linda helped you with your business plan. You just need to register your business name and you'll be set."

"There's a bit more to it than that," I answer wryly. Not to mention that launching will require money. I've saved a lot by staying with Dani, but my coffers are still nearing empty. If I'm going to launch a new business, it would probably be wise to at least get a part-time job while I do it.

Then I run a hand over my stomach. A spear of anxiety rams through me. Who would hire me? Employers aren't supposed to discriminate against pregnant women, but they do. What kind of job would hire a woman who will need time off work in a matter of months? I'm not showing yet, so I could lie in any interview I get, but then what?

And what if this whole business idea is a pipe dream? Soon, I'll have an infant to take care of. How can I start a business while I do it? What am I even *thinking*?

As if my thoughts conjured a solution all on their own, my phone rings. I pick it up from the arm of the couch and frown at the number. I was expecting Linda's name to flash on my screen, since apart from the ladies in this room, my doctor, and my lawyer, she's the only one who calls me, but I don't know this number.

"Hello?"

"Is this Bonnie Delmar?" a gruff male voice asks.

"It is," I confirm, hesitant.

The ladies around the room lean toward me. They want to know what's happening. I shrug in response.

"This is Chester Holt calling," the man says.

In the middle of my shrug, my shoulders stay frozen up around my ears. My eyes widen. The ladies exchange meaningful looks, then turn to me again.

"Oh," I squeak. "Mr. Holt. What can I do for you?"

He lets out a long sigh. "This would be easier if you came into the office, Bonnie," he says, and his voice sounds tired. "It seems we have a few things to talk about."

My heart takes off at a gallop. I shake my head. "That won't be necessary," I tell him.

"I think it will," he responds.

"No, really, I'm fine."

"Bonnie, we know about Galen Deely. We know where he got the spreadsheets and systems that got him the promotion."

I fall back against the sofa cushions and stare out the windows, seeing nothing. "I see."

"Are you free to come into the office this week?"

"I'd...have to check my calendar," I hedge. It's a lie; my calendar is entirely free, other than figuring out how to launch a business that doesn't exist yet.

"Hilda will schedule you in. See you soon."

The phone clicks, and a woman speaks next: "Hi, Bonnie. I've got Mr. Holt's calendar here. Are you free tomorrow at eleven a.m.?"

I blink. "Um."

"The only other possibility is five o'clock, but you know how he gets around that time. Next week is tougher, since he's out of the office for the holidays."

"Tomorrow at eleven is fine," I hear myself answer.

"Great! We'll see you tomorrow. You know your way around the building, of course, but you'll have to check in at reception for a visitor's badge. Ta-ta!"

Another click, and the line goes dead. I pull the phone away from my ear and stare at it. What the heck?

"Who was that?" Nikita tilts her head, frowning at me.

"That was Chester Holt, the director of Holt & Holt."

"Your old company?" Dani asks.

I nod. "Yeah. They want me to come in tomorrow at eleven o'clock."

"Tell them to go to hell," Layla answers, scowling. "After what they did, they have some nerve to tell you to run right back to them."

"They know about Galen," I tell my friends.

Silence settles over the room.

I bite my lip. "I'm tired of running away," I admit. "I kind of want to hear what they have to say."

"You think it's a good idea?" Dani says, brows drawn. "They were such dicks to you."

"Well, I think it's great," Penny says, beaming. "You can waltz in there like Julia Roberts in *Pretty Woman*."

"'Big mistake,'" Layla quotes. "'Big. Huge!'"

"They're not offering me my job back," I say with a snort.

"You don't know that," Penny singsongs.

"I kind of do," I answer. "They'll probably attack me with a pack of lawyers and try to intimidate me into signing something just so I don't sue them."

"I think they'll grovel," Layla says, an evil glint in her eyes, "like the dogs they are."

"You're all delusional," I say with a smile. "But it is a nice fantasy."

"Mark my words," Penny says, wiping her palms against each other. "They're going to beg you to come back and work for them."

Nikita laughs like an evil overlord. "Yes," she agrees, standing. "Let's figure out what you're going to wear!" Then she drags me up to my feet and we all tromp to my closet together.

THE NEXT DAY, at ten minutes to eleven, I wipe my damp palms on my thighs as subtly as I can and walk through the sliding glass doors of my old employer's building. My friends decided that a look they dubbed, "Corporate Beeyotch" was required, so I'm wearing a black blazer, black skirt, and silky black blouse. My hair is slicked back in a low, sleek bun.

My heels click as I walk across the marble floor toward the reception desk, and I try to ignore the fact that my ankle is throbbing like crazy. I don't know the woman sitting behind the desk, which is no great surprise. It's been nearly a year and a half since I worked here. She signs me in and gives me a visitor's badge, then instructs me to head to the elevator and take it to the thirty-second floor.

I'm ejected into an elegant lobby that I've only seen a handful of times; I used to work on the seventeenth floor with the rest of the junior staff, and I rarely ever had a reason to come up here.

Hilda is there waiting for me. She's about my age, with black hair tied back in a low bun. "Bonnie," she says with a small, professional smile. "Welcome back. Please come with me." She leads me to a glass-walled conference room and sweeps her hand toward the chairs for me to sit. "Coffee? Tea? Water?"

"Water would be great."

She disappears with a nod, and I sit in the fishbowl, wishing my palms didn't insist on sweating so much. The girls' groveling theory doesn't seem very likely from where I'm sitting.

Thankfully, I don't have to wait long. Hilda reappears with a pitcher of water and a few glasses, and Mr. Holt isn't far behind. He bustles in behind his assistant and drops a zip-up folder at the head of the table before thrusting a hand toward me.

I stand and shake his hand. "Mr. Holt," I say with a nod.

"Bonnie. Thanks for coming in."

Hilda backs out of the room and I'm alone in the fishbowl with my former boss's boss's boss. I try not to think about that too much as I sit back down and fold my hands on the table in front of me.

Mr. Holt splashes some water into two glasses and passes one to me. I accept it with a nod and sip delicately, ignoring the nerves slowly tightening my ribcage around my lungs. Being in this building is slowly wearing me down. Memories of working here—of Galen—press down on me, no matter how hard I work to push them back.

"Listen, Bonnie," Mr. Holt says, "I don't want to waste your time. We want you back."

I jerk. "What?"

He holds up a hand. "I know what you're thinking, and I want to assure you that Galen Deely has left the company."

That's not what I was thinking. I was hearing Layla's voice say, *"Big mistake. Big. Huge!"* in my head on repeat.

Mr. Holt stares me down. "I wanted to personally apologize for the treatment you endured here and recognize the contribution you made to Holt & Holt. There's no excuse for the way we over-looked your work."

It takes all my self-control not to shift uncomfortably in my seat. I was not expecting this, no matter what Penny and Layla said.

"I have here an offer of employment for you." Holt unzips his folder and passes me a sheet of paper. My eyes bulge at the salary written there. "I know it can't make up for the way you were treated before, but I want to assure you that we are well aware of all the contributions you made before. You should be rewarded for them."

I stare at the sheet, and I see an old version of myself. I wonder if two months ago, I might've been happy about this. Maybe it would have been a gift, to know that I didn't have to start over at zero. It would have been a lifeline out of rock bottom.

Now that I'm here, in this glass box, sitting across from an old man who never once spoke to me while I worked for him, it feels hollow.

Chester Holt slides another stack of papers toward me. "This is the agreement our legal team has put together, to ensure that what happened before won't be repeated."

Ah-ha. I bet. More likely, the legal team is covering the company's posteriors to make sure I don't try to sue them.

I stare at the two pieces of paper, and I know it's an easy way forward. A job I was good at is being handed to me, and all I need to do is reach out and take it.

Arlo took everything away from me when he tossed me out of his house. I've spent the past month studying for an exam that will help me build my own business. I've read three baby books and started shopping for strollers and baby clothes.

Am I terrified of what's to come? Of course. Do I feel like I'm in over my head with a human growing inside me? No doubt.

But I also feel like all the pretense has been stripped away. I don't have a billionaire lover to rely on, but I do have friends, and more importantly, I have myself. I've had time to think about the kind of life I want to provide for my child, and I'm not sure it's the life of a parent working on Wall Street.

Not that it isn't admirable. I'm sure many women do it, and do it well; I just don't think it's for me.

Still, it feels good to see the offer written in black ink on the piece of paper in front of me. It's a tangible piece of evidence that I *am* good. I *am* worthy.

I don't have to start over once again...unless I choose to.

The realization rocks me to my core. I've spent so long lamenting all the stuttering starts I've had to make in my life that I haven't realized that they've also been gifts. Now, when I look at the mountain I need to climb to start my own financial advisory business, I feel like I've already done it twice before. What's one more time? Yes, it'll be difficult. I'll be launching into the unknown. I'll make mistakes.

But I can succeed.

The papers make a soft scraping noise as I push them back toward the old man on the other side of the table. "Thanks, but no thanks," I tell him, and I stand. "Goodbye, Mr. Holt."

A little smile curls my lips as I leave him sitting in his fancy fishbowl. My heels click as I strut my power-suit-wearing butt all the way back to the elevators and press the down arrow. Glancing around the offices of Holt & Holt, I say a silent goodbye to the hedge fund—and to the woman I used to be.

THIRTY-SIX
BONNIE

NIKITA MEETS me in the lobby café of the building where she works. She throws her arms around me and cackles uproariously before even saying hello.

"I knew they'd be begging you to come back," she crows. "Those idiots."

I giggle, slumping down in my seat. I feel exhausted—and elated. Nikki squeezes my forearm, then goes to the counter to order herself a drink. I sip my hot cocoa and smile as she comes back to the table.

"Okay," she says, sitting down as she waits for the barista to make her drink. "Start from the beginning. Tell me everything."

I do, and Nikita is the perfect audience. She laughs and gasps exactly when she should, her love for me pouring off her with every reaction. Speaking to her makes me feel like I made the right decision.

"You're such a badass," she tells me, then darts over to the counter to grab her drink. She comes back and drops into her seat, beaming at me. "I love you, Bonnie."

"Right back atcha." I grin, ignoring the twinge in my chest.

I've done a good job ignoring the twinges since I left Arlo's place. I've buried myself in work and responsibility. I've thought of the baby and what's to come. I've worked on my business. I've studied for the financial advisor certification test. I've operated on the principle that if I just keep moving, I won't have to think about how much Arlo hurt me. I still worry that Nikki will be able to read it in my eyes, so I shift my gaze away from her.

Oblivious, Nikki stands up again. "I'm going to run to the bathroom," she tells me.

I nod, not wanting to meet her gaze, still trying to wrestle the monster of my emotions.

Across the fancy lobby of chrome, marble, and rich timber, I let my gaze wander. People in business suits scurry across the space, wearing black, gray, and navy. They stare at their phones, frown, and do their best to look important.

My gaze snags on a dark-red shirt. It covers the broad back of a man deep in conversation across the lobby. For the first time since I left Arlo's place, I feel something akin to attraction—or at least attraction's distant cousin. I watch the man shift his weight from one foot to the other, his body coiled with strength. Even from the back of his head, I can tell he's good-looking. It's evident from the set of his shoulders and the way everyone's eyes dart his way.

Maybe this is a good sign. It means that Arlo didn't ruin me completely. I can still feel these tiny sparks in my gut and acknowledge that there are men out there who make my heart beat faster. It gives me hope that one day, I'll be able to peel open the lid on my heartbreak, let it fly away, and move on.

Maybe—*maybe*—I'm on my way to healing. I'm edging closer to making it, instead of purely faking it.

Until the man turns around, and I see who it is.

As soon as I see Arlo's face, all the hope inside me drains away.

Did I really think there would be someone else? Did I actually believe I'd feel attracted to a man who wasn't him?

Arlo stands across the room from me, surveying the lobby like it's his own personal antechamber. He nods to the man he'd been speaking to, then starts striding across the gleaming marble floors.

Toward me.

From ten feet above my head, I watch myself like it's an ultra-slow-motion car crash, and I can't look away. I see the moment Arlo feels my stare and stumbles. I watch myself freeze in response, the power of his gaze like manacles around my wrists.

Then he moves.

Long, powerful steps carry him across the room in mere seconds. I snap back into my body and rocket to my feet, gripping the back of my seat to steady myself just in time.

"Bonnie," he says.

I suck in a breath. He's here, in the flesh—and I'd forgotten.

I'd forgotten how beautiful he is, and how the press of his energy feels like heaven on my skin. I'd forgotten how dark his eyes are, and how much I love the way they roam over my face.

Over the past month, I'd buried my feelings for Arlo under a slab of concrete, and he's just punched through the hard gray stuff like it was nothing. Wobbling, I curl my fingers into the back of my chair and try to survive the onslaught.

"Arlo," I breathe.

A breath gusts out of him, like his name on my lips is the sweetest thing he's ever heard. He opens his mouth, watching me, then closes it and gulps. His hands wipe on his pants once, twice. He clears his throat, letting his eyes drop to my chin, then to my collarbone.

"How are you?" Arlo finally grates. His eyes meet mine again, and I wish they hadn't.

I was fine, up until ten seconds ago. I would have said despite the odd twinge in my heart, my life was on the way up. I thought my concrete barrier was secure, and I wouldn't have to peek at the heartbreak and fear looming beneath.

I was wrong.

"I'm..." It's my turn to swallow.

I wish I were Nikki right now. She'd have a snappy response or ten. She'd pop out her hip and arch a brow, and she'd breathe fire until any man who wronged her was burned to a charred crisp.

But I'm not her. I'm the one who's burning up—especially when Arlo reaches over and takes my hand in his. He grasps my fingers and lets out another shuddering sigh, squeezing gently.

A simple touch of his fingers around mine almost undoes me completely. I pull away, straightening my blazer as I try to grasp the fleeting remnants of my mind.

"What are you doing here?" I manage to say.

He tilts his head toward the elevators where he'd been standing with the other man. "Catching up on some business," he says. "You?"

His gaze feels like a physical touch, roaming around my face like the ghost of his fingertips. I stare into the dark depths of his eyes and become unmoored. He's so beautiful. I want him so much. I *ache* for everything I thought we had.

"Visiting Nikita," I croak.

He nods, and the weakest part of me wishes I hadn't pulled my hand away from his. I remember just how good it felt to be wrapped up in his arms, and heartbreak rises up like a wave about to crest.

Moments before I'm knocked off my feet, I manage to straighten my spine. "We shouldn't... The lawyers..."

Arlo stiffens. His gaze shifts to the side, and a tightness enters his expression. "Yeah."

Whatever existed between us is broken beyond repair. I feel it in the distance that separates us, in the stilted sentences and the aborted touches. There will be a child shared between us in the future, but if there weren't, we'd probably never see each other again.

He looks at me again, and for just a second, I let myself enjoy the feel of his attention. He smiles sadly. "Take care, Bonnie."

"You too." It comes out as a whisper, and judging by Arlo's grimace, it looks like my soft words hurt.

He tears his gaze away from me and walks away. The yawning void within me opens wider with each step he takes, but I don't have the courage to run after him.

How could I, after what he did? How could I trust him again?

I'm finally building myself back up again. I'm starting over, but I'm embracing it. I can't crawl back to him and put myself at his mercy. I just can't.

But I still watch him walk away, and I let my heart splinter with every step of his shiny, black shoes on the shiny, marble floor—

Until he stops dead in his tracks and snaps his head up at the sound of his name, snarled from behind one of the potted plants blocking my view of the lobby's entrance.

THIRTY-SEVEN
ARLO

GALEN DEELY LOOKS like a different man from the slick, smooth-talking hedge fund manager he'd been only a few weeks ago. He's wearing dirty sneakers, ripped jeans, and a wool pea coat over a dirty hoodie. His fists tighten as he thrusts a finger in my direction. "You. God. Damn. *Bastard.*"

I freeze, widening my stance. With every ounce of my self-control, I stop myself from immediately turning to Bonnie and tucking her behind my back. As long as this asshole doesn't see her, everything will be fine. I just have to keep his attention on me, and—

"Galen?"

I close my eyes for a beat. Shit.

Deely's gaze swings away from my face and lands on Bonnie. His lips lift into an ugly snarl.

Bonnie, the only woman I've ever truly loved. The mother of my unborn child. The woman I'll never deserve.

And this dickhead—this piece of absolute *scum*—is looking at her like he wants to hurt her. A red haze starts to blanket my vision, and I do all I can to keep it at bay.

I'm in Rome's lobby. I can't get in a fight, even if Deely is asking to get socked in the mouth.

"You bitch," he hisses, and yep, he's just begging for a punch in the face.

I step to the side to block his view of Bonnie. "Don't talk to her. Your problem is with me."

"Is it? From where I'm standing, my problem is with the bitch who stole my job."

"Is that what happened?" I ask in a low voice, drawing curious gazes from half a dozen people around us. I ignore them. "Seems to me you're the one who stole her work over a year ago. It just took your company a while to realize it."

Deely clenches his jaw, his muscles coiled. He's itching for a fight—and I welcome it. This is the guy who hurt Bonnie. He deserves every bit of retribution I intend to extract.

Yeah, I did too. I know I messed up. But I'm trying to fix it. This asshole only wants to hurt her more.

And that's unacceptable.

"She got me fired and tried to weasel her way into my position," Deely spits.

Bonnie lets out a little squeak of surprise.

"She did not," I answer, voice dark.

"Oh?" Deely scoffs. "Right. So they just happened to look through the company emails randomly? They went on a hunting expedition for no reason at all?"

"There was a reason," I tell him, desperate to get his ire away from Bonnie and aimed at me. "And the reason was *me*."

It works. Deely frowns, wild eyes meeting mine. "What?"

"What?" Bonnie repeats, a strange lilt to her voice.

"Bonnie, baby, back up. Get behind the café counter, okay?" I keep my eyes on Deely.

I don't hear her moving, which is just like her. Stubborn woman.

"You," Deely says, his eyes taking on a dangerous edge. "You're telling me you called us into your office, told Chester you weren't hiring us, and then got me *fired?*" The last word echoes around the lobby.

We have a full audience now. Distantly, I see security guards speaking into their radios as they approach us from the opposite side of the lobby.

And Bonnie fucking walks *toward* us. "Is that true?" she asks softly, eyes on me.

"Bonnie," I bark. "Get behind the café counter, *now.*"

"You took everything from me," Deely says. "You both did."

Then he *moves.*

I'm not sure if he's aiming for Bonnie when he lunges toward us, but I'm not willing to give him the chance. With a shout, I intercept him, and his shoulder hits my middle with surprising force. I let out a grunt and am swept off my feet, landing on the hard floor an instant later. My tailbone explodes with pain.

Bonnie stumbles back with a cry.

Galen isn't done. He rises up above me and balls his hand into a fist. I duck my head at the last minute, and his punch grazes my cheekbone. More pain.

Distantly, I hear Bonnie shout. Boots running on the floors tell me security guards are rushing for us—but I know they won't get here in time. Deely winds back again, and I use the mere breath of a pause before he punches to twist my legs around and grapple with him until we spin around and I'm above him, my hands curled into the lapels of his wool coat.

That's when I see Bonnie sprawled on the floor, her face twisted in pain, her hand on her ankle.

The red haze takes over. My lips curl into a snarl as I cut my gaze back to the piece of dirt lying on the floor beneath me. Grabbing his jacket with my fists, I slam him against the floor with both hands.

He grunts, then gets three good punches in, hitting me in the eye, the cheek, and finally on the lip. I spit blood, spattering him with it as I slam him on the ground again. And again. I realize I'm screaming when two security guards haul me off. Another two land on Deely, securing his hands before he can do any more damage.

"I'm fine," I snarl, shaking off the men trying to haul me back. "Get off me."

"Sir—"

"Arlo!" Bonnie's standing. She rushes toward me, limping, blue eyes wide. She puts her hands on my cheeks and it feels so good to have her skin against mine, I barely even feel the pain when she touches my bruising skin. She searches my face, breathing heavily. "What... What just happened?"

"Are you okay?" I shake the last security guard off and put my hands on her shoulders. "Get off your ankle. You're hurt."

"I'm fine—" She squeaks as I pick her up, stalking to the nearest chair.

A wordless yell makes us look at Deely, who's writhing around on the floor as another security guard tries to jump on him. I tense, standing up between Bonnie and the action. The security guards finally overpower him, dragging him across the lobby to the security office by the elevators.

I turn back to the woman sitting behind me, dropping to my knees. "Your ankle. You were holding it." It's hard for me to make words. My hands are trembling as I grab Bonnie's shoe. She's wearing patent leather heels, and I grip the shiny black material and tear it off. My hand wraps around her hurt ankle, gripping it gently, wishing I could heal it with a touch.

"Arlo," she says, and from the tone of her voice, she's been repeating it for a while.

The last of the haze clears from my gaze as I meet Bonnie's eyes. Her hand touches my jaw. "I'm fine, Arlo."

"Your ankle," I grunt.

"I landed on it funny. It's fine. You're the one who's hurt."

I growl, mindless, and Bonnie's other hand slides over my jaw. Her thumb nudges the edge of my lip and I hiss when she touches it.

She arches a brow. "You need to get patched up, Arlo. My ankle is fine. I just stumbled when Galen lunged, and I jarred it. I promise."

Finally believing her, I let out a breath. "Okay."

"What," a woman's voice says from the hallway leading to the bathrooms, "the *hell* did I miss?"

THIRTY-EIGHT
BONNIE

ODDLY EMBARRASSED, I pull away from Arlo's arms and spin on my chair to face Nikita. She comes stomping toward me, eyes full of glee, staring at Galen being dragged across the lobby, then glancing at Arlo's split lip and rapidly growing shiner. I try to stand, but Arlo plants his hands on my hips and keeps me in my seat.

"Hi, Nikki," I say stupidly.

She looks utterly amazed as she scans the space once more. Her eyes land on Arlo. "What are you even *doing* here?" She points at Galen before he disappears behind a door. "What is *he* doing here?"

"I had a meeting," Arlo explains, voice gruff.

A woman runs up with a bag of ice, which he presses against the side of his face Galen was punching. My heart slowly returns to a regular pace, and I put a hand to my forehead.

Suspicious, I frown at Arlo. "Was he telling the truth? Did Mr. Holt investigate Galen's and my emails because of you?"

Arlo scowls at me, then tears his gaze away and looks at the door behind which Galen disappeared. "You didn't deserve your reputation to be tarnished, Bonnie."

Warmth buds in my chest. He did that...for me?

But it's not enough. One good deed doesn't make up for the way he treated me, the way he threw me out without even a backward glance. I can't trust him. No way.

"That doesn't explain why you're both *here*, though." Nikita crosses her arms, gaze narrowed.

"I can't do business with a friend?" Arlo asks, sounding almost petulant as he sweeps an arm toward the elevators.

As if on cue, they open, and Arlo's friend Rome comes rushing out. He jogs across the lobby, and Nikita goes oddly still beside me.

Rome comes to a stop in front of Arlo and lets out a short huff. "I can't leave you alone for five minutes, Noble. What the fuck."

"He was going to attack Bonnie," Arlo growls, eyes flashing.

Rome throws his hands up, then his gaze lands on Nikita. A dark eyebrow arches. "And why aren't you at work?"

She gives him an evil smile. "My apologies, Majesty. If I'd known you required the office coffee wench's services, I wouldn't have taken my lunch break." She curtsies for extra emphasis.

I whip my head from her to Rome. *He's* the boss she's been despising all this time?

My head spins so fast, I'm glad I'm already sitting. Arlo must notice my reaction. His hand slides from my hips to my thighs as he kneels in front of me, dropping the ice bag to the floor. His other hand grips my other thigh. "What is it?" he asks. "Are you okay? Do you need an ambulance?"

"What? No." I close my eyes. His hands feel so good on my legs, as warm and broad and magical as I remembered. "It's just a lot, is all."

"I'm calling a doctor."

"Arlo, stop. Unless you're calling a doctor for yourself, which seems like it'd be a good idea."

He isn't listening. He's already got his phone out, but it must have gotten damaged in the tussle because the screen is just a starburst of broken glass. He clenches it in his fist, swearing.

I'm in a daze. Half of me wants to throw my arms around Arlo and make sure he's okay. I want to thank him for trying to fix my reputation, even if I don't want my old job back. And the other half wants to curl up in a ball and go back to living how I was this past month, numb and clear-headed and alone.

"Before I forget," Rome says, stomping over toward us, "I'm sending you the final invoice for the Delmar account tonight. And I'm including the damage to that potted plant." He points to a plant that got knocked over when Galen tackled Arlo.

Then his words sink in.

"The Delmar account?" I ask, straightening.

Arlo's hands tighten on my thighs. "Bonnie…"

"Um." Rome clamps his lips shut. "I mean…"

"Stop touching me." I peel his hands away, and Arlo lets his arms drop by his sides. "What is he talking about?"

"I, uh, have to get back to work." Rome backs away with an awkward smile, then narrows his eyes at Nikita. "And so do you."

Nikita arches a brow. "You're not the boss of me."

"I literally am, though."

She rolls her eyes and walks over to me, putting her hand on my shoulder. "Are you okay? Do you want me to get him to leave?" She looks at Arlo, who's still kneeling in front of my chair.

Arlo scowls at Rome, then at Nikita, and finally meets my gaze.

"What's the Delmar account?" I ask, voice frosty.

Arlo sighs, then stands. I hate him towering over me, so I stand too and take a big step back. My stupid ankle twinges, and based on the tightening around Arlo's eyes and the way his gaze flicks to the joint, he notices. He watches me for a beat, then shakes his head. "You weren't supposed to find out about this."

"What are you talking about?"

If he lied to me again...

Breaths come short and sharp, until Arlo puts up his hands.

"I hired Rome to put together an advertising campaign for me," Arlo says after a pause. He won't meet my gaze. He stares at a spot on the floor between us, then rakes his hand through his hair. "For your sister's childcare agency."

Horror ices my veins. "Excuse me?" If this guy went on a hate campaign against my sister's business, I will *never* speak to him again.

Arlo snaps his head up and meets my gaze. "No, Bonnie, it was..." He spreads his arms. "I just wanted to help. I knew she was short-staffed, and there were all the whispers of what happened between us... I thought I could get Rome to do a viral online campaign to try to attract some staff for her. That's all."

Confusion warms the edges of my icy rage. I frown at him. "Huh?" I glance at Nikita, who just shrugs. Then I think about the influx of applicants Linda has gotten, and how relieved she's been to be attracting good staff. I straighten. "You advertised my sister's agency? To help her?"

Arlo spreads his arms, like he doesn't know what to say. "I did everything wrong with you, Bonnie. I was just trying to fix some of it any way I could. I know... I know it's not enough."

Blinking rapidly, I don't know how to process the information coming at me. Arlo went out of his way to help my sister, and neither of us were ever going to find out about it? He spoke to Chester Holt about me, and got me a generous job offer without ever wanting to take credit?

A shout draws my attention to Galen, now firmly behind the

security office door. There's a cop car outside. I blink, mind whirling.

"You..." I gape at Arlo.

The part of me that wants to run into his arms grows a little bit stronger. Maybe...maybe I could trust him again? If I'm happy to start over with my own business, maybe I could start over in my personal life too?

Then my phone rings.

Numbly, I pull it out of my purse and swipe to answer. It's Dani's lawyer—my lawyer.

"Bonnie?" The woman on the phone says in my ear.

"Yes?"

"We just heard from Noble's legal team. He's set up a trust in the kid's name, and he's prepared to meet all our demands about child support and custody." She blows out a breath. "I almost can't believe it. They've rolled over on everything."

I drop the phone to my side and stare at Arlo. He gazes at me with deep, dark eyes, and in that moment, I realize I'm seeing the real him.

The man who will take punches to the face for me. The man who will try his best to make my life easier, without ever expecting thanks in return. The man who will do what's best for me and my child, even if he hurts himself in the process.

He stands before me, stripped bare, with a split lip and a soon-to-be black eye, and I realize I'm sick of fighting it. My phone and purse clatter to the floor, and I'm sprinting to close the distance between us. He catches me, wrapping strong arms around me, crushing me to that broad, strong, irresistible chest of his.

I sob in the crook of his neck, clinging to his shoulders while he says my name over and over again, like he can't believe I'm real. Pulling away, I put my hands on either side of his face, careful to avoid his injuries.

"I'm so sorry, Bonnie. I acted like an idiot. As soon as you left, I realized I'd been blaming you for what another woman did." His voice cracks. "I punished you for something you didn't deserve. I'll spend the rest of my life making it up to you, whether or not you accept my apology. I promise."

"Stop it," I say, letting my thumb drift over his lips. He kisses it. "Stop it, Arlo. I forgive you. I love you. I can't live without you."

A shudder passes through his body, and his hold on me tightens. Eyes glassy, he meets my gaze like he wants to make sure what I'm saying is true.

"I love you more than life itself," he tells me. "I love you so much, I've been ready to tear apart everything I've built if it means I get to give it to you, piece by piece. I never want to be the one who hurts you. I never want to be the reason you have to start over again, Bonnie. Never, ever."

My lips tilt. "Really? Because I kind of feel like starting over one last time..." I press a kiss to the uninjured corner of his lips. "With you."

EPILOGUE
BONNIE

IF I WERE A CAUTIOUS WOMAN, I would keep living with Dani and take it slow with Arlo. We'd date, truly get to know each other, and try to rebuild our relationship from the ground up before the baby arrives.

Unfortunately, I'm utterly reckless, and head-over-heels in love. I move back in with Arlo the very next day. To my surprise—and delight—he's cleared half of his walk-in closet for me, so I move right in to the master suite on the second floor. Arlo refuses to hear of us ever sleeping apart again.

While I unpack, a figurine catches my eye on Arlo's bedside table. "What's this?" I ask.

Arlo huffs and picks up Mr. Freeze, pointing the villain's gun at me. "This is a reminder I've been keeping near me."

"Reminder of what?" I curl an arm around his waist, smiling.

"How easy it is for me to stay frozen," he says, pressing a kiss to my temple. "I was stuck in the past, Bonnie. My heart was a block of ice. Until you came along and thawed it."

I smile and turn my head for a kiss.

Unpacking my bags takes a lot longer than planned; we end up getting distracted by more pressing matters that require us to be horizontal for an hour or three.

After that, Arlo insists on icing my ankle and making an appointment with a physical therapist. Even though his black eye is clearly the worst injury between us, it feels good to be taken care of.

WHEN WILL GETS home from kindergarten, he lets out a happy scream when he sees me, then comes barreling toward my legs. I catch him and try to toss him up in the air, but he's too heavy. We land in a heap on the floor.

Arlo rushes over, clucking about the baby, so I tackle him right down to the ground beside us. Will hops on his father's stomach, eliciting a low *oof* and a groan.

A rush of happiness overwhelms me. As I lie on the carpet beside Will and Arlo, I thread my fingers through Arlo's and stare up at the glittering light fixture above. It would have been so easy to keep my heartbreak locked away, to not bring the hurt out into the light.

But as Will chatters excitedly, I let some of the hurt ease out of me, healed by the love that surrounds us.

We still have a long way to go, but as Arlo brushes a kiss across my knuckles, our hands intertwined, I know I'm making the right decision by being here with him.

GALEN IS ARRESTED and then released, but not before the news of his actions makes the circuit around the city. I'm not sure if Arlo is involved in how much bad press occurs, but the vindictive parts of me are glad that my ex-boyfriend gets his comeuppance. A year after he tried to destroy my reputation, his own reputation forces him to tuck tail and leave the city for greener pastures. Hopefully far, far away from me and mine.

MY BUSINESS UNDERGOES a soft launch six months later. I decided to keep things quiet since I'm eight months pregnant and I know I won't have the time or energy to do a big splashy launch and take on a zillion clients. I just want to get things going, get my name out there, and see if anyone is interested in my services. Scrolling through my brand-new website, I recline on the sofa in the second-floor living room and let my lips curl into a smile.

"It looks so good," I brag.

"I know." Arlo rubs my feet, digging his thumb into my arches as I groan in satisfaction. "You did amazing, Bonnie. Any client inquiries yet?"

"I launched two hours ago," I tell him, brow arched. "So no."

Then my phone dings. I gasp, opening the email. "Wait! Wait, wait, wait! One of Beth's artist friends is interested! Help me up!"

I stick my arms up, and Arlo heaves me to my feet. Then I do a little dance, and Arlo laughs and kisses me on the lips, his hand coasting over my gigantic bump. His arms still feel like heaven around me, even if I don't fit quite as perfectly against his chest as I used to.

Lifting my shirt, Arlo kisses the stretch marks lining my belly and croons to our baby. "Your mom is amazing," he says.

I laugh, digging my fingers in his hair. "She is," I confirm. "Super duper amazing."

In the past six months, Arlo and I have confessed everything about our pasts. When he told me about his ex-wife's manipulations, the last of my anger faded, and I was able to forgive. It helped that Arlo found a therapist and started working through the pain of his previous relationship. It's not a magic potion, but it's yet another piece of evidence to show that he's trying and we truly have a shot at making things work. He hasn't let me forget that he understands how much he hurt me, and he's done everything to make it better.

All I can do is trust him, and with every day that passes, that bond grows stronger. I feel loved and cherished and safe when I'm with Arlo and Will. Now all that's left to do is welcome our new baby into the world, and our family will be complete.

OUR BABY GIRL is born the day before her due date, after a grueling twenty-seven hours of labor. The memory of it is a haze. The pain was unimaginable. I got stitches in places that don't need to be discussed. I don't even want to talk about how many times I've peed myself. Childbirth is *not* glamorous—but it's all been worth it.

Now, three weeks postpartum, I sit in the nursery and feed my baby daughter while Will and Arlo watch on. It's the room directly across the hall from Will's room, which he was very excited about. The love that little boy has for his sister brings tears to my eyes.

I still feel like an emotional wreck who just got hit by a train. Then Arlo sits beside me on the loveseat, curling an arm around my shoulders. His touch settles something in my heart, and I find myself running a finger over Becca's impossibly soft cheek.

"She's beautiful, just like her mother," Arlo says softly, tiredness lining his face while bright happiness floods his eyes.

"She's a little milk monster, is what she is," I mock-grumble.

Distantly, I hear the elevator ding. A moment later, Beth appears, and Will jumps up in excitement. Arlo's sister has been a great help, and I'm not surprised to see Linda appear behind her. Both of Becca's aunts are going to spoil her rotten.

I shift my daughter when she's done feeding so I can burp her, her little body squirming against my shoulder.

Arlo reaches for her. "Let me help."

Grateful, I put a rag over his shoulder to protect his no doubt disgustingly expensive bespoke shirt from baby vomit, then watch my daughter settle in his arms as he pats her back with his broad palm.

My sister and Beth chat with Will and then fawn over Becca, and I don't realize I've fallen asleep until Arlo tucks a blanket around my body and I realize the room is empty. Distant voices tell me our guests and children have moved to the living room.

I start to get up, but Arlo gently pushes me down. "Sleep, Bonnie. You were up all night."

All the fight leaves me, and my eyelids are already closing. Arlo settles at my feet, hauling my legs into his lap. The soothing stroke of his hand up and down my calf lulls me to sleep.

When I wake up, I'm alone. Rubbing my eyes, I sit up and try to get my bearings, then follow the smell of food to the kitchen. Arlo is at the stove while Will is regaling Beth and Linda with stories from his latest birthday party. He's excited to start first grade in a month.

Linda's holding my daughter, but she shifts the baby into my arms as soon as I reach for her. Becca is wiggling happily, and I press a kiss to her soft, downy hair. I sit down in the corner booth seat, surrounded by easy conversation, laughter, and love.

It's a good day. A perfect day, full of all the things that are truly important. By the time our sisters leave and the kids are in bed, I wrap my arms around Arlo and let out a happy sigh. He leads me out to the living room and tucks me against his chest as we look out over Central Park and the vastness of the city.

"Bonnie," he says, his voice rumbling through me.

"Hmm?" I'm pleasantly sleepy in our quiet house, warm in Arlo's arms.

"Will you marry me?"

Blinking, I stare up at the man I love. My heart starts to thump. "What?"

He pulls a ring box from his front pocket, keeping his other arm wrapped around my lower back. With his thumb, he flips the top of the box open and reveals a glittering diamond ring. There's a big honking oval-shaped diamond surrounded by lots and lots of small ones, all around the oval and down the sides of the band. His lips brush my temple. "Nikki helped me choose it."

My voice stops working. Happiness floods through me as my eyes turn watery. I gulp and finally manage to squeak, "I don't know what to say."

There's laughter in Arlo's eyes when he responds, "Say yes, Bonnie."

My lips finally curl into the smile that's been lurking beneath my shock. I let out a breathless laugh and sway in Arlo's arms. "Yes," I whisper.

He slips the ring over my finger, then cups my cheeks and kisses me like he wants to make another baby already. I laugh against his lips and nuzzle his nose. "It's way too soon to have sex, Arlo. I hope you remember that."

"I can't kiss my future wife?" he growls in response, nipping at my bottom lip.

"Well, when you put it that way, I guess I'll allow it."

Arlo wraps me in his arms and kisses me again, and again, and again. Then he grabs a remote from a nearby shelf and presses a button. Salsa music starts playing over the speakers, and Arlo sweeps me into his arms.

He takes me through salsa steps I've never taught him, and I laugh in delight. "Have you been learning?"

"I decided that if my wife is going to be dancing salsa, I'd better be the one to do it with her."

I grin, letting him twirl me. We dance for the rest of the song, and then another. Arlo moves well—he's definitely been taking lessons. The thought warms me down to my toes, especially when I remember the first awkward dance steps he took all those months ago, in a sweaty club surrounded by other dancers.

When I'm breathless and laughing, Arlo wraps me in his arms and kisses my lips.

I let out a happy sigh. "You know that I'll be asking you to come dance with me every chance I get now, right? I hope you know what you've gotten yourself into."

Arlo kisses me again, his eyes shining. "I love you, Bonnie. I'll take you dancing every single night, if that's what I need to do to keep you by my side. I'll build you your own private salsa club. I'll fly you to—"

"Okay, okay, I get it." I laugh, curling my hands around Arlo's neck. "You love me. Sheesh."

He grins. "Just making sure you understand."

My heart turns to goo. I pull him down until his lips are hovering just above mine. "As long as you know that I love you just as much."

His searing kiss is answer enough for me.

Bonnie gets a very special wedding present from her friends. Want to find out what it is?

Tap here to get your exclusive bonus chapter!
(URL: http://www.lilianmonroe.com/subscribe)

EXTENDED EPILOGUE
BONNIE

WHITE SAND STRETCHES OUT in both directions. Behind me, palm trees sway in the Caribbean breeze, the soft scent of salty water wrapping around me. My dress flutters around my ankles as I shift my weight from one foot to the other.

"Knock, knock," Dani says behind me, stepping into the pavilion I've been using to get ready. She ducks under the curtained door and smiles at me. "Wow, Bonnie," she says. "You look beautiful."

Spilling into the pavilion behind her are Layla, Penny, and Nikita. They're all wearing matching bridesmaid dresses, and they clasp their hands at their chests in unison.

I spread the fluttery skirt of my dress. "You like it?"

My dress has an A-line skirt that falls all the way down to the ground. The bodice is fitted with an open back and a sweetheart neckline. Delicate lace flowers fall over the chiffon, placed in intricate clusters all over the bodice and skirt. It's fluttery and delicate and feminine. My hair is in a low chignon, which the hairdresser recommended in case the beachside outdoor venue was particularly windy. I smooth a hand over my hips and smile at my friends.

"You're a vision." Penny beams at me.

"I have a present for you," Dani cuts in, lifting a bag.

"You shouldn't—"

"Hush," Dani interrupts, smiling at me. "Open it."

From the bag, I pull out a velvet box. My hands begin to tremble at how familiar it is. "Dani..."

She clicks her tongue, urging me to open it with a wave of her hands.

But I already know what's inside.

I flip the lid open and see the necklace Arlo gave me for the Noble Foundation Gala. A lump forms in my throat as light bounces off all those twinkling diamonds and sapphires...and then I notice the matching earrings pierced into the velvet beside the necklace.

"I gave this necklace to you, Dani. You were meant to break it apart and sell it."

"Ha. Right. So," Dani says, almost businesslike. "We figured this covers all your bases. Something old—the necklace. Something new—the earrings. That leaves something borrowed and something blue. I knew you'd be all weird about the necklace, so here's the deal. You're borrowing it—indefinitely. So that covers that. And the blue part is obvious."

"Eight hundred grand's worth of obvious," Layla adds with a grin.

"I can't—"

"Of course you can." Dani lifts the necklace and undoes the clasp while Penny spins me around. Nikki grabs one of the earrings, handing it to me to put on while Layla grabs the other and waits on my other side. When both earrings are firmly in place, I spin around to look at the full-length mirror resting against one of the pavilion's pillars.

I suck in a deep breath, running my fingers over the gemstones. "It's perfect."

Dani smiles at me in the reflection, her eyes glassy. "I know."

"Come on, now," Nikki says, blotting my forehead lightly to get rid of the shine that's already poked through my makeup. "Let's get you out there and get you married, already."

A small string quartet begins to play the wedding march. My heart takes off in a flutter. I poke my friends out of the pavilion and find a group of people waiting to walk down the aisle in front of me. First are Beth—who carries a squirming one-year-old Becca—and Will. Penny winks at me, heading out to walk down the aisle beside her husband, followed by Layla, Leif, Dani, and Emil. Nikita and Rome are the last in line, and then it's my turn.

My sister waits for me near the curtained entrance of the pavilion. "Ready?" she asks, extending her arms toward me.

"As I'll ever be."

Linda walks me down the aisle, proud as any parent. As I step to the beginning of the aisle lined with flower petals, my eyes lift, and I catch my first glimpse of my soon-to-be husband.

He's wearing a sharp black suit with a white shirt and white waistcoat. His gaze crashes into mine, and it feels exactly like that first day in his living room. The world tilts, freezes, and nothing exists but him and me. I suck in a deep breath, and a smile breaks over my lips.

It takes all my self-control not to sprint down the aisle. Linda holds me firmly by her side, but she grins at me when she hands me off to Arlo. She could feel me urging us faster.

Arlo's gaze drops to the necklace glittering against the base of my neck, and I watch him gulp. "I thought you got rid of that," he whispers.

"I did," I admit. "But apparently my friends had other ideas."

His smile is the most beautiful thing I've ever seen. He clasps my hands in his as the officiant begins the ceremony. I hear none of it. All my attention is captured by the man in front of me. His broad shoulders, his dark eyes, the smile lines around his lips. The kindness and love and trust pulsing from him like a living thing.

We seal our vows with a kiss, and I pull away from Arlo, laughing. His eyes shine bright, and he steals another kiss for good measure.

"You're stuck with me now," I tell him. "For better or worse."

"I was going to say the same thing," Arlo admits, laughing. He kisses my knuckles and leads me to the reception with all of our family and friends.

We—and by "we," I mean Arlo—decided to rent out an island in the Bahamas for our wedding. The reception takes up the ball-room of a huge mansion where our guests are already milling, dancing, drinking, and eating. They cheer as we enter, and I couldn't wipe the smile off my face if I tried.

Our first dance is set to salsa music, of course. In the past year, Arlo has kept to his word and taken me dancing as often as I've wanted. He's only improved, and dancing with him is a special kind of joy. When our friends crowd onto the dance floor with us, happiness floods through me like a never-ending well bubbling up from the earth, warm and pure.

We dance until my ankle aches. Arlo notices immediately and sweeps me up into his arms, carrying me out of the room to the delight of all of our guests.

"I can walk," I protest, but the way I've wrapped my arms around his shoulders belies my words.

Arlo grins at me. "I know, love, but you're my bride, and I'm going to carry you to our wedding bed if it's the last thing I do."

We head out the front door and over to a smaller building. It's tucked behind palm trees and lush foliage, a cabana looking out over the pristine waters all on its own. Arlo steps into the air-conditioned space and sets me down on my feet with the utmost care. His hands slide to my hips as he spins me around, resting his cheek against mine as we look over the space.

"What do you think?" my new husband asks softly.

I take in the flower petals strewn over the bed, the champagne chilling in its bucket of ice, the waves crashing on the beach just outside the big doors on the other side of the room. I lean into him, letting a smile curl my lips. "It's so perfect, Arlo."

"Just like you."

I snort, turning in his arms. My fingers coast over his temples, stroking into his hair. I pull him down for a kiss that warms me through and through. Arlo groans as he licks into my mouth, deepening the kiss as he guides me to the bed.

My dress has a row of six buttons down the lower back. Arlo flicks them open one by one as he kisses me, then slips the shoulder straps off. The dress puddles at our feet in a white froth, and I'm left wearing a strapless white bra, white panties, white heels—and the necklace.

Arlo's eyes darken as his fingers touch the edge of the precious stones ringing my neck. "I never got to do this before."

"Do what?" I ask, even though I know the answer.

"Make love to you when you're wearing nothing but this necklace." His fingers flick open the clasp of my bra, and one more item of clothing drops to the floor.

I bite my lip. "Well, tonight's as good as any—" I squeal as Arlo tosses me onto the bed. I bounce twice, laughing, and then my panties are being torn off.

"I'll leave these on," Arlo says, touching my shoes.

"You're the boss," I say, placing one of those shoes against his chest. I nudge one of the buttons of his shirt with the pointy, white toe. "But you're also wearing too many clothes."

Grinning, my husband kisses my ankle and gets to work rectifying that problem. As soon he's as naked as I am, he joins me on the bed—and I forget about everything except him, me, our bodies, and the love that binds us together.

———

WANT MORE?

ROME AND NIKKI ARE UP NEXT...

ONE

NIKKI

ON THE SEVENTH day of my employment at the Blakely Advertising Agency, I found myself locked in a room with a giant dildo. That was unfair; it wasn't really a dildo—at least, not in the sense that I was familiar with them—but it *was* distinctly phallic. And huge.

As the minutes bled into one hour, and then two, I stared at the giant bottle of perfume that was to be the star of an advertising campaign for an emerging luxury fashion house, and I saw dick.

"I think it's the slight curvature," I told my friend Penny, who was busy wrangling her toddler. "And there's a texture to the bottle that if you squint, looks almost...vascular. And the shape of the bottle itself doesn't help. Like an elongated bullet with a bit of a flared tip to accommodate the spray nozzle. They've put it on a little trolley with some fake clouds clumped around the base that are very testicular."

The phone ruffled and a child squealed in the background. Penny huffed into the microphone and said, "Why the clouds?"

"The theme of the shoot is celestial sensuality. Models

wearing gauzy dresses and shimmer all over their bodies reclining in the clouds while they hug this thing."

"So it's intentional."

"You'd think so, but no one has mentioned it."

That seemed to get Penny's attention. "You mean you've been working on this shoot for a couple of days, and no one has mentioned that the bottle is a giant cock?"

"They keep talking about the freshness of the scent and the aspirational nature of the campaign. Taking people to heaven."

"Let me guess. A man came up with this concept?"

I barked out a laugh, leaning against one of the wire shelves behind me. "Yep. They say Mr. Blakely himself was the brain behind this one."

"The guy who owns the company?"

"Yeah. Apparently the client loved the idea, and they've run with it ever since. Yesterday they shot with smoke and glitter, hence me having to wash and polish this thing."

Penny giggled. "So you've been stuck in a room for two hours rubbing down a giant—"

"Yep."

"And no one's mentioned it."

"Nope."

"How long did it take for you to figure out you were locked in?"

"About twenty minutes."

"What's taking so long? Why aren't they getting you out of there?"

"Took forever to find the keys, then they figured out the lock was broken, then their usual locksmith was on vacation, so they had to call around to get someone over here quickly. Now the longer I look at this thing, the more it looks like a huge dildo."

"Maybe it's all in your head. Maybe you need to get laid," she suggested.

I considered Penny's words. After all, it had been a while since I'd been with a man. I let my gaze trace the six-foot perfume bottle and said, "No. It's definitely a huge cock."

Penny giggled, then gasped and told me, "Nikki, I need to go. Timmy just spilled juice all over our kitchen floor." Her four-year-old was cute as a button and also happened to be an absolute terror with more energy in his little toe than I had in my entire body. That she'd been able to chat as long as she had was a surprise.

"All right. Thanks for entertaining me for a while."

"I wish I could talk longer. Any word on when you're getting out of there?"

"The locksmith should be here any minute."

"Text me when you're out."

"Will do," I replied, staring at the giant penis. It had to be intentional. There was just no way dozens of people could design and approve this bottle without knowing they were mass-producing perfume-filled phalluses. Just no way.

"Nikki?" a voice called out through the metal door. "How are you doing?"

It was Eleanor, the prop stylist for the shoot. She was a few years younger than me, in her mid-twenties, and she'd been the only person to befriend me on set so far. Over the whole of the studio was a thick sense of urgency, a palpable fear of messing up. Thankfully for them, I was here to take the fall for everyone as the daily screwup.

"I'm okay," I answered.

My prison wasn't the worst place to be. The storage room had light and air, and I'd been able to sit on one of the tables on the back wall. One side of the room was covered in shelving that held various props and cleaning supplies. I'd been tasked with polishing the penis before its big moment on stage. It wasn't until I was done rubbing it down with a microfiber cloth that I realized the door behind me wouldn't open. I had to call Eleanor before anyone even noticed something was wrong. That had been nearly two hours ago.

"The locksmith was stuck in traffic but he's down with security as we speak, so it won't be long."

"Thank you. Is everyone freaking out about the shoot being delayed?"

There was a pause. "It's not too bad."

I snorted. "Be honest."

Through the door, I heard Eleanor's soft huff. "Ophelia's losing her mind. She's rushing around trying to get everyone to get back to work, but there's nothing to do until we can get the perfume bottle out. The last shot we need is with the big one."

I eyed the proverbial big one through slanted eyes. "Right. Why is she so worried all of a sudden?" And where was this urgency two hours ago, when the lock on that stupid door first jammed? It took them nearly forty minutes of messing around with keys before they even contacted a locksmith.

"Well..." Eleanor dropped her voice so I had to press my ear to the door. "I heard someone say Rome Blakely is on the way down."

"Ah," I answered. "That explains it."

"Ophelia's worried he'll fire her on the spot. It's costing them a hundred thousand dollars an hour to hold the talent here for this project." They'd hired famous models for the shoot, but the number still staggered me.

"That's a lot more than I get paid in a year," I noted.

"You and me both, girl."

Cringing, I tried the door handle again, just in case. It rotated into nothing, not engaging the latch to open the door.

"Would he really fire her for something that isn't her fault?"

"Well…he's been known to fire people for less."

I heard the subtext of her words and swallowed thickly. "So my new job might be over a lot faster than I expected, is what you're saying."

"This wasn't your fault," she protested, but her voice lacked conviction.

"Right."

"Ophelia's calling me. The locksmith will be here soon."

I grunted halfheartedly. The minute that door opened, my employment at this advertising agency would be over.

New York is an at-will employment state, so if Mr. Blakely did see fit to pin this disaster on me, it wouldn't be the first time I was let go for less-than-scrupulous reasons. The whole reason I was working this crappy job in the first place was because my previous boss decided he didn't want to follow through on his promises to promote me. When I finally worked up the nerve to ask him about it, he fired me instead. That was *after* I'd paid for a business management certificate out of pocket after he'd told me he'd reimburse me once I got promoted.

Like an idiot, I'd bought his bullshit. Had the debt to prove it.

A consultant had informed my former boss it'd be cheaper to replace me than to pay me what I was worth, and that was the end of that.

Life hadn't exactly been going according to plan lately. The loss of my job seemed to be the first domino in a long line of increasingly alarming events. First, the promotion turned into a firing, leaving me high and dry with a useless certificate and a lot of debt. Then the landlord for the rent-controlled apartment I'd been living in for years told me he wouldn't be renewing my lease, so I had three months to find somewhere halfway affordable if I didn't want to end up on the street. That was just over two months ago, so time was ticking.

Then, the cherry on top of the crap sundae, the guy I'd been half-seeing told me he met someone else.

It nearly broke me, which hadn't made sense to me at the time. I didn't love the guy, and he didn't love me, but his rejection stung. It was so patently clear that I'd been a placeholder for him while he looked for a woman he wanted to keep. And maybe I'd been a placeholder for my landlord, so he could make some money off his place while he lived his life elsewhere. And, hell, maybe I was a placeholder for my old boss, who let go of me without so much as a reference.

And now I was stuck in a room with a giant glass cock filled with pink perfume.

One of many dicks that had done me wrong lately.

Grimacing at the pink phallus, I admitted the truth: It was the loss of my job that had really hurt. I'd been working for a vintage clothing store as a manager and buyer. I'd go out and purchase all kinds of treasures, then care for them and put them for sale in our store. Looking back on it in the weeks of unemployment that followed, I realized that the owner had taken advantage of me for a long time.

I had started as a sales associate and quickly started taking on tasks outside of my job description. Much of the time I spent trawling through online consignment shops and thrift stores was unpaid. I told myself I enjoyed the activity—and didn't I want the shop to be as good as it could be?

But the truth was, I should have been paid for that time. I should have *demanded* to be paid for that time. Instead, I drank in the empty promises of a promotion that included health insurance, dental, and a 401k match that would see me through my golden years, and the reimbursement of the school fees I'd incurred for upskilling.

What a bunch of bull.

I'd been a placeholder. A convenient person who went above and beyond because she thought she was appreciated, but really, she was a chump. Maybe that's what I should've put on my resume to get people to hire me. Nikita Jordan: Will go above and beyond for free because she was, in fact, born yesterday.

A knock at the door drew my attention.

"Hello?" I called out.

"Locksmith," an older man's voice proclaimed. "Give me a few minutes and I'll get you out."

My shoulders dropped in relief. "Thank you." I moved toward the table and crossed my arms to wait for the locksmith to do his thing.

But instead of the door opening and sweet relief flooding my veins, I stared at the dull gray metal of the door and listened to the old man's frustrated grunts.

I moved closer. "Is everything okay?"

"Lock won't budge. Have to take it apart."

I jumped back when there was a bang on the door.

"Stupid thing," the old man grumbled.

Then, another voice. This one younger and more commanding. "Why isn't this door open? What's the holdup?"

"Buddy, I'm trying here," the locksmith protested.

"Try harder," the other man said, danger laced through his words.

"Sir, he only just arrived," I heard Ophelia simper from a little farther away.

And I understood. The second man was Rome Blakely, billionaire, entrepreneur, and dick-loving advertising mogul. My gaze narrowed on the steel door, then shifted to the pink penis.

I'm not sure what came over me then. It was some kind of deep, seismic shift in the very core of me. I'd been tossed aside by so many people so many times recently—and not so recently—and I was sick of it. Facing down the end of my employment, I discovered that this arrogant man being rude to a poor locksmith was pushing me closer and closer to the edge.

Blakely said, derision dripping from his voice, "How hard could it be to get a simple lock open?"

The locksmith said nothing, and the silence on the other side of the door turned oppressive.

My boss's boss's boss said, "Well?"

And I couldn't take it anymore. Who was he, to treat this nice, grumpy, old locksmith like he was dirt under his shoe? I didn't see Rome Blakely picking up the tools to get me out of here. And besides, I was about to get fired anyway! It was just another injustice in a long line of injustices delivered by men who were far wealthier and more privileged than me.

And I was sick of it. "Back off, Blakely," I snapped. "He's just trying to do his job."

The silence thickened, but I was filled with too much righteous fury to let it bother me. I crossed my arms and glared at the door. "Well?" I said, echoing his rudeness.

"And who do we have hiding on the other side of this door?" he finally said, voice slithering through the gaps around the door toward me.

"Like you care," I responded. "Just let this guy do his job and get out of the way."

"I'm finding that I do care," the billionaire on the other side of the steel barrier responded. "After all, you know my name. Shouldn't I know yours?"

"Sir, it's Nikki Jordan. A new hire. Don't worry about her. She'll be gone before the end of the day."

I heard the man hum. "And how did Nikki Jordan get herself locked in the room with the single most important asset for this campaign?"

Somehow, I knew that despite the way he'd phrased the question, it was directed at me. So I responded accordingly. "Nikki Jordan did what she was told and buffed the giant perfume-filled dildo to a high shine"—the gasps on the other side of the door should have been a warning that I'd gone too far by mentioning the unmentionable, i.e., the fact that we were advertising male genitalia instead of fragrance, but outrage had buoyed me, and the man was just a faceless entity on the other side of a locked door. At that moment, he couldn't hurt me. Nothing could hurt me. So I continued—"only to discover that Rome Blakely failed to maintain the operation of the locks in the building that bears his name, and she found herself locked in a small, windowless room for"—I checked the time on my phone—"two hours and seventeen minutes."

The only sound I heard was the rushing heartbeat in my ears and my heavy breaths filling the small space.

But hey—I'd already lost my job. What did I care if I made an enemy along the way?

"Got it!" the locksmith exclaimed, and something metallic clattered on the other side of the door. "But—" He grunted, and there was a muffled thump on the other side of the door.

"What seems to be the problem?" Mr. Blakely asked in a slow drawl.

"It's jammed somehow. Hey, lady, is the hinge on the door okay in there?"

I took a step to the side and inspected the hardware. "One of them seems wonky. When I first opened the door to get in here, it was a bit sticky."

"I think the hinge failed," the locksmith explained, "and it put pressure on the locking mechanism, snapping this piece here. You really should go for higher-quality locks, especially somewhere that's getting this much traffic. I would never recommend a hook lock like this for this type of door."

"Fascinating," the jerk who owned the building replied. "Now get it open."

"That might require a pry bar of some sort."

"I'll get maintenance up here," Ophelia said, then called out, "Ben! Get maintenance up here."

I pursed my lips and moved away from the door to lean against the table on the back wall again. In a strange way, I didn't want the door to open. Once it opened, my job would be over. And I'd have to face the man I'd just sassed. The man who would fire me on sight. The man who would make me start all over again, because once again, they hadn't hired me for me. They'd hired me to be a placeholder until they found someone better.

As my temper cooled, I began to dread the prospect.

The paycheck wasn't much, but it was keeping the loan sharks at bay.

The sound of voices on the other side of the door faded and then increased again. I heard the sound of metal on metal, and the locksmith called out, "Stand back, lady!"

"I'm clear," I replied, straightening.

There was a bit of grunting, the sound of a tool scraping against the door, then a horrible squeaking sound. After a moment, all was quiet except for the locksmith's panting.

"Give me that thing," Mr. Blakely ordered.

"Sir, we'll get one of the grips—"

"Give me the pry bar," he snapped.

My mouth went dry. I gripped the edge of the table with both hands, waiting for the noise of the tool being propped between the door and its frame. There was a scrape, then a beat of silence before the door was flung open with far more force than I expected.

I jumped, letting out a yelp, as the door swung open and flew toward the metal shelving.

And here's where I might have messed up. The giant perfume bottle was on a wheeled dolly since it weighed a few hundred pounds. But as I'd vigorously buffed it, I'd found it hard to get some of the scuff marks out while the caster wheels let it move around. I'd tried hugging it with one arm while my free hand buffed, as unpleasant as that had been, but I kept leaving marks on it with my supportive arm. They didn't have any locks on the dolly's wheels, so I'd jammed it into the bottom of the metal shelves.

So the door flew open, and I caught a glimpse of Rome Blakely's silhouette. He was in his shirtsleeves and tie, with a big metal bar grasped in strong hands. A dark lock of hair had fallen over his forehead, and his eyes were filled with a violent sort of victory.

Then the door hit the dick. The giant phallus, with its base jammed into the bottom of the shelving, was forced to bear the brunt of all of Rome Blakely's considerable strength. The door slammed into the perfume bottle with enough force to make it rebound toward its frame.

Then a few things happened at once.

Mr. Blakely put his foot in the opening and stopped the door from closing again. I didn't have time to be grateful, though, because the giant perfume bottle, being tall and slender, began to wobble.

Had the testicle-clouds been made of something solid, they might have been strong enough to hold the penis-bottle upright. Being made of fluffy cloud-like material, however, they failed to stop the bottle from wobbling.

In retrospect, I should have let the thing smash on the ground. Maybe the bottle wouldn't have broken. Maybe all the drama that followed could have been avoided, if I'd just sat back and let things happen the way they would.

But I was a good girl. I was a little worker bee who always jumped in to help when I was needed. That's how I'd ended up doing the job of four people for my old boss, and why every romantic interest seemed to slowly learn to take advantage of me. Why I always had been, and always would be, a stepping stone that people used while they were waiting for something better.

So, when the six-foot-tall cock began to tip toward me, I leaped forward to catch it. It, however, had the advantage of being taller and heavier than I was, and already on the way down.

I felt a sharp pain in my finger as it jabbed against the glass phallus. Then I tried to divert the thing's descent but only managed to slam it against the shelving and nick the edge of it.

I heard a roared, "Get away from it!" and finally had the good sense to listen.

Cool glass kissed my leg as I stumbled and fell back, and then several hundred pounds of cock-shaped perfume fell to the concrete floor and shattered. A glass shard embedded itself below my knee while another slashed across my calf. Blood gushed.

A gasp slipped through my lips as I watched my clothes become soaked with the pink perfume flooding the room. A patch of dark-red blood diffused into the puddle of pink as I stared, not quite understanding. My hand throbbed.

The smell was horrendous. The bottle had actually been filled with perfume, and not some colored water. Why, I had no idea. I didn't know why anyone thought that was a good idea. It was like a scented bomb went off, and suddenly I was dizzy and bleeding and the pain in my finger was unbearable.

It all must have happened within a couple of seconds. Distantly, I heard the clatter of the metal pry bar on the concrete floor, and then strong arms clad in a crisp white shirt were siding beneath my knees and around my back, and my boss's boss's boss was picking me up.

"I'm bleeding on your shirt," I noted.

"Quiet," he barked.

"It's white. It looks expensive."

"I don't care about the shirt. You! Call an ambulance. You, Ophelia. Get a towel. Bring that table over, we need to set her down. And open a damn window."

The edges of my vision were going fuzzy. The fingers of my uninjured hand felt clumsy as I reached up to feel the fabric of his shirt between my fingers. "Good-quality cotton. The fil-a-fil is a nice touch. Subtle blue tinge." I glanced up, then my head lolled when I couldn't keep it up. "Like your eyes."

He had beautiful, startlingly blue eyes. His eyelashes were thick and very black, almost making it look like he wore eyeliner. Some people had all the luck.

Those remarkable eyes met mine. He was angry for some reason. "Will you stop talking?"

"Why?" I asked, surprised to find my voice was slurring.

I was jarred when he kicked something, and a chair went flying. Then, more gently than I would think him possible, he set me down on a hard surface. Glaring, he said, "I told you to be quiet. You're bleeding."

"Sorry about your shirt," I said, pouting at the red stain on his arm. "But I already know you're going to fire me, so it's okay."

"Just—don't die, all right?"

"Firing me will be your loss," I told him. I was a star employee, after all. They'd only had me for a week, and they'd put me on dick-polishing duty. "Big mistake for *sure.*"

The last thing I saw before everything went black were the dark slashes of his eyebrows drawing together, his full lips pursed in displeasure.

ROME HAS A PROPOSITION FOR NIKKI. A JOB OFFER SHE CAN'T REFUSE.
SHE'S ABOUT TO BECOME HIS OFFICIAL PLUS-ONE...AND HER LIFE IS ABOUT TO GET A WHOLE LOT MORE INTERESTING.
HTTPS://GENI.US/ForbiddenBoss

ABOUT THE AUTHOR

Lilian Monroe adores writing swoonworthy heroes and the women who bring them to their knees. She loves making people laugh and is eternally grateful to have found people who share her sense of humor.

When she's not writing, she's reading (or rereading) a book, walking, lifting weights, or attempting to play the guitar with very limited success.

She grew up in Canada but now lives in Australia with her Irish husband. He frequently asks to be used as a cover model for her books, and she's not quite sure whether or not he's joking.

ALSO BY LILIAN MONROE

For all books, visit:

www.lilianmonroe.com

<u>Manhattan Billionaires</u>

Big Bossy Mistake

Big Bossy Trouble

Big Bossy Problem

Big Bossy Surprise

Forbidden Boss

The Wrong Boss

Dirty Boss

<u>More surprise babies!</u>

Knocked Up by the CEO

Knocked Up by the Single Dad

Knocked Up...Again!

Knocked Up by the Billionaire's Son

Yours for Christmas

Bad Prince

Heartless Prince

Cruel Prince

Broken Prince

Wicked Prince

Wrong Prince

Lone Prince

Ice Queen

Rogue Prince

<u>Small Towns are the best towns</u>

Four Steps to the Perfect Revenge

Four Steps to the Perfect Fake Date

Working with the Enemy

Faking It with the Firefighter

Conquest

Craving

Combat

Calamity

<u>Small Town + Later-in-Life Romance</u>

Dirty Little Midlife Crisis

Dirty Little Midlife Mess

Dirty Little Midlife Mistake

Dirty Little Midlife Disaster

Dirty Little Midlife Debacle

Dirty Little Midlife Secret

Dirty Little Midlife Dilemma

Dirty Little Midlife Drama

Dirty Little Midlife (fake) Date

Filthy Little Midlife Fling

Merry Little Midlife Matchmaker

<u>Brother's Best Friend Romance</u>

Shouldn't Want You

Can't Have You

Don't Need You

Won't Miss You

<u>He'll do anything to protect his woman</u>

His Vow

His Oath

His Word

<u>Enemies to Lovers/Workplace Romance</u>

Hate at First Sight

Loathe at First Sight

Despise at First Sight

<u>Fake Engagement Romance</u>

Engaged to Mr. Right

Engaged to Mr. Wrong

Engaged to Mr. Perfect

<u>Mountain Man Romance</u>

Lie to Me

Swear to Me

Run to Me

<u>Doctor's Orders</u>

Doctor O

Doctor D

Doctor L